JAN KELLY ANDERSON

THE LOVERS' CRUSADE

Black Rose Writing | Texas

This is a work of fiction. Names, characters, businesses, places, events, and incidents are either the products of the author's imagination or used in a fictitious manner. Any resemblance to actual persons, living or dead, or actual events is purely coincidental.

ISBN: 978-1-68513-551-5
PUBLISHED BY BLACK ROSE WRITING
www.blackrosewriting.com

Printed in the United States of America
Suggested Retail Price (SRP) $23.95

The Lovers' Crusade is printed in Minion Pro

*As a planet-friendly publisher, Black Rose Writing does its best to eliminate unnecessary waste to reduce paper usage and energy costs, while never compromising the reading experience. As a result, the final word count vs. page count may not meet common expectations.

This is dedicated to Mary Ellen and Cathy;
we were young wives and moms together.

Thank you to our daughter Kay for her helpful suggestions and edits. Madre is so proud of the kind, generous and loving person you have become.

THE LOVERS' CRUSADE

CHAPTER 1

May 1095

The sound of girlish laughter echoed through the forest, dancing off the spring leaves. Christian stopped and listened. In the background he could hear the splash of water as they frolicked. He knew who they were and where they were. They had gone to the lake every spring for years for the first swim of the year. He knew the water was icy cold from the winter melt. His sister, Felise, would leave the water first leaving Emely, her serf companion, and friend behind. They had been eleven when he returned to his father's manor after fourteen long years away. He had trained to be a warrior at the castle of Duke Leonard. Fourteen years of learning how to distinguish every out of place sound wherever he was. Fourteen years of learning the sword and lance. Fourteen years of sleeping on hard cold stone floors, eating meager rations, wearing clothing reeking of sweat, filthy with mud, and the droppings of horses and men in battle. Fourteen years growing from a boy of seven to a man of twenty-one. The last seven learning what men did with women be the woman willing or not. Fourteen years of being at battle as his lord took town after town, increasing his domain. When the towns had fallen, the nobles took whatever women they wanted and let the knights and squires have the rest. To some age made little difference, young and untouched was the preferred to some conquerors. He had taken his share of women as had others but now he was home and had seen Felise and Emely grow. He was sickened at the thought of what he had done.

The sound of Felise and Emely's laughter brought him back to the present. He smiled to himself remembering them as the young girls they had been when he first came home six years before. They were eleven years old, all arms and legs hidden under their tunics. Both girls trying so hard to act mature. He had tried not to laugh in front of them. When had they changed? Now they were young women on the brink of becoming wives.

Emely, he thought, was by far the prettier. Her long hair was the color of wheat, her eyes the color of a clear summer sky, her skin pink and soft. She was always smiling, a brightness about her, a warmth. They had kissed at Christmas and Easter when everyone kissed as part of the celebrations of Christ's birth and his rising. Innocent kisses but as she grew those kisses had lit a fire in him. He stayed away from her for he had nothing to offer her. She needed to marry a good serf from their manor. He, however, looked forward to those kisses. He waited for the time when he could hold her just a few seconds more than was necessary, feeling her soft warm body pressed to his. She never resisted or tried to pull away from him and if the kiss lingered just a bit longer, she never ended it and sometimes leaned into him as he pulled his lips away as if wanting to savor more.

In the years since he had come home, they had danced at celebrations. Times when their hands had touched, and their eyes had met. Times when she came into his arms with joy and excitement when dancing and he had been happy she was in his embrace. Times when he wished they could be alone if only for a few seconds so he could kiss her as he wanted to kiss her, so she would know his desire for her. Times when they had argued about bible passages and their meanings laughing and teasing each other. Times when they had talked about passages in the old testament as he tried to guide her to the realization, they could be together like Boaz and Ruth. Times when he could have asked her if she cared for him. So many times, he wanted to know her heart and let her know his.

The sound of her laughter echoing through the forest drew him to her. He could see her eyes dancing with amusement, her soft mouth lifted in a smile, her cheeks flush with mirth. At seventeen she was a prize. So many young men in their village followed after her when she walked through with Felise. She talked with all of them and laughed at them. She teased them and flirted with them. She must have been taken by now. The village boys would be fools if they had not tried. Around him she had always been shy. He had seen her eyes follow him at dinner each night. He had seen the adoration in her eyes. Did she feel about him as he felt about her? Could they have a future? Would his father allow him to marry a serf? Would her father give her hand in marriage to him? He cared not if she had been taken. He wanted her, her warmth, her laughter, her caring. He wanted to see his child grow within her. He wanted to grow old with her. He wanted the last thing he saw each night and the first each morning to be her face.

Both girls, at seventeen, were getting old for a first marriage, but his father had resisted giving away Felise, his youngest child and only daughter, waiting he said for the right man to asked for her hand. Emely's father must have the same reservations about the match he would make for her. He would speak to his father, he would still have to have his permission and blessing, there were still rules and obligations limiting his freedom. He needed to be sure of her. Would she want him, did she want him? He thought he knew but he needed to be sure. He reined in his horse so he could watch the two girls play. They laughed as they splashed each other, so free of cares.

"Enough, I am freezing," Felise said wading out of the water.

"Wait, I will come with you," Emely said swimming toward the bank.

"No, stay and enjoy your swim."

"You should not go through the forest by yourself" Emely protested.

"No one would dare harm me on my father's land," laughed Felise. "Stay!"

Emely watched the other girl go to her clothes and dress before Felise headed back toward the manor house. Emely debated whether she should follow her friend or not and decided Felise was right no one would dare touch the lord's daughter on his own land. Knowing Felise was safe, Emely turned and looked at the shimmering water she had all to herself, a rare gift to be treasured and enjoyed. Smiling to herself she dove under the water, savoring the pinpricks of the icy cold silken feel of the water sliding over her skin. She stayed under water as long as she could, pushing her limit before coming up gasping for air. She turned and smiled at how far she had gone. She swam back to her starting point, savoring the feel of the water flowing over her body. She saw him then. She lowered herself in the water to cover her nakedness as he dismounted.

Emely watched him, tall and muscular. To her there always seemed to be a glow around him. From the first time she had seen him when he returned from his training, dressed in newmade mail reflecting the spring sun like the light of a thousand candles, she had fallen in love with Christian. He had his father's dark brown hair and his mother's green eyes. When he spoke, his voice was mellow and restrained. He was a warrior bred and trained. No movement wasted, no words spoken without thought, no feelings revealed for that would make him vulnerable. Warriors fought like savages but knew when the fight was won to release all anger and find inner peace.

"Where is my sister?" Christian asked trying to sound annoyed at Felise for leaving Emely alone and unprotected yet again.

"She is going back to the manor, milord."

Christian gave a deep sigh.

"You must be getting cold. Come out now."

"I would, milord, but modesty requires I wait until you leave."

Christian stared at the young woman in the water before turning his back to her.

"Now I cannot see you. Get out and dressed before you freeze," he ordered.

Taking a deep breath Emely walked up the bank looking for an escape with every step. Her long hair covered her firm young breasts. She stopped when the water was around her waist.

"Are you dressed yet?"

"No," she muttered.

"Please hurry. I have a few words to say to my sister and I am only getting angrier as I wait."

Emely hurried to her gown and slipped it over her head, not bothering with her under garments.

"I am dressed milord."

Christian turned back toward her and saw her long hair still dripping and knew she would still be chilled as her gown got soaked. He took his cloak and walked toward her. He wrapped it around her and pulled her hair outside the cloak. Emely looked up at him and their eyes met. When, he wondered, had she grown up. When had the awkward girl become this graceful woman. He took a breath and kissed her.

Emely was startled at first but then kissed him back. She had dreamed of this so often, had adored him for so long. She had loved him almost from the minute he returned from his training, and she had seen him for the first time. Her love had grown as she listened as he talked over the years, as she watched him at family celebrations, as she heard him laugh even when he was teasing Felise and her. He had authority over her but never before had used it to take advantage of her. He had always treated her with respect even at times when she would have gone to him, kissed him, held him, touched him. Now he lingered over the holy day kisses, holding her just a few seconds more than he should. She had cherished every moment and wanted them to last a few seconds longer. She wanted to be in his arms, feel his lips on hers, wonder at the swirl of sensations she felt when with him.

"Emely," he said as he pulled his lips from hers.

"We should go," he whispered knowing he would stay holding her for as long as she would let him.

"Yes," she agreed but neither took their arms from around the other. They stared deep into each other's eyes before he lowered his lips to hers again.

She tightened her arms around his neck and felt him pull her closer as he deepened the kiss. The kisses deepened as both Christian and Emely sought more. Neither was quite sure how it happened, but his cloak was on the ground, and they were lying wrapped in each other's arms. Her gown was tossed aside as was his jerkin and leggings. Christian was touching and tasting every inch of her and then came back to her lips. Emely opened herself to him, all of herself. Then came the intrusion into her womanhood. Emely gasped as muscles were stretched.

"Emi!?!" Christian gasped and tried to pull away but she held him to her.

"I always wanted it to be you," she whispered, pushing her pain aside. She looked up at him. How often had she dreamed of being with him this way? Of giving herself to him? Of loving him not only with all of her heart and soul but with her body? Becoming his in every way possible? She reached up and caressed his hair loving the feel of it under her hand.

He studied her looking for some sign of reluctance or withdrawal to their joining. He saw none and lowered his lips again to hers. He was gentle with her at first, then as their need arose, his passion demanded her complete surrender. Her response was ardent and complete. Her body opened and welcomed him seeking to take him deeper into her, to be joined and become one with him. Their desire took them to fulfillment as he poured his seed deep into her womanhood. She cried out her satisfaction as her body throbbed to pull him and his seed even deeper into her. He collapsed onto her, their passion fulfilled, their breathing ragged.

They lay entwined for several minutes, each taking pleasure in the feel of their bodies joined as one. Then he raised his body away from her and looked deep into her eyes.

"We will go to my father," he said. "Ask his permission to be wed."

"I . . .. We cannot be seen together. Not yet," she countered.

"Eme," he said using her childhood nickname.

"No. You must go back alone and talk to him. I will follow. If we go back together, the whole village and manor will know before him, and he would be offended and humiliated."

Christian sighed, knowing she was right. He looked into her eyes and saw their future together, their children. He smiled and knew he loved her. With his father's permission they could be together here. He would be one of his father's knights and after his father's death a knight of his older brother, Benoit, who would inherit all his father's possessions.

"I must go now," he said pulling from her. "Will you be safe going back alone?" He forgot his anger at Felise for leaving Emely here unaccompanied. She was sending him away the same way she had sent Felise.

"I have walked these woods most of my life. I know every tree, bush, and sound. Nothing and no one could surprise me," Emely said smiling up at him finding joy in his unwarranted concern.

"Emely," he said turning to her after they were dressed, "I love you." Emely smiled at him.

"You love me?" She asked in wonderment.

"Yes," he said smiling down at her. Wondering how she could not have known.

"And?" he asked.

She laughed. "Of course, I love you. I think I have since the first moment I saw you. All bright in your mail, sitting so tall on your horse as you came back a full knight."

"I am a younger brother. I have nothing to give you or offer you except what I earn as a knight. It may not always be easy."

"We will be together," she said caressing his face. "We will have each other and our children. We will grow old together, living, loving, till God calls us to our eternal home."

"And then for all eternity," he said before kissing her one last time.

"Go," she ordered. "Felise will be looking for me and you have an important conversation to have with your father."

"I love you," he said one last time before kissing her and leaving.

Emely watched him disappear into the woods and smiled. She was having a perfect day. The best day of her young life with the hope of many more perfect days to come. She straightened her gown one last time and started to walk back to the manor, smiling and hugging herself in happiness.

CHAPTER 2

Christian smiled to himself as he rode back to the manor house. She loved him. They would marry, with his father's permission, and live here among the people they loved and who loved them. He would be the leader of his father's army and after his father's death his older brother's. They would have children and be happy. When he reached the courtyard there seemed to be an unusual amount of activity. He stabled his horse and went into the manor house. The activity was much greater here. Extra tables were being set up and places set. 'A feast tonight,' he thought, 'why?' He moved past the controlled chaos to find his father.

Lord Bryce was talking to Benoit, his older son when Christian found them.

"We will need provisions for the trip to Rene's. You need to select what villagers will be going to the new manor," Bryce was instructing Benoit. "I will have your mother take care of household items and clothing. Lord Duran will be joining us in a few days and travel with us to Rene's. We just got this message so there is more to be done but we have a few days to work out the rest of the details. Start on the list of villagers. They need to be told so they can prepare," Bryce finished. "Aha Christian," Bryce said smiling at his younger son. "We have great news. Duke Marcel has agreed to the marriage of Felise to his oldest son, Duran. They are to be married within the month."

"That is good news. Felise needs to be wed. Father, I want to talk to you," Christian said.

"Oh yes there is good news for you also. Rene has sent word. He will let Arianna be married," Bryce said.

"Why good news for me?"

"Because she is your betrothed. Do you not remember? When you were eleven, we held the betrothal ceremony. She was only a year old then, but Rene and I have long wished to join our two houses. Since he has no sons, Arianna is his heir so as her husband you will inherit all his titles and lands. You will have a great manor of your own."

"No. I love . . . ."

"Love? No. It has been decided. You will marry Arianna," his father said allowing no disagreement. "Rene and I have planned this for years. Benoit is already married and only ten years separate you in age."

"Father, please listen to me!"

"No! You will marry Arianna within the month." Bryce said in a tone that allowed no disagreement before softening. "If you love another take her with you, let her be a companion to Arianna and a comfort to you. Younger sons and their women must accept their lives will be decided by others."

Christian stared at his father. He would never debase Emely in such a way. Make her his comfort woman? No. Now how did he tell her they could not be together as they dreamed? How did he leave her? He turned and left the room. He had to find her. He had to be the one to tell her. They had to hold each other. He searched for her but was told after searching for several minutes she was with Felise. He knew Felise would tell Emely of his marriage. He wanted to be with her, hold her, share their sorrow. He started toward Felise's room, but Benoit stopped him.

"I need you to help me with this list of serfs who will go with you to your new manor."

"What new manor?" Christian ask.

"Father and Lord Rene have both contributed land to create a new manor as a home for you and Arianna. You will have your own manor until Lord Rene dies then you will move to his manor. A younger son getting his own manor is a unique opportunity. You are a lucky man."

Emely entered the manor house through the garden door and was engulfed in the whirlwind of activity. Serfs rushed from table to table to fill **trenchers with vegetables.** The smell of bread baking mixed with the aroma of meat roasting in the huge fireplaces. Kegs of wine and mead were on racks as large jugs were filled. A great feast was being prepared.

"Emely, Lady Felise has been asking for you," the head cook called to her.

Lord Bryce must be hosting important visitors or planning a major announcement for this night. Emely hurried up the stairs to Felise's chamber. Several serf girls were moving around the room as Felise shouted orders. Seeing Emely, Felise ordered all the other girls from the room.

"At last, you must help me, these serfs know nothing of how a lady should be dressed. Father is planning a great celebration and making, mother says, major announcements about the family's future. It will be a marriage contract and an alliance with another noble family. I wonder who father will have picked for Christian."

"Christian?" Emely questioned, a stab of pain going through her heart. How could they have been so stupid? Of course, Lord Bryce would make a marriage contract for Christian and Felise with other noble families. A simple serving girl would never be an acceptable wife for the son of such a high ranking lord and Lord Bryce was high ranking, a friend of the king from their years of conquest.

"Who else? He will need a manor to support himself. Father is too high ranking for his son to be a warrior in service to another even Benoit. I wonder who she will be. Maybe someone of a high ranking, even higher than father. How wonderful for Christian."

Emely moved around the room bringing Felise things she needed. Felise continued her happy speculating about Christian's future, a future without Emely. She would have to live her life content with the memory of one short time together. She would not have to see him every day at least. Perhaps in time the pain would end, and she would be left with only the memory. A knock at the door announced dinner was ready in the great hall. It was then Felise looked at Emely but without realizing the agony Emely was suffering.

"Come on," Felise said as she swept out the door.

"Why would I go to table?"

"Have you not heard a word I said? Father summoned not only the family but all household staff to the table. You will of course be below the salt but still in a conspicuous place. What is wrong with you? I cannot be late. Come on," Felise said as she hurried from the room.

Emely watched Felise go but had no wish to attend a feast or hear any announcement, so she did what she always did after helping Felise get dressed: she straightened the room and turned down Felise's bed. With nothing more to keep her in the room, Emely walked with great unwillingness down the stairs. She followed the sounds of laughter and music. The great hall was lit with a hundred torches. The family and even the serfs were dressed in bright colored gowns and tunics. The music was joyous, and the mood was one of great celebration. Such festivities were rare. The last time had been when Benoit, the eldest son, had married seven years ago. Emely took her place by her parents, only smiling when they greeted her. The tables were piled high with food and every villager would share in the bounty tonight. Even the wine was abundant. Emely looked toward the dais where the family sat, Lord Bryce, Lady Martha, Benoit and Marilee on the lord's right and Christian and Felise on Lady Martha's left. Emely took a carrot and an apple from the trays in front of her, but it was more to just have something before her rather than to eat. Everyone was talking and laughter filled the room. Emely looked at Christian and realized he was not eating either. She realized he was looking around the room as if searching for someone then he fixed his gaze on her. She returned his gaze and nodded her head in acknowledgement. Still, he watched her, a strange, anguished look on his face.

"Friends," Lord Bryce said standing, "I call you together tonight to join my family in celebration of two marriages that will take place before the next full moon. Daughter Felise, I have arranged a match for you with Lord Duran, the eldest son and heir to my old friend and comrade in arms, Duke Marcel of Gaston. They will arrive for the marriage three weeks from today. Please rise and declare your acceptance of the match."

Emely could see the panic on Felise's face. She tried to remember Lord Duran but if ever she had seen him, it would have been years ago when neither of them were thinking ahead of being married.

"I … am honored … milord. When will the betrothal ceremony be held?"

"Twas celebrated a week ago," Lord Bryce replied. "You sent him a fine handkerchief you had embroidered."

"Oh. I pray he was pleased with … my gift and I look forward to our life together."

Emely watched Felise. She had said all the right words and with the well trained deference expected of a maiden of her station. Emely could tell by Felise's rigid stance she was not well pleased with this news.

"Since he will be coming to stay with us so you can become acquainted you will be able to ask him. After your wedding of course you will be leaving us to live at the Duke's manor and in a few years, you will be the lady of the manor. There is another announcement to be made," Lord Bryce said lowering his gaze to Christian. "Sixteen summers ago, Christian was betrothed to the daughter of my oldest and closest friend, Lord Rene. She is now of an age to be a wife. We leave for Lord Rene's manor after Mass on Sunday and the wedding will take place Saturday next. Lord Rene and I have agreed to each give a grant of land from our manors so you will have your own estate and Lord Rene has agreed to name you as his heir."

Christian looked as unhappy as Emely felt. He looked at her, longing to go to her and take her from this place. Knowing he could not, he stood fighting the personal struggle of having to accept a future he had not chosen. He knew he never would have understood Felise's unhappiness if he had not been subjected to the same destiny.

CHAPTER 3

"I will honor my betrothal vows as I honor you father," Christian said. "I have only a vague memory of the ceremony and nothing of … my betrothed."

"Stand," Lord Bryce ordered, "raise your cups and rejoice at the happiness our family will celebrate this summer and hope these unions will be fruitful. To Christian and Felise!"

"Christian and Felise!" Everyone cheered. Everyone except Christian, Felise, and Emely.

While the crowd was still standing Emely rose from her place and left the great hall. She searched for someplace where she would not hear the music or laughter, someplace where she could cry without anyone coming upon her, someplace where she could find peace and solace.

How could she have been so stupid, she wondered. Lord Bryce would never have approved of a marriage between a serf and one of his sons. Marriages were arranged with protecting and securing the family manor as the first and most important consideration. Lucky couples came to love each other, easing the mating required of them to have heirs. Love was the last and least consideration of noble marriages. Christian would never be hers. The words of love they had said to each other meant nothing now.

It was late when she accepted, she would live her life without Christian. She stopped crying and knew she had to return to Felise's room. The sound of music from the great hall still floated through the halls, echoing through the empty spaces. Felise had not returned. Emely could imagine her friend dancing, a last joyful celebration. Would Felise see her future as an opportunity or an obligation? Emely smiled to herself. Felise had always found a way to turn every situation to her advantage. Her father and brothers had indulged her. Only Lady Martha had scolded Felise and when necessary, punished her. Emely prepared the room for their night's sleep as she had every night since she had first been brought to be Felise's companion. They had shared their lives, their dreams in this room in the stillness of the night when they were alone. Would she go with Felise? What would be her place and where would she be settled? Felise's future was changing and so was Emely's.

Laughter in the hall woke Emely. Felise came into the room swirling as if still dancing to the music floating through the manor. Felise's warm sunny disposition had returned. Emely knew the other girl well enough to know Felise was finding the thought of having her own household, being able to give orders to her own serfs appealing. Emely helped Felise undress as the other girl continued to talk about her plans for the future in her new home and Lord Duran, trying to remember what he looked like. Once Felise was in bed Emely moved around the room blowing out the candles until the fire cast long shadows putting the corners and much of the room itself into darkness. Emely lay down on her mat next to Felise's bed. Both were exhausted so they went to sleep quickly. Morning would come soon enough.

Emely was up early in the morning before the first light of dawn crept through the windows. She splashed some cold water from the bucket on her face. She added wood to the fire and put a kettle on to warm water and laid out Felise's clothes for the day. She gathered a cloth, towel, and soap so Felise could wash her face and hands when she woke. Felise stirred in her bed and Emely smiled. The other girl had never been an early riser. When she ran her own household, she would have to be up early because morning set the pace for the rest of the day. Lady Martha had ensured Felise knew how to run a household and insisted her daughter be educated and able to read, write, and do mathematics so she would be able to maintain her household accounts. Since Emely was Felise's constant companion, she too had learned all these skills even though the likelihood of her ever making use of them was small.

Felise stirred again and Emely put warmed water in a small pail and took it and the cloth and towel to the side of Felise's bed.

"Good morning," Emely said with a cheerfulness she did not feel as Felise sat up.

"Tis morning? I had the strangest dream," Felise said stretching. "Father announced my marriage."

"Twas no dream," Emely assured her.

"So, I will have my own household, my own serfs and best of all a husband to take care of me."

"As you will take care of him," Emely reminded.

Felise made an unhappy face but then smiled. She washed and then Emely helped her dress. Felise left to go to breakfast and Emely completed her morning routine. Something was beginning to haunt her. According to the church and social code, Emely had sinned in laying with a man who was not her husband. She knew she had to confess and receive absolution. When she was done, Emely left to join the other serfs at their morning meal. She had not walked but a few feet when Christian stepped from the shadows in front of her.

"Good morn, milord," Emely said dropping into a curtsey.

"Emi," he whispered, "there is no reason to curtsey to me. I . . . we need to speak . . . .."

"No, milord, we do not. You are betrothed to another. No words between us can change the past."

"Emi, I . . . the ceremony meant nothing to me at the time."

"Promises were made and cannot be broken. You are committed to another."

They stared at each other, both knowing whatever they felt could never be fulfilled. Emely moved past Christian fighting to keep her tears from falling.

"I love you," Christian said as she passed him, but Emely did not acknowledge him.

CHAPTER 4

Down in the Great Hall there was activity everywhere as Lord Duran was to arrive today. Lady Martha assigned tasks for the day. The morning passed as all the women worked at cutting and sewing. Emely managed to slip away and go to the village church. She found Father Bernard in the church. Father Bernard greeted her with a warm smile until he saw her face.

"Emely, what has happened?"

"Father Bernard, may I give you my confession?"

"Why?"

"Please, may I?" she questioned again, in a near panic.

"Yes."

She knelt before him and waited for him to begin the ceremony. She heard the familiar prayers in Latin and began to respond as she had been taught as a child.

"Forgive me Father. I have mated with a man who is not my husband."

She could hear Father Bernard's sharp intake of breath but ended her confession in the usual way and waited for the priest to give her absolution, but he was silent for several seconds.

"Emely, who is the man?"

This was the question she had feared. How could she tell anyone it had been Christian?

"Tis my sin, not his," was her reply whispered so the priest did not hear it.

"Emely, who is the man?"

"Father Bernard, this I cannot tell, please grant me absolution."

"Emely, did you do this willing or were you forced?"

"I . . . I did it willingly. Words of love were said but . . . he belongs to another. Please father give me absolution and my penance."

He said the words she had begged for, and then gave her a penance, knowing nothing could equal the one she was giving herself.

Emely went to the statue of the Virgin to say her prayers. Father Bernard watched her praying. He knew the carefree girl was gone, lost forever in a single act of love which should have been joyous between a husband and wife. She looked more grown up, almost weary of life. He watched as Emely rose from her prayers.

"Emely, if you should decide to name the man, please let me know, so I can be of help to you."

Emely nodded her head, her heart breaking at the secret she knew she had to keep. She left the church and returned to the manor house. She slipped back into her place working with the other women. The household was preparing for the midday meal when the outriders announced the arrival of Lord Duran. The household moved to the main entrance of the manor house, arranging themselves by station.

An older man accompanied by three knights came into the courtyard. They dismounted and he stepped forward to greet Lord Bryce and Lady Martha. He was introduced to the family with Felise being last. Emely saw the flicker of dismay on the other girl's face. He was not a handsome young knight who had come to rescue her and sweep her off to a life of passionate love. He was a man solid and experienced. Emely remembered him now. His wife had died in childbirth a few years before. His mourning at her loss had been spoken of with wonderment for the deep love they had shared. She knew little else of him as he was twice their age. He would be a good match for

Felise, Emely thought, because he was older and would help her mature. Since his father's manor lay to the north of Lord Bryce's. Emely understood the strategic importance of this match. Lord Bryce has secured his western lands by Benoit's marriage to Marilee. He would secure his eastern lands through Christian's marriage to Arianna. Now he would secure his northern lands through Felise's marriage to Duran. While girls looked for love in their mates, male relatives looked to secure their lands and provide peace and safety for their serfs and descendants.

Emely watched Felise. The other girl still looked sullen even as she invited Duran to sit with her at the midday meal. His smile was warm and genuine. The family returned to the Great Hall where food and drink had been placed on long planks set upon sturdy braces. Emely kept watching Felise and Duran as they ate. He remained polite and seemed to be trying to engage her in conversation, but Emely could tell Felise was not making any effort to be more polite than good manners required. Finally, Duran gave up and turned his attention to Lady Martha. It was then Felise reacted. She was even more upset because he was no longer paying attention to her. Felise introduced Emely to Duran after the meal. Up close Emely could see the lines on his weathered face. He was warm, polite and was trying to engage Felise in conversation.

"Please excuse me as I have work to do," Emely said.

"No" said Lord Duran. "You must join us to chaperone us. Perhaps a walk in your garden."

Emely looked to Felise for a sign of her agreement and the other girl gave a slight nod. In the garden as they walked, Emely found herself talking to Duran.

"You have many of the same medicinal plants and herbs as my mother grows," he said looking at the extensive garden.

"Lady Martha takes care of making sure we always have a good supply," Emely said.

They talked about the various plants and herbs. He was very knowledgeable.

"Where did you train?" Emely asked looking at Felise as these were questions, she should have been asking.

"At the king's court. It was a great honor to have been selected." He then shared stories of being a young squire. He had a subtle sense of humor and seemed to enjoy using unique words. Soon Emely found herself enjoying Duran's company and Felise seemed to sulk more as the afternoon progressed. Emely managed to excuse herself an hour later telling Duran she had work to do. Emely heard Duran try again to get Felise to talk to him as she left them in the garden, but the answers Emely heard continued to be brief and basic. Emely knew Felise's pettiness would not serve her well. The betrothal ceremony had taken place, the marriage ceremony was all but performed.

Minstrels provided music for dancing at the feast later. Needing to get away, Emely left the manor house and went to the village where the music was louder and far less sedate. Kegs of mead and ale were consumed and replaced swiftly as the village men enjoyed this rare generosity. Many a villager would have trouble rising in the morning. The talk and laughter was louder and happier. While Emely had grown up in the manor house, she was still a serf and knew the villagers well. She had shopped at the marketplace, played among the children over the years, and helped tend the sick alongside Lady Martha and her mother. She was greeted by villagers and offered ale, a place to sit among the other young women, and asked often to dance by the young men of the village. She was swept into the joyous celebration of the village and found herself a popular dance partner. For a time, she could forget Christian and her future without him. She could be free and happy here among the villagers. It was late when several village young men escorted her back to the manor house. They laughed and teased each other pushing and shoving so they could be the one walking next to Emely. A figure emerged from the shadows as they approached the manor house door. Christian. with a scowl on his face. ended the merriment of the group.

"Felise is looking for you," he said. "And you," he said glaring at the young men, "morning will be here soon, and you will be needed in the fields. You best get to your mats and sleep off your drunkenness!"

The young men backed away with uncertainty as one by one they said 'good morrow' to Emely and disappeared back into the darkness. Emely did not watch them go but stared at Christian.

"Felise!" he growled at her.

"Yes, milord," Emely said as she moved up the steps toward the door.

He reached out and caught her arm as she passed.

"Did they . . . have you?"

"What?" Emely asked and then realized what he meant. "No, milord, you did! You belong to another and should care not who . . . has me." She replied angry that he would even think she would ever be with another man. She pulled her arm from his touch, turned and walked away from him. She wanted to be as far from him as she could. For the first time in her life, Emely was rude to a noble, somehow, she knew it would not be the last.

Christian stood, his face turning stone hard as she walked away. He wondered how she could forget what they had meant to each other, how they loved each other. He, however, knew she had not forgotten. She was doing what she had to do, moving on, seeking warmth and affection from others who were uncommitted and free to marry and build a life with her. His heart ached to think of her in the arms of another, but he understood and knew he had to let her build a life without him as he would have to build a life without her.

The next day in the courtyard wagons were loaded with supplies and the possessions of those serfs who would go with Christian to his new home. Felise, Lord Duran, and Emely spent the day together riding through the woods. Emely and Duran did most of the talking despite their best efforts to include Felise in the conversation.

Everyone was up early the next morning. The carts were loaded, and the women settled. Emely watched as the manor gates disappeared behind the procession. The men, Lord Bryce, Benoit, Christian, and

Duran, all rode ahead to ensure the safety of the caravan while some of Lord Bryce's knights followed the last cart to protect the supply wagons. The four women rode in silence as they worked on their sewing, completing the last of the ornaments on the new or reworked gowns the family would wear during the marriage festivities. Even with the front and back of the cart uncovered it was warm and all four women were soon dozing. The cart hit a bump jarring them awake. Felise moved to the front and called to her father.

"Father, may I ride awhile? I need fresh air and it will help cool the cart for the others," asked Felise when Lord Bryce came to ride beside their cart.

"You may but take Emely with you and stay in sight of the carts," he agreed.

Two horses were brought to the back of the cart and the girls climbed on. Felise urged her horse to a canter as Lord Bryce reminded her to stay within sight of the caravan. Ignoring her father's words, Felise urged her horse to a gallop forcing Emely to do the same. Within a few minutes they were out of sight of the caravan and Felise slowed her horse to a walk.

"I cannot marry him," she said.

"You have no choice," Emely reminded her friend.

"I could run away, disappear at least for a while then when father has given up on this ridiculous idea I would come home. He would forgive me, he always does."

"Felise, your reputation would be ruined. You would never be able to marry. You would live your whole life as a dependent of your father or Benoit. If your father even let you come home. He could well send you to a convent."

"It would be better than being married to that old man. Really Emi he is old enough to be my father."

"He seems to be a very nice man."

"Then you marry him," Felise said pouting.

"You know it is not possible. He is betrothed to you and far above me in station."

"He likes you; I can tell."

"Felise, he is to be your husband. Nothing will change that."

"I thought you would understand," Felise whined.

Emely said nothing more. They rode in silence letting their horses walk slowly; both girls lost in thoughts. The little caravan caught up with them a short time later. The two girls returned to the confines of the cart after a scolding by Lord Bryce.

The caravan found a small clearing and camped for the night, noble women sleeping in the cart and everyone else on the ground. Emely watched Christian and Lord Duran as they sat by the fire late into the night taking the first watch. They seemed disinclined to talk. When sleep came to Emely it was filled with nightmares of hands pulling her down into darkness and despair. In the morning it appeared many had experienced the same fitful sleep.

The second day of traveling passed much as the first had but when Felise went riding Lord Bryce insisted, she stay with the nobles. When they stopped for the night, Emely ate and went to arrange Felise's sleeping space in the cart, before crawling onto her mat underneath the cart as soon as was polite. She turned her back to the fire and hoped for a more peaceful sleep than the night before, but sleep did not come. Most of the men had gone to their mats, she turned over seeking a better position and saw Christian and Duran had again taken the first watch and sat by the fire. Tonight, they seemed to be in deep conversation. Were they discussing Felise? Was Duran trying to get to know the girl through her brother?

When they woke in the morning, everyone looked forward to the end of their journey. Lord Rene's manor was less than a half a day away. They would feast and sleep under his roof this night. The sounds of shouted greetings indicated they had entered a village. Emely watched out from the back of their cart as they passed through the manor village. Once their cart entered the courtyard and stopped the women were helped down and the noble women joined their lords to be greeted by Lord Rene, his wife and young daughter.

CHAPTER 5

"Welcome to my manor, my friend, and all who travel with you on this joyous occasion, the joining of our families," Lord Rene said hugging his old comrade in arms.

"It is both an honor and a privilege to visit your illustrious manor and to the joining of our families. Please allow me to present my wife, Lady Martha, my sons, Benoit and Christian, Benoit's wife, Marilee, my daughter, Felise, and her betrothed, Lord Duran of Gaston."

It was the same formal greeting they always exchanged when visiting each other over the years. The real greeting, the handshakes and hugs would take place inside the manor house. It was not considered proper for the nobles to display deep affection for others who were not members of their immediate family in front of serfs.

"I am honored to present my wife, Lady Gracen and of course, my daughter, Lady Arianna whose marriage to your son, Christian, will join our families."

Lady Gracen stepped forward and dropped to a deep curtsey before Lord Bryce. When she rose and stepped back, a small dark haired girl stepped forward, giving Lord Bryce the same deep curtsey as her mother had. Emely looked at the girl who would be Christian's bride and wondered at her passive demeanor. When the girl stood, she moved not back beside her mother but in front of Christian where she again dropped into a deep curtsey.

"I welcome my betrothed and hope I please him so we will have a long and . . . successful marriage," said the girl in a voice so soft Emely barely heard her. Emely studied the girl. They had been betrothed sixteen summers ago and she would have passed her first birthday before such a ceremony would be held, so Arianna was perhaps seventeen, the same age as Felise and Emely. Emely studied the girl, noting a remoteness as if she was not an important part of what was happening. Arianna seemed more suited to the cloister than as a wife. Emely wondered if Arianna knew what would be expected of her so their marriage would be considered successful.

"Please enter my house and take your ease," Lord Rene invited as he offered his arm to Lady Martha.

The members of the household followed them into the manor, nobles to the great hall for the midday meal and the personal serfs of Lord Bryce followed Lord Rene's steward to the rooms allocated to their nobles. Emely unpacked the box containing Felise's things. Once satisfied everything was in order, she went in search of the kitchen to get a piece of bread and a ladle of porridge. Her mother, father and several of the other personal family serfs were already gathered around the table being questioned by some of Lord Rene's household.

"She's a quiet little girl, always has been," one of Lord Rene's older women said. "She will take any rowdiness out of him with her gentle ways."

"Lord Christian is not rowdy," defended one of Lord Bryce's serfs.

"They all are," replied the woman. "Tis their training, they never learn the gentle arts."

"No and be thankful for that," added one of Lord Bryce's serfs. "They protect us all. I would rather a rowdy knight than a noble whose greatest skill was the singing and reading of poetry."

"He can be rowdy with me," one of Lord Rene's young female serfs said.

"Be quiet girl," said the older woman. "You know nothing of being with a man rowdy or otherwise."

"So, you say," the girl said flippantly before flouncing from the kitchen.

"Silly lass, she will soon find herself taken and tossed and end up a camp follower," the older woman said shaking her head.

Emely felt a sharp ache go through her heart. Without knowing it, Emely thought, the older woman had described her future. She left the room without finishing her meal, wandering through the manor house not knowing where she was going, nor caring. The sound of a door opening ahead drew her attention. She saw Arianna walking away from her. Emely looked around and realized this was the private family area and moved toward the door Arianna had emerged from. Emely pushed open the door and discovered a small chapel. It was dark with little of the afternoon light piercing the window high on the wall behind the altar. Emely walked into the chapel closing the door behind her. She moved to the dais the altar sat upon and knelt, closed her eyes, and brought her hands together in prayer. She was not sure what she was praying for. She only needed the comfort of speaking to God in this way. She did not hear the door open or his footsteps as he came to kneel beside her. It was the warmth of his body next to hers making her aware of his presence. Emely opened her eyes and looked at Christian beside her, praying. Then as if aware of her study he turned and looked down at her.

"I am asking God's forgiveness for taking your innocence," he said. "I do not expect yours."

"I am as much to blame as you. I . . . I wanted to be with you, to know you, to have you know me," she replied.

"Not like that," he said. "We should have wed. We . . .."

"We, there is no we, and there never can be now" she answered, with a conviction she did not feel. She stood and left the chapel.

"Emely," he called to her as the door closed behind her.

She found a stairway up to the roof. Outside a breeze swept across the parapet as Emely looked out over the courtyard and watched as more nobles and their entourages arrived. She stayed on the roof long after the last arrival of the day, long after the sun had gone down, and the fires of the village cottages were visible. The sound of music from the celebration taking place in the great hall floated up and on occasion the sound of laughter. Wine and ale would flow unstopped until the wedding celebration. The moon was high when Emely finally left the roof to go to Felise's room. She would be coming to bed soon and would expect Emely to be there waiting as she always was.

Sometime later the door flew open, and Felise danced into the room, humming some tune to herself as she skimmed across the floor.

"You had fun," Emely said smiling. Felise loved to dance, loved being with people her own age, hearing the latest gossip and romances.

"Oh Emi" Felise babbled. "It was so much fun. Even mother and father were enjoying themselves and not frowning at me. They were too busy fawning over little Arianna. I suppose I will have to endure lectures of comparison all the way home but not tonight. Tonight, I danced and laughed and flirted."

"With Lord Duran I hope," Emely said smiling.

"Yes, even with the old man."

"Felise!"

"Well, he is."

"He will be your husband old or not. You need to show him the respect his rank and title require."

"Not his age?"

"Felise!"

"Oh, Emi please. Will I not have to endure enough lectures from mother and father? Please not tonight, not from you."

"Alright. Now into bed with you, dream about your new life at your new home."

Once Felise was tucked in, Emely lay down on the mat next to Felise's bed. She was still awake when the blackness of the room became gray and then silver as the sun rose bringing the morning light. Felise's soft stirring was Emely's signal to rise like the sun and prepare for another day. Once Felise was up, washed, dressed and out the door to break the fast, Emely followed her morning routine, but the rest of her day was spent not as usual in Felise's company but rather on the fringes of the household staff watching the arrival of yet more wedding guests. Emely watched Christian closest of all. She knew his moods, when his pleasure at greeting a true friend was sincere and when he was only doing his duty. He had trained to be a warrior not a court pretty boy.

He looked up and seemed to be searching until he saw her. The smile left Emely's face. She turned and moved away from the arrivals. She went again to the chapel seeking solitude and solace but there was none. Work, she needed to work, to be busy even if it had no purpose. Something to keep her mind free of the memory of their time together and the awareness of her future without him. Emely went to Felise's room and found cloth, needle and thread and began to sew without purpose, producing a handkerchief and then embroidering it with Felise and Duran's initials. She would present it as a wedding gift to her friend. Hours had passed when Felise returned. Felise burst into the room allowing the light from the torch outside the door to brighten the room.

"Was it not thrilling?" Felise gushed. "The music, the dancing, the men, I could have stayed for hours more but mother was giving me one of her disapproving looks" she said then giggled.

Emely said nothing moving with silent stealth. She did not listen to the other girl's monologue. She did not want to hear of the fun and happiness others were enjoying. Then she heard the words she least wanted to hear.

"Did you see Christian and Arianna dance? They did not look happy. Her unhappiness is beyond my understanding. I would be happy to be marrying someone like Christian; young, handsome, a warrior. I wonder what is wrong with her."

Emely stared at her friend. Felise had been no happier when she had met Lord Duran. While he was neither as young nor as handsome as Christian, he was a good man who wanted Felise to be happy. Emely was not sure Christian would wish the same for Arianna. The girls were both to be married to men they did not know. Neither seemed to take much joy in the future planned for them by others. They had that in common, but Felise had never been aware of her own faults or tolerance of those of others.

CHAPTER 6

Sleep came after hours of staring as the flames of the fire faded to embers. Dawn's first light streaming through the window brought Emely to full wakefulness. Today on Christian's wedding day Felise would attend Arianna, meaning Emely would be on her own the rest of the day. The Great Hall was aflutter with activity as household serfs set up tables and covered them with green cloths, Lord Rene's heraldry color. In the kitchen the activity level was even higher as twenty or thirty people scurried about in the oppressive hot cavern. Finding the head cook, Emely asked if she could help but was told no, there were already too many people falling over each other. Emely went out into the garden. Everywhere people were busy scurrying from one place to another, shouting orders to whoever would listen, but no one was. When she tried to help, Emely was shood away by Lord Rene's serfs.

Emely walked out of the manor enclosure and down the road to the serf village and to the commons where the men of the village toiled in the fields. Reaching the far end of open manor lands, Emely stopped and turned back toward the manor house. It would be foolish of her even in her unhappy state to venture out of sight of other people. The forest was not somewhere village or household people went unless they were very sure of their safety. Bands of villainous persons were said to be living in forests who would attack anyone unwise enough to enter the forest unprotected. The only reason Felise and Emely could do so at home were the patrols Lord Bryce had riding through the forest every day. She started an unhurried walk back to the manor house. Wondering about her future again, she hoped she would be chosen to accompany Felise to her new home.

Emely slipped once more back into the house through the kitchen and remembered she had not yet eaten. She asked the cook for a small piece of bread and a piece of fruit before going to Felise's room. Felise came bustling in a short time later somewhat out of breath and flushed.

"What a morning," she gasped. "Everyone is so excited." Felise gushed. "Everyone but Arianna," she added. "She is so distant, removed from everything, like this is the last place in the world she wants to be. She is like a guest at her own wedding, taking little part. Not the kind of bride Christian wants, I am sure. She will either have to learn to speak up for herself or be nothing but an afterthought in her own marriage. Not what I ever imagined Christian's wife would be. He needs someone with the same fire and strength. Someone who will stand up to him and not just do whatever she is told."

Emely listened to Felise's description of what she thought Christian needed in a bride and knew she was what he needed. Except she was not of the right station, she was not the daughter of someone who owned land adjacent to Lord Bryce's, not someone whose father commanded warriors who could be called upon in time of need to defend Lord Bryce's shire.

"Emely!" Felise said, "what are you daydreaming about? Help me, I am needed in Arianna's room. We must all attend to her this day, do her hair, add ornaments to her gown, change her shoes. It is like dressing a child. She just sits and seems oblivious to everything around her. It is like she is somewhere else. Anywhere else," Felise added with a giggle. "She is not of this world, poor thing."

Emely shook herself out of her stupor and gave Felise her full attention. Once Felise had washed her face, Emely tidied Felise's hair and added a pink ribbon to adorn her forehead. Her long braid was adorned with another pink ribbon and a few pink wildflowers were interwoven into the braid as Felise had requested. Felise admired herself in the polished silver disk. Satisfied with her reflection she sailed from the room after reminding Emely more ornaments would need to be added in a few hours for the ceremony and feast to follow. Emely smiled. Felise was sweet by nature but sometimes acted much younger than her seventeen years.

Once the room was straightened again Emely left and found a small niche overlooking the great room where much of the celebrations were taking place and watched the lords and ladies below as they moved about greeting old friends and meeting their now grown children.

Emely watched from her niche above them and could tell from the way Christian was acting and reacting to all the people who were greeting him, this was the last place he wanted to be. Trained as a warrior he was not accustomed to the genteel meaningless talk he was expected to engage in with the wedding guests. Watching Arianna, Emely noted the girl looked no more comfortable than Christian. Felise had been right, there was something ethereal about the girl. Her expression was indifferent to all that happened around her. She neither smiled nor frowned as she spoke. Emely turned her attention to the other guests. Laughter, smiles, and hugs were exchanged with old friends; exclamations of joy and surprise at new babies and young children not seen before. Happy exclamations at the growth of children, some of whom would be celebrating their own betrothals and marriages in the next few years.

The sounds coming from the great room were getting quieter, Emely realized. The number of people was decreasing as lords and ladies left to go to their assigned chambers to change for the wedding ceremony and the feast to follow. She left her niche and went to Felise's room and not a moment too soon. Felise bustled in behind her. out of breath, her cheeks flushed with excitement. Emely helped Felise out of her surcoat and tunic and into the much more expensive and elaborate garments she would wear tonight. Emely removed the pink ribbon and flowers from Felise's head and replaced them with a gold ribbon. When

Emely was done, Felise again admired herself in the polished silver disk and then again left the room. She came back a few seconds later.

"You need to dress also," Felise told Emely.

"Why?"

"Father has ordered all of our family serfs to attend the wedding. You will sit with Lord Rene's serfs but at least you will get to see Christian and Arianna get married," Felise said as if Emely would take great joy in watching Christian marry someone else.

If it was anyone else but Christian getting married Emely would be happy for them, but she could not be happy for Christian's marriage to someone else. She also knew she would have to attend, to not do so would have resulted in questioning, Questions she could not answer without facing unthinkable consequences.

"Do you want me to send someone to help you change?" Felise ask.

"No, no thank you. I can manage by myself."

"Hurry, the wedding will start soon, and you must be there," Felise said as she swept from the room again.

Emely sat on the side of the bed staring at the door for several minutes. Attending Christian's wedding to Arianna, anyone but herself, would be painful but she had to attend. Standing she opened the small bag she had brought with her containing the new blue tunic Lord Bryce had provided. In the great hall. Emely entered and went to stand with her parents and the other members of Lord Bryce's household. Her mother smiled at her and then turned her attention back to Lord Bryce's family. Lady Gracen stood a few feet away. Arianna and her father would not appear until the whole assemblage was in the chapel.

CHAPTER 7

Lady Gracen offered her hand to Lord Bryce as a bell rang out from the family chapel. They began to move toward the door. The other nobles fell in line behind them. They proceeded to a large chapel. Once everyone was standing in their appropriate place the doors closed and a small choir in the little loft began a Gregorian chant. Then the doors opened, and Arianna was escorted into the chapel by her father. While he smiled at the guests, Arianna never raised her gaze from the floor. She was dressed in deep green silk. The light green veil covering her long lose flowing hair was sheer and transparent. Lord Rene handed Arianna's hand to Christian at the altar and stepped back to stand beside Lady Gracen.

"We come together this day to witness the joining of Lord Christian of Tabow and Lady Arianna of Asque. You as their family and friends by your presence here are required to hence forth help and support them as they go forth from this day forward. Do you all pledge before them and all present you will fulfill this requirement?" the family priest opened the ceremony.

The gathering in unison pledged as expected. The priest then turned his attention to Christian and Arianna.

"You come to fulfill your betrothal promise made by your fathers many years ago. Do you Christian come of your own free will to take

Arianna as your wife and promise to live with her, honor her, protect her, beget children with her, and to live with her until the time when one of you is called to join our savior and all the angels and saints in heaven?"

"I do so come of my own free will to fulfill my betrothal promise and vow to live my life with Arianna until we are separated by death," Christian said with conviction and loud enough so all could hear. Then Arianna repeated the same vow but much quieter, so few could hear her. She must have spoken as anticipated because there was no unexpected reaction from those who could hear her.

"Christian and Arianna have vowed to live together as man and wife before this gathering and so they are declared to be joined as one in the sight of God and this gathering. Let us celebrate their joining with the sharing of the bread and wine of our lord Jesus Christ," the priest said before turning to the alter and beginning the mass.

Emely could feel the tears slipping down her cheeks, but she made no move to wipe them away fearing it would draw attention to her and again raise questions she did not and could not answer. She watched as the mass progressed, there was nothing she could do. She went when it was her turn to receive the host and sip the wine.

"We have witnessed the vows of Christian and Arianna and shared the body and blood of our savior," said the priest, "Now we go to share in the wedding feast as Mary, the mother of Jesus, his apostles and our savior did at Cana. Let the food we are about to eat and the wine we are about to drink be blessed as they were at Caan. Go in peace to love each other and serve our Lord. I bless you in the name of the father, the son, and the holy ghost, amen," finished the priest making the sign of the cross in the air.

Christian and Arianna turned and proceeded out of the chapel followed by the rest of the nobles and then the family serfs. In the great hall Christian and Arianna and their parents were seated on the dais with the guests seated at tables around the outside of the room. Tables had been set up for the family serfs who had attended the wedding. Lesser serfs would be celebrating in the courtyard, feasting on food and ale provided by Lord Rene. The celebrations both in and outside of the manor house would go long into the night.

Happy chatter filled the large room. the making of toasts brought Emely's attention back to the celebration in the great hall. Benoit, Lord Bryce, and Lord Rene each offered words of welcome, love, and support to the newlyweds. Lord Rene announced the many wedding gifts he was giving the young couple including a small manor and all the supplies needed to support the newlyweds. The manor would be close to functioning when Christian and Arianna arrived.

The meal finished, the celebration would begin with dancing and tables of fruits and sweets. Wine, ale, and mead would flow, and house serfs would be kept busy keeping the guests refreshed as they celebrated long into the night. Emely danced several times when asked by other serfs.

Christian watched Emely as she was swept across the floor even as he danced with his bride, mother, new mother-in-law, and his sister-in-law, all proper dance partners. Then he did something unusual, he approached Emely and her mother.

"Mistress Grace," he said bowing to Emely's mother, "may I have the honor of this dance?"

Emely's mother stared at the man before her in shock.

"I . . . I would be honored, milord," she said taking his outstretched hand and standing.

Christian swept Grace away in a swirl as many looked on in surprise before several other nobles followed Christian's lead and asked serf women of their household to dance. More surprisingly, Lady Martha asked Stuart, Emely's father, to dance. Lord Rene followed Christian's lead and asked Lady Gracen's personal serf to dance, and Lady Gracen asked their village reef to dance. When the music ended Christian escorted Grace back to her seat and thanked her. Then as the music started again, he turned to Emely.

"Emi, may I have this dance?"

"I . . . I am fatigued milord so thank you but no," Emely said smiling as best she could.

"I can make this an order," he said.

"Milord, please, no."

"Emi! Come dance with me," he cajoled using her childhood nickname. He put out his hand.

Emely took a deep breath before taking his hand and rising. They walked to the center of the floor and concentrated on each other, moving in harmony as if they had danced together many times before.

"I want you to come with us," Christian said as they made one turn passed each other.

"As what?" Emely countered.

"As handmaiden to Ariana. So, we can be together. So, I can watch over you and protect you."

"I am sure Ariana has her own handmaiden already. She does not need me."

"I need you!" he said.

"As what? Your woman of pleasure?" Emely asked.

"Lower your voice; others will hear."

Emely stopped dancing. forcing Christian to do the same.

"Thank you, milord, but I am tired and will retire. I have no interest in . . . dancing with you." Emely said angry with him for embarrassing her. She turned, leaving Christian standing alone in the middle of the room.

Christian watched her walk away. hurt and angry. Angry more at himself for his suggestion than at Emely for refusing. He turned to walk back to Arianna and met the angry glare of Lord Rene. Christian sighed and then turned to look at his bride. She looked at him expressionless, as if she cared not what he did. He smiled at her hoping to find a glimmer of warmth, but her expression remained unchanged.

Christian walked to their table still smiling, fake as it was.

"It is time for us to . . . retire," he said to her hoping to not frighten her.

"As you wish milord," she replied. "Good morrow father, mother," she said kissing each on the cheek before taking Christian's outstretched hand so he could lead her from the great hall to their bedroom.

It was long after dark when Felise returned to her room where Emely was waiting.

"Good night," Felise snapped at someone in the hall as she opened the door and stepped into the room.

"Good night, Felise. Sleep well," Lord Duran said.

"Oh, he is insufferable," Felise whined as she closed the door. "He treats me like I am a child who has to be protected everywhere I go. He is smothering me!"

"He is being attentive and respectful of your person," Emely said.

"You are supposed to be my friend. How can you defend him?"

"I am your friend. He is your betrothed. It is his responsibility to take care of you."

"I wonder if his first wife died of boredom. He is . . . boring. He does not like to dance, tells no funny stories, laughs not at the humor of others. Boring!"

Emely knew there was nothing she could say to change Felise's mind. So, she said nothing.

CHAPTER 8

Dawn was breaking and Felise began to stir. The morning routine they had shared for years followed. Then Emely again took her place in the niche above the great hall and watched the lords and ladies below continue the celebration from the day before. Christian and Arianna were there and once again the center of attention. Emely studied the other girl's face and expression. Arianna had dark circles under her eyes that had not been there before. Her skin seemed pale, almost white. On this the first full day of her marriage she should have clung to her new husband. Rather she seemed to recoil whenever he spoke to her or even looked at her as if she was afraid, he would pounce on her. Emely also noticed she was not the only one who observed Arianna's behavior toward Christian. Lord Rene looked none too happy with his daughter's reaction to Christian. He turned and said something to Lady Gracen. She looked at her daughter and new son-in-law and responded. It must have satisfied Lord Rene because he smiled and turned back to his guests.

Emely kept watch over Arianna and Christian. The younger girl said little and smiled even less. Her other worldliness was gone, and she seemed not to know her place in this new reality and the life she would now have. More interesting to Emely was how Christian was reacting to his young wife. He seemed to speak just above a whisper to her, smiling at her, and touching her arm with a gentleness warrior seldom demonstrated. He always included her in the conversation with the guests. Emely noted the change in his behavior. Could one night with Arianna change him, Emely wondered. She had never seen Christian this gentle before.

Two more days passed before Lord Bryce, his household, Christian and his new household departed Lord Rene's manor. Arianna hugged her parents and wept as if she would never see them again, before Christian helped her into the covered cart, she would ride in on their new home. Lady Martha, Felise, Emely, and her mother all took their places in their cart. Finally, all the good-byes were said, and the two parties left Lord Rene's courtyard. After they had stopped for the midday meal, Felise requested permission to ride, and it was granted on the condition Lord Duran accompany her and Emely. Felise was not happy but agreed as Lord Bryce made it clear there would be no repeat of the two girls taking off like they had on the way to Lord Rene's.

It was a beautiful late May day with a clear sky and a bright sun, a gentle breeze kept it from becoming too warm and the tall trees gave the path shade, helping to cool the path. The three rode in silence for some distance before Lord Duran spoke.

"You have asked me nothing of what will be your new home. Surely, there is much you want to know."

"Will I be mistress?" Felise asked, knowing Lord Duran's parents were both very much alive and it could be years before Felise would have any power over her new home.

"No, but my mother is eager to turn over much of the household responsibilities to my wife."

"Oh," Felise said sarcastically, "I will be able to arrange the household as I wish, chose the food that comes to the table, the chores for household serfs each day and the other ladies of the manor?"

"Well not quite all that," Lord Duran said, "but daily activities of my sisters and their serfs and your own, yes. My mother does not expect you to take on all household responsibilities at once. More will be added as you become accustomed to our manor and the relationships among our people."

"So, sewing, tapestry, and other decorative arts will be my responsibility. How demanding!"

Lord Duran, as if realizing nothing he said would pacify her, smiled.

Emely gave a short sigh knowing such tasks were far more than Felise had to do now. Emely had little doubt there was a lot more planning and preparation to be done than either she or Felise ever imagined.

"I need more exercise," Felise said after several minutes and gave her horse a kick sending it into a gallop.

Emely and Lord Duran had little choice but to follow. The wind streaming through Emely's hair felt good as if clearing all cares from her mind and spirit. Lord Duran caught up to Felise before Emely, so she did not hear what he said to the other girl but the look on Felise's face told the story. She had been reprimanded for her foolish action and it was clear Lord Duran would not allow her any more leeway. He had taken her reins from her and had turned their horses back toward the rest of their party by the time Emely reached them. They returned to the carts at a slow walk to allow the horses to cool down. Lord Bryce gave them a questioning look when they returned.

"We had a good gallop," Lord Duran said smiling at the older man.

Felise gave him a quick look, surprised he had not told her father of her careless action. Emely recognized Lord Duran was already protecting Felise both from herself and whatever punishment her father would have imposed. The party stopped for the night several hours later at a small clearing Christian and Lord Duran had found earlier. Everyone gathered around the fire and talked of home. In small groups over the next hour or two, everyone left the fire to take their rest until again only Christian and Lord Duran remained. The two men were in deep conversation. Christian asking as many questions as possible. It seemed Duran also had a number of questions about Felise. Emely presumed Lord Duran was trying to get some knowledge of the girl who was to be his bride in less than a fortnight. Perhaps he was giving Christian some advice on how to deal with a young and inexperienced wife. He had been through these first difficult days already and knew something of what Christian was going through. Then they fell silent again and Lord Duran took to his pallet leaving Christian alone staring into the flames. Emely watched him looking for some expression and was surprised when he looked up at her. For the first time since she had left him on the dance floor, she saw his expression change, soften. Then a hint of a rueful smile as if in acknowledgement neither of them would ever be happy because they would never be able to build a life together. Emely shook her head and turned away from him, this was only a dream, she knew.

At dawn all were up again and after eating a quick meal they were on their way again. When the sun was high in the sky, they stopped to say their good-byes to Christian and Arianna as they would be turning off to follow another small cart path to their new home. Hugs and promises to see each other in a week were exchanged. Christian and Arianna would come to Lord Bryce's manor for Felise and Lord Duran's wedding. Then Christian came back to Emely and again hugged her.

"I will always love you, Find someone worthy of you and be happy," he whispered before releasing her and turning to walk away.

Emely watched him mount his horse. Without a look back at her he turned and led the cart on the small path away from the rest of the group.

"Emely," Lord Bryce almost whispered beside her. "Is there something between you and my son?"

"No milord. He belongs to another and is far above me in station."

Lord Bryce stared at the girl he had known all her life and wondered but said nothing more.

The next day they arrived home and returned to an almost regular routine except for the increase in activity around Felise's upcoming wedding. Clothes she would take to Lord Duran's after the wedding had to be prepared. Serfs well trained in sewing worked from early morning to late in the evening. Emely, however, was not free to do as she wished. Felise often turned to Emely seeking confirmation of how beautiful she looked in her new finery.

CHAPTER 9

By the end of the week Felise had an almost new wardrobe, far too much to take to her new home so she gave it to Emely, as she had for years, things she no longer wanted. Emely supposed Felise planned only taking her to Duke Marcel's and Emely would be expected to be dressed in proper attire. The clothes were simple and not reflective of what would be Felise's new position.

Lord Duran had left to escort his father and mother back to Lord Bryce's, Duke Marcel and his family arrived two days before the wedding was to take place. Lord Bryce extended a welcome and the rest of his family greeted Felise's new family. Felise said all the correct things to Lord Marcel and his family even if she remained reserved toward Lord Duran. The next day Lord Rene and Christian and their parties arrived. From her place behind Felise Emely studied Christian. The weeks since his marriage had not been kind to him or to Arianna from the look of her. She still shied away from him when he spoke to her or tried to touch her in any way. The dark circles under her eyes remained. She now had a haunted look about her. Her other world tranquility was gone, and she looked like she had seen too much of a much less than perfect world. Not the happy union Lord Bryce and Lord Rene had hoped for but there was nothing any of them could do about it now.

The next day more guests arrived and the routine of welcome and greetings continued without any unpleasantness until the day before the wedding. Felise had sneaked away from the other ladies and sought out Emely.

"We must go riding," Felise insisted.

"Where are the other ladies?"

"I got away. I have to get away. I cannot marry him," Felise whined.

"Felise, you have no choice," Emely told her friend trying to be the voice of reason.

"I do. I can run away. I will run away but I want you to come with me."

"We can go riding," Emely offered, "but not off the manor and not without an escort."

"No!

"Felise, to run away would be the end of your life as you know it. You could never return, and no one would accept you into their manor. You would be sent to a convent at best, worst is beyond imagination. Think what you would be sentencing yourself to."

"I care not! I cannot marry him. I would rather die!" the other girl said before bursting into tears.

"You fear your future. Lord Duran seems to be nice, and he cares about you. He has made that clear by his words and actions."

"If you think he is so wonderful, you marry him," Felise yelled as she opened her chamber door.

At the door stood Lord Duran, his hand raised as if he were about to knock on the door.

"You again!?! Are you following me? Give me some peace. Go away. I hate you!" Felise screamed at the startled man as she pushed past him.

"Felise!" Emely called. Realizing the other girl was not stopping, Emely ran toward the door.

"She is running away. We must stop her!"

Lord Duran hesitated a moment before moving to catch the fleeing Felise followed by Emely.

They caught up with her halfway across the courtyard. Lord Duran wrapped an arm around Felise's waist and lifted her off the ground before turning back toward the manor house.

"I am taking her to her chamber. Bring her mother to her," Lord Duran ordered Emely.

"Go up the side stairs not through the main hall," Emely cautioned knowing the sight of Lord Duran carrying Felise would draw attention to them. Gossip would spread through the guests spoiling Felise's reputation and embarrassing both Lord Duran and Lord Brice. Wars had been fought over such incidents.

They separated just inside the great door and Emely found Lady Martha in the great hall. Emely told Lady Martha she was needed in Felise's chamber without going into detail. When Lady Martha and Emely arrived at Felise's chamber, they could hear Felise sobbing. Lady Martha went in, and Lord Duran came out into the hall looking ashen. It was evident Felise had continued her tirade against him. Once the door closed behind him, he leaned against the wall and closed his eyes before taking a deep breath. Emely turned to leave but then he spoke.

"Should I break our betrothal?"

"What?"

"She is so young. So unprepared for what is to come, for what will be expected of her."

"There must always be a first time. You . . . you understand. You will be . . . gentle."

Lord Duran studied her for several seconds as if trying to figure out how much Emely knew about life.

"I could make it sound like it was my . . . unwillingness. Her reputation would be safe."

"No," Emely said. "You are what she needs. Someone who will be patient and careful of her person. She will marry you on the morrow because she must. She will be your wife. Give her time. Your patience will be rewarded."

Lady Martha came out of Felise's chamber and Emely turned to enter.

"No, Emely. She needs to be alone. She needs to prepare herself for tomorrow and to realize how foolish she was being. Sometime alone with her own conscience is what she needs. I am sure your help would be appreciated in the kitchen or chapel as it is decorated."

"Yes, my lady," Emely answered curtsying before turning to leave.

Emely heard Lady Martha telling Lord Duran he must be patient before she was out of earshot of their conversation. In the kitchen Emely told the head cook Lady Martha sent her to help. She was sent to help prepare the vegetables and fruits for the next day's feast. In the kitchen, there was hardly any room to move as every available serf was put to work, It was long after dark before Emely and the other kitchen help were allowed to leave to take their rest. Most would be back in the kitchen before the sun was up.

Emely slipped unseen and unheard into Felise's chamber and lay down on the mat next to Felise's bed as she had every day since she was seven. Somehow this night was different. She had not been the one preparing Felise for bed; she had always been the one who said the last 'good morrow' to Felise. She was not, however, the one who would attend Felise the next day, the day which would change Felise's life from one of a carefree young girl to a wife and someday a mother. Emely fell into a fitful sleep long after she had taken to her mat. She was wide awake as light from the morning sun slipped into the chamber. Emely got up as she had for so many years and prepared the room for Felise's morning routine. Emely laid the new clothing out onto a bench as Lady Martha, Lady Marilee and the other ladies would be arriving soon to attend Felise. She would need to have her mother near to keep her calm. When she heard Felise beginning to stir, Emely went to Lady Martha's chamber and let her know Felise was waking. She returned to Felise's chamber. Lady Martha and Lady Marilee arrived a short time later. Emely was sent to help elsewhere in the manor house. She spent most of the day again helping in the kitchen. It was hours later when Emely's mother came looking for her.

"You must dress for the ceremony. We are to be included as guests," Emely's mother told her.

"My clothes are in Felise's chamber."

"No, Lady Martha has placed your things in one of the serf chambers; second at the top of the stairs."

Emely let the head cook know she was leaving and was thanked for her help. Walking through the manor, Emely noticed flowers had been cut and woven into long boughs and hung from pegs in the walls where normal weapons and battle flags were displayed. Musicians had arrived who would provide music for singing and dancing during the celebration; all was in readiness.

In the chamber a white tunic and light blue surcoat had been laid across one of the beds. Emely put on clean clothes after splashing water on her face, hands, and arms. She left the chamber and went to the great hall to join her parents. Everyone was waiting for Lord Bryce and Felise to come and head the procession to the chapel. Lord Bryce and Felise entered a few minutes after Emely arrived. Emely watched her friend and saw the strain on her ashen face. Lord Bryce led Felise followed by the rest of her family and Lord Duran's to the family chapel. Everyone took their place and Emely saw Lord Duran lean down to say something to Felise. The bride looked up at him and gave a weak smile as the priest began the ceremony joining them.

Lord Duran and Felise led the procession back to the great Hall after the ceremony. There a feast had been laid out. Lord Bryce and Duke Marcel's families took their appropriate places on the dais then the rest of the company sat in their proper places to partake in the meal before them. Emely nibbled at the food in front of her, watching Felise. In all the years they had spent together, Emely had never seen Felise so withdrawn. She barely touched any of the food offered and drank little of the fine wine being served. Emely watched as Lord Duran whispered to Felise and was rewarded by an occasional slight smile. Over the hours of the feast, Felise seemed to warm as her face softened and she responded to his obvious warmth and caring nature. However the reality of her situation must have occurred to Felise, and she slipped once again into moodiness, Her expression again became serious. The feast was over, and the musician began playing music for dancing. Lord

Duran led Felise to the floor so they could lead the first dance. They were soon joined by the other lords and ladies including Christian and Arianna. Even now, as Emely watched Felise, her expression changed little with only a rare smile for Lord Duran who continued his gentle sweet, charming, whispered chat. Dancing was one of her favorite activities and yet her unhappiness was obvious. Lord Duran was very attentive to her, but nothing seemed to lighten Felise's mood.

CHAPTER 10

After an appropriate amount of time, Lord Duran stood and offered Felise his hand, an indication it was time for them to retire for the night, their wedding night. The look of fear on Felise's face prompted her mother and Marilee to rise and move to attend to her. Emely followed the ladies to Felise's chamber. She reached it before they had and stood outside the chamber waiting for the others. When the others arrived, Felise was crying and clinging to her mother.

"Look, Emely is here to help you," Lady Martha said to her daughter trying to sooth the hysterical girl.

"No! I do not want her anywhere near me. She wants him for herself. She loves him!" Felise wailed.

"Felise," her mother said admonishing the girl.

"It's true and he wants her. I heard him offer to end our betrothal so he could marry her. She is not my friend. I hate her. I hate them both," Felise screamed.

Emely looked at Lord Duran who was as shocked as she was by this outburst. Then he took a deep breath and spoke.

"You are my wife; I want no other than you. Emely has been your true friend and has given me good council toward our future together," he said. "Ladies, my wife and I need to be alone," he said with a little more force, dismissing the noble ladies.

The ladies looked at each other before turning in unison and leaving the chamber. Emely hesitated a moment more before leaving also.

"I hate you," Felise screamed as the door closed behind Emely. It was not going to be a pleasant night for either of them. Emely returned to the Great Hall and the celebration. Seeing Christian with Arianna was just as uncomfortable as had been the scene in Felise's chamber. Emely returned to the serf's chamber where her clothes had been laid out and presumed she should spend the night there. Dawn was long passed when she woke. She went to wait outside Felise's chamber. Lord Duran emerged a short time later looking ashen.

"Emely, she needs her mother," he said.

Emely hurried toward Lord Bryce and Lady Martha's chamber. Her mother was just emerging, and Emely relayed Lord Duran's message. Emely's mother returned to the chamber and a few seconds later Lady Martha emerged and hurried toward Felise's chamber followed by Emely. Once there, Lady Martha entered the chamber but after a few minutes she returned.

"Emely, please get Felise a small repass and then asked the other ladies to join us here."

Emely curtsied and went on the errands. When she returned with the small plate of food, Lady Martha told her to see if she could be of use in the kitchen or elsewhere in the house. Emely went to the kitchen and again was assigned the task of cleaning vegetables. The head cook realized the finery Emely was wearing was not appropriate for the work she would be doing and suggested she get a serf tunic. For the first time in her life Emely looked like the other serfs working in the service of their lord. After hours of scrubbing and pealing vegetables the head cook came to Emely and told her to get some food. She took a small piece of bread and a tankard of watered down wine and went out into the courtyard. The sun was high, and the weather was warm. In days passed she and Felise would have been riding or at the stream to swim. Or at least enjoying a walk around the village to the edge of the clearing, enjoying the beautiful late spring day. Now she had no idea where Felise was or what her position in the manor would be. When she returned to the kitchen there were more vegetables to clean which kept her busy for several more hours. Finally, the day was over, and the kitchen staff could take their rest. Emely had no idea what was happening in the Great Hall for the next two days. The entire household was called to the Great Hall a week after the wedding.

Lord Bryce and Duke Marcel's families were seated on a dais. Emely noted Christian and Arianna were not present and most of the other guests were no longer here either.

"Tomorrow my beloved daughter Felise leaves our manor to go to her new home at Duke Marcel's. Some of our manor serfs will be going with her as part of her dowry. They have been informed of this. Tonight, for the last time as a daughter of this house we celebrate her marriage to Lord Duran. You who have served us so well and put forth the best our house has to offer are invited to join us in celebration tonight. Partake of our food and drink and share with the new couple your good wishes for their happy future" Lord Bryce announced.

A cheer went up from the staff. They moved toward the food laid out on tables around the room. While Lord Bryce and Lord Marcel and their wives left the great hall, Lord Duran and Felise stayed and moved through the staff. Lord Duran accepted the good wishes of the staff while Felise remained silent with a small smile on her lips. When they came to Emely, she curtsied and expressed her good wishes for them. Lord Duran smiled at her.

"You have been missed," he said with a gentle smile which surprised Emely.

Emely looked at Felise waiting for the unpleasant reaction she had displayed on her wedding night. It did not happen. Instead, Felise's smile deepened.

"Yes, you have been missed. I . . . I am sorry for what I said to you," Felise said. "I . . . I was scared . . . confused. Please forgive me."

"You are my friend. I knew it was your unhappiness speaking," Emely said.

Felise moved forward and wrapped her arms around Emely.

"I was such a fool. I . . . I did not request you come with me."

Emely signed knowing that they would continue their lives divided by time, space, and status as they had never been before. Felise released her.

"You will have many people looking after you at Duke Marcel's and your husband to take care of you. I will not be needed."

"Emely . . . I."

"Worry not. I have been working in the kitchen and learning so much."

"The kitchen?!" Felise exclaimed.

"Yes, you know where the food comes from," Emely replied half laughing.

For the first time in weeks Felise smiled a real smile. The happy light-hearted girl Emely had grown up with returned for an instant.

"We must move on," Lord Duran said regretting he had to separate the two friends.

The smile left Felise's face.

Emely saw Felise look back at her a few times before they lost sight of each other. The household serfs ate and drank to their fill and then in small groups returned to their work. Emely's mother came later to get her to be among the group bidding Duke Marcel and his family farewell. The required formal goodbyes were said at the manor house entrance. More touching were the hugs and tears of Felise and her mother at this partying. Emely saw Felise seem to search the gathering as if looking for someone until she saw Emely. Felise gave a small wave before turning and climbing into the back of the cart carrying her mother-in-law and sister-in-law. The cover had been removed so they could enjoy the sunlight as they traveled home.

CHAPTER 11

After the last cart was outside the courtyard gate Lord Bryce and his family went inside the house and the rest of the serfs returned to their work. Emely stood as a lone figure staring at the open gateway. Long after the cart had disappeared into the forest, she returned to the kitchen and the vegetables. Her life slipped into a new and very different routine than anything she had ever known. It was rare when she saw any of the lord's family or even her parents. Over time she made friends with some of the other young serfs who worked in the kitchen. Wearing the same clothes, doing the same work, sleeping in the same room, they came to accept her and include her in their gossip. Spring became summer without her realizing it. What she did realize was her once flat stomach was no longer flat; she got tired more easily. Then came the first of the fluttering in her belly. She knew something was happening, but she was not sure what and sought out her mother. Once Emely had told her mother what was happening to her, her mother's face went ashen, and a look of worry Emely had never seen before was there.

"Who . . . who did this to you?" her mother asked.

"Did what?" Emely asked.

"You are with child," her mother said.

"No," Emely protested then with less belief "no. How?"

"You have been too sheltered. I always thought there would be time to tell you when you became betrothed. I would have time to prepare you for marriage and what happens between a man and his wife."

Emely stared at her mother. Emely thought back to the day by the stream when she had lain with Christian the way wives laid with their husbands. Emely realized she was not a wife. She would, however, have a child. She would be alone and could never tell anyone who she had laid with.

"Who is the father? Lord Bryce and Lady Martha will insist he marry you."

"I . . .He does not matter. He is gone." Emely said.

"Emely you cannot do this alone. You need a husband to protect you and your child."

"No! I will do this on my own. He is gone. I will have and raise my child," Emely said. Her life was changing again. She would make decisions about her life and the life of her child on her own. She would do whatever she had to do to protect herself, her child and in due course Christian from any consequences to come.

"Emely! You have no choice."

"I have made my confession as to lying with a man when it happened. Who the man was is between God and me, I will tell no one else."

"Emely, you could be sent out of the manor house. You could be banished from the manor completely. Lord Bryce is a good man, but he cannot allow a woman without a husband who is with child to remain. The example would be unacceptable, you are too close to Lord Bryce's family. He cannot this let violation of God's law to go unpunished. He cannot allow you to stay in his house. You must tell so arrangements can be made for your marriage to the father."

"No! Whatever the penalties I will not speak his name."

"Emely!"

"No mother, no. I must get back to the kitchen." Emely turned and walked back to the kitchen with uncertainty, one hand protective over her abdomen, a slight smile on her lips, a child, his child. If she could not have Christian as she knew she could not, at least she would have his child. Then she stopped: not his child. Her child, hers alone for he belonged to another and would have children with his wife.

In the kitchen she returned to her work, but her thoughts were on the future, a future with her child, watching him grow into a fine young man. Her child would be a boy, she had no doubt. She would try to give him the kind of good education she had received. He would be different. He would be able to read and write. He could move to the city and become a merchant or tradesman. He could become wealthy. His children would be serfs to no one. They could rise even higher. Then Emely stopped her thoughts and laughed at herself. She was making plans for a far distant future. She smiled. It was good to have hopes and dreams for her child and his future. If there is no hopes, no dreams there could be no future, no goals to be achieved and she wanted her child to have goals, to have a future. It was her job to start him on his way.

The days passed. Emely worked in the kitchen making friends with the other serfs. Working hard and earning the praise of the head cook. She kept her secret as long as she could. Loose tunics and loose tied aprons covered her swelling belly, and she could always claim her enlarging waist as weight gain from being around food all day and tasting each new dish the head cook allowed her to make on her own. Cooks were always heavier than the rest of the serfs. Summer turned to autumn and on the few days she was given off from working in the kitchen; Emely spent wandering the manor as she had done all of her life.

"Emely," the head cook said. "You are wanted in the great hall."

The fall harvest was coming in. It was a busy time in the kitchen with everyone working longer hours than usual. It had to be important if she was pulled away from her work. She turned and headed toward the stairs leading to the main floor.

"Emely, your apron," said the cook.

Emely looked at her, knowing she could not hide her growing belly under the extra layer of cloth. She untied the apron and handed it to the head cook.

"Thank you for all your kindness," Emely said not knowing if she would be returning.

She climbed the stairs knowing her secret was a secret no longer. She entered the great hall and felt the tension in the air. Lord Bryce and Lady Martha were on the dais. Benoit and Marilee were standing to one side. Father Bernard was on the other side. Her parents were also there standing and facing the dais. Emely's mother gave her a look confirming Emely's fear. They knew.

"Emely," Lord Bryce started. "It has come to our attention you are with child." He spoke. "Who is the father? We would have him take you to wife."

Emely thought. What she said next would change her life.

"It matters not who he is," she whispered. "This is my child, and I will raise it by myself."

"That cannot be," Lord Bryce said.

"It must be," Emely countered.

"Emely, I have known you all your life. Watched you grow into a fine young woman in my house!" he said. "I will not let you be alone during this time. You need a protector; you need a husband."

"I have no husband and will never have one. I will protect myself and my child. Thank you for your care and the advantages you have given me. this I must do alone!"

"To lay with a man without the blessing of the church is a sin. You are in jeopardy of damnation," Lord Bryce said trying a different appeal.

"I have confessed my sin and received absolution. My soul and my conscious are free."

"Is this true? Did she confess?" Lord Bryce asked, turning to Father Bernard.

"Yes. The child came to me when . . . when she laid with the man. She gave her confession and did her penance, more than even I imposed on her."

"Who is the father?"

"I know not. She did not reveal his name."

"What? Did you ask?"

"Yes, milord, I ask. She said . . . he would have to seek his own absolution and make his own penance. It was not her place to reveal the sins of another."

Lord Bryce looked at the priest and then turned his attention back to Emely.

"Your father is the shire reeve. Surely, you went to him. He would have brought the man to justice."

"Milord," her father began before Emely cut him off.

"No, I did not go to my father," Emely said with spirit. "There . . . was . . . no crime."

"You lay with a man willingly?" Lord Bryce almost shouted causing everyone to gasp in surprise as he came to his feet. Emely had never heard him raise his voice before to anyone no matter how angry he might be. Lady Martha reached out to put a hand on his arm as if to remind him this was one of their own.

Emely closed her eyes to gather her composure. "Yes," she answered staring at the floor as tears began for the first time to well in her eyes. "Yes," she repeated.

The great hall was silent except for the soft weeping of her mother. Emely looked up at Lord Bryce. His face was white with shock. Then as she watched, it turned red with rage.

"And how many more have there been? Lord Bryce exploded. "You who have been like a daughter to me. Do my friends laugh at my expense because an easy woman lives in my house, sits at my table, and sleeps under my roof? Do you provide them more hospitality and warmth than is proper?"

"Bryce," Lady Martha gasp.

"Silence wife. You should have known. She attended to our daughter. And you!" he continued, turning toward Emely's mother. "What lessons did she learn from you?"

"Bryce," Lady Martha said trying to restrain her husband. "The sins of the child are not the sins of the parents."

Lord Bryce took several seconds to calm himself before he spoke again. "True. She has brought shame to our house. Because she will not reveal the name of the father, her absolution is in question. The almighty will be her judge. My responsibility is her earthly life. You can no longer live under my roof," he said turning to Emely. "You must be punished so others do not follow your example."

"I understand milord," Emely uttered.

"Go to the chapel and spend the night there in prayer and consider with care your refusal to reveal the name of the father. I will ask you again tomorrow the father's name and if you do not tell it I will tell you what your punishment will be. Leave my sight, now!" Lord Bryce said before sitting down again.

Emely curtsied before turning and leaving the great hall. The sound of her mother weeping followed her out the door. The chapel was empty as Emely knew it would be. She knelt in prayer and when it grew dark in the room she lay on the hard, cold floor to take her rest. Despite the conditions, Emely slept better than she had since finding out she was with a child. The secret was out; she no longer had to hide her swelling belly. She no longer had to make up lies. It was a relief, the weight off her mind. Now whatever happened she would deal with it in the open.

CHAPTER 12

When she woke in the morning someone had brought a bowl of water and a cloth so she could wash the sleep from her face. She said her morning prayers and then sat and waited to be called to face Lord Bryce. It seemed like hours later, but she could tell from the sunlight it was only an hour after she woke when her mother came to take her back to the great hall. They were all there again.

"Emely, I will give you one more chance to tell me the man's name so this can be made right," Lord Bryce said.

"If it would serve some good purpose, I would tell you, but it would change nothing for me or him. So, no I will not speak his name, not today, not ever."

"You leave me no choice. You cannot continue to live under my roof. I have found someone in the village who will take you in. You will have to work there like all the other village serfs to make your way."

"Thank you, milord. It is considerate."

"Your father will take you to your new home. You may take all your things with you."

Emely and her father went to the serfs' room as she changed out of the serf's tunic into one of the Felise's castoffs. She bundled the rest of her clothes into a sack. She also took with her the small purse where she had put all the coins she had been given at Christmas, Easter, and her birthday each year. She had never spent any because she had needed nothing. Emely did not know if they would be helpful in the village but just having them might be useful.

"Time to go," her father said.

Emely took one last look at the room. She had been happy here. For the first time she had friends who were her equals. She turned toward the door and smiled at her father as she left the room. No one was on the stairs or in the entrance as they walked through the manor. Emely thought it strange. Serfs were always moving about the manor, going about their daily chores. Even in the courtyard there was no one about. No men were standing watch on the battlements. Emely realized Lord Bryce had ordered no one to say goodbye to her. It was part of her punishment. Out in the village it was different, serfs went about their daily chores barely looking up as Emely and her father passed. They walked past the church in the center of the village and then several huts before Emely's father turned into a yard. The hut was small and in need of repair. The oiled cloth in window openings were dirty and stained. The door shook on its hinges when her father knocked. The woman who opened the door was old.

"Well come in," she snarled as if angry at the disturbance.

"Wilona, this is Emely," her father said.

"I know her name," Wilona sneered. "And I know why she is here. Done wrong girl! Now you have to come live with the low ones. Well, there will be none of your loose woman ways here my girl. You will work to stay under my roof."

"I understand," Emely said as she looked around the small hut.

A small fire in the middle of the hut with a pot hung over it was cooking the day's meals. The sticks and twigs making the walls were held together with twine but there were gaps between many of them, some bigger than the sticks. The ceiling was a thatch laid years before and was dry and brittle. Emely doubted it kept out much rain but kept in a thin layer of smoke from the fire.

"Not what you are used to, is it girl," Wilona scoffed.

"I will be content here," Emely gave Wilona a weak smile.

The old woman was taken aback, and it showed on her face. Then she smiled.

"Got a backbone. You will need it."

"I must return to the manor house," Emely's father said. "Your mother and I will come to check on you when we can. If you change your mind and will tell the man's name, Lord Bryce will let you . . . come home."

"No, my decision is made. My child will only be my child," Emely said knowing how much pain she had caused not only her parents but also Lord Bryce. His outburst the night before, she knew, was not really anger at her but at whoever had lay with her and then abandoned her.

Her father nodded, his sadness at the difficult conditions his beloved daughter would now be living under obvious in his expression. She had been brought up to live a life of comfort if not luxury. This was far from what he had wished for her. He left the small hut.

"That is your mat," Wilona said pointing to a small thin mat in one corner of the hut. "Food later," she added.

"How may I help you?" Emely asked, knowing anything she did would ease the woman's life.

"Stir the pot."

Emely did as she was asked even as she was looking around the inside of the hut. She could make this woman's life easier. She created a list in her head: a bench to sit on rather than the floor, a table to take their meals on, wooden bowls rather than holding their bread in their hands, more twigs for the walls and new twine, a second pot so this one could be cleaned. She had something to spend her coins on after years of saving them. Emely smiled to herself. Her life of ease and comfort gone, now by helping this old woman she would build a new life. Her son would be born here, and she wanted it to be better for him as well as Wilona.

"Enough," Wilona said. "Go get our daily bread from the baker. Tell him it is for me. He always gives me a left over loaf from the day before. Once soaked in the stew it is like fresh."

Emely nodded and started toward the door then turned.

"Where is the baker?"

"At the oven. Have you ever gotten bread before? What did you do all day, sit around gathering dust? Lazy girl."

Emely smiled. Wilona was not far from wrong. Felise and she had spent their days sitting around sewing or working on tapestries. Everything she had ever needed had been provided. Until she had gone to work in the kitchen, she had no clear idea what all the household serfs did. she had learned and now she would learn what the village serfs did. One of the household serfs, Lynnet, was getting the household bread for the day at the oven, Emely smiled at the other girl but rather than the greeting she expected, Lynnet turned away. Emely thought they were friends but then realized Lord Bryce had ordered her exclusion from the manor house to be complete. Other than her parents no other house serfs would associate or even talk to her. Emely sighed and then squared her shoulders and lifted her chin. She had made new friends once; she would do it again. Once she got the bread and returned to Wilona's hut, they ate their midday meal.

"Wilona, may I . . . improve your hut? Winter is coming and better walls and roof will make it warmer," Emely said with care hoping not to offend the old woman.

"Improve? Only burning this place down and building anew would improve it."

"Where would we live?" Emely asked with a small smile at the old woman's ironic response.

"This old place is beyond improving. It was my parents and theirs before them."

"Then we could build a new hut next to this one," Emely offered thinking about her coins.

"No," Wilona said. "Someone would take it from us. Better to have the old. No one wants it."

"So . . . we fix the walls and roof?"

"How do you expect to pay for such things? Remember none of your loose woman ways here. I will send you out into the cold rather than have shame come to my door."

"I will pay for the repairs. I have some coins . . .."

"You have coins!?" the old woman said in shock. "Tell no one. If the others knew, we would be killed on our mats."

"I will be careful." Emely said half laughing. "We can improve the hut, if you are willing to let me help."

"Do what you want," Wilona said distressed not at the changes the girl would make but at the jealousy the improvements might provoke among her neighbors. Emely was not taking her warning seriously.

"Your coin will be wasted on this old shack."

CHAPTER 13

Emely smiled. Wilona would be happy when all the work was done. They finished their meal then Emely followed Wilona out into the field where the other village women were helping with the harvest. The men were cutting the rye and barley, and women were picking up the grain tops. Wilona and Emely joined the others and although her size made it difficult, Emely tried to work as hard as the others. Whatever each family harvested from the common village field was theirs. Other fields were worked by specific families where they grew their own vegetables. Wilona showed Emely her section. It was not overgrown with weeds but had not gotten the attention other families had given theirs. Wilona also showed Emely her pigs and the goat which provided her with milk each day. By bartering some of her piglets each year, Wilona had been able to supplement her meager vegetables and grain and still have meat. There, however, was never enough extra to barter to cover the work needed to improve the hut. Emely knew she would have enough work to keep her busy and free to raise her son.

After they were done gathering grains for the day, Emely took one of her coins and found the villagers who did most of the hut building and upkeep. Emely tried to use her coins to negotiate a price for his work on Wilona's hut, but he would not accept them.

"We have no need for coins," he said. "Food and clothing are what are needed. Got any of those to offer me?"

Emely admitted she did not. It was the same at the iron monger and wood wright. What Emely thought would help ease their lives was of no use to the villagers. The wood wright's wife, however, was studying Emely's tunic. It was the one she was wearing when she left the manor house. The clothes Felise had given her were still tucked in the sack she had brought with her.

"Perhaps a new tunic for your wife," Emely suggested to the man.

He turned to look at his wife and saw the desire in her eyes. He looked back at Emely before agreeing. She agreed to return with the tunic later in the day. Emely then returned to the iron monger and carpenter and made the same offer. Both accepted after their wives expressed their excitement. Emely could not use her coins, but she realized she had things she could barter. Emely negotiated an addition onto Wilona's hut: a second room and a shed to house the pig as well as new bowls at the carpenter's. His wife would have both a new surcoat and a tunic. Emely smiled as she walked back to Wilona's. The women of the village would soon be wearing more than their usual drab brown tunics. Wilona's hut would now be big enough for both of them and the child Emely was carrying. She had no need for fancy surcoats. The remaining tunic would be made into swaddling clothes and gowns for the baby.

The next day the builder and his son arrived before Wilona and Emely left to go to the field. Emely explained what she wanted done to the hut and the additions to be made. The man smiled and nodded agreeing with her plans. It would take him a few days but everything Emely wanted would be completed. The new pot arrived from the iron monger and the wooden bowls and spoons from the wood wright. Wilona taught Emely how to milk the goat. This would be her job each morning. Then they went to the fields. While Wilona picked vegetables from her patch, Emely gathered grain. When the sun reached its highest point, they returned to the hut where the improvements were already obvious. They ate their midday meal after storing their morning gatherings. Emely walked to the baker's and got a loaf of bread. Then it was back to the fields. The following days were the same except Wilona took Emely to the forest where they gathered wild strawberries and rhubarb. Then they went to the orchard where they picked apples, pears, and plums.

The days passed. Emely was busy, too busy to think about her future or her past. she was content in her new life as she had said she would be. For the first time in her life, she had work to keep herself busy. She missed some of the freedom she had enjoyed with Felise but not as much as she once thought she would. She was learning something new every day. When the sow gave birth to her last litter of the year, Emely had watched as the piglets came one by one. Emely had never seen an animal give birth before. She wondered if her child's birth would be this easy. Three weeks later the piglets were weaned, and most were traded for a new pair of boots for Wilona, some wheat flour, and a few other 'luxury' items.

Fall was becoming winter. Emely had taken one of her fine linen tunics and cut squares from it to be oiled. The dirty window covering were replaced by these new pieces. The rest of the tunic was made into swaddling clothes for when her child came. What at first had been weak movement inside her now became stronger. She smiled as she rubbed her swollen belly and spoke to her child often as if he could understand all she said to him. She talked of his future and her hopes and dreams for him. He would not be a warrior if she could prevent it. She dreamed of better things for him.

The first snow of winter came and while there was no field work to be done, there was still sewing, salting, and animals to be cared for. The harvest was over, Emely had more free time. She walked through the village being greeted by the other villagers. She thought of herself as a villager now, she was one of them. Christmas was coming. The village would go to mass in the village church and give small gifts to the 'baby' Jesus, Wilona had told Emely. The gifts would then be distributed among the women in the village who would have children in the coming year.

Christmas was only a few days away when after she had milked the goat, Emely went to get their daily loaf of bread. Walking back to Wilona's several villagers were in a group outside the neighboring hut and were giving her strange looks. Emely smiled and greeted them, but they said nothing to her, which was strange. Often, they would smile back and invite her to join their conversation. She shook her head then looked at Wilona's hut. Four village men were walking out of the gate. They smiled and nodded at her as they passed but said nothing.

"Something strange is going on in . . .," Emely started to tell Wilona as she came through the door. Then she stopped. Lord Bryce was sitting on the bench.

"Milord?" Emely said curtseying while looking from him to Wilona who was huddled in the far corner away from Lord Bryce.

"Emely," he said in soft tones, studying the woman who stood before him.

Emely realized she had changed since last they had seen each other. Her face was thinner while her body was now heavy with child. Her clothes were a simple tunic covered by the one thick cape she had brought with her. She put the bread on the small table before removing her cape and laying it on her mat on the floor.

"Milord," she said again turning to face him. "Why have you come?" she asked. He was still her lord and could still banish her off the manor.

"You have been here for several months."

"Three, I came in September."

"Yes. Will you tell me the man's name? You should not be here. You should be at the house among those who love you."

Emely shook her head and smiled to herself.

"No, I will not tell. I … I am among the people who love me. Wilona has opened her home to me. The villagers welcomed me. I . . . belong here now."

"Emely, tell me his name!"

"No," she answered. For the first time she realized he was in pain as her parents were. They came to see her as often as their responsibilities allowed, with small gifts.

"Emely," he pleaded once more.

"I . . . honor you, milord. I . . . love you as a daughter of your house would. I would give my life to protect you and yours. I will not reveal his name. It will die with me, whenever death's dark hand comes to take me." She said as tears slipped down her cheeks at the pain, she caused the people who loved her. Her first tears since she had come to live in the village, and she vowed the last she would cry. She sighed, wiped the tears from her face and faced him with her chin held high. She had become stronger than she had ever believed possible. To defy her lord was not a wise thing to do.

Lord Bryce stood. He looked older than Emely had ever seen him before. Her time in the village had aged them both. She had grown into a woman through experience, he had grown old from the weight of the punishment he had imposed on her. Neither would nor could change the decision they had made.

"I had heard of the kindness you have shown Wilona and can see the improvement of this hut. I have also heard of your generosity to the other villagers. The village ladies are much more colorful than in the past," he said with a smile. "Such care and concern for others at your own expense should be rewarded. I have brought you a Christmas gift from Lady Martha and myself. It should help ease the time to come."

Emely looked around the room but nothing new seemed to have been added.

"In the new room," Lord Bryce said as he turned to leave.

Emely walked to the addition and there was a bed: crude by manor house standards but still it would keep her off the cold hard ground. She stood looking at it for several seconds. She went back to the main room, but Lord Bryce was gone. She ran out the door unmindful she was dressed only in her tunic. She caught him at the edge of Wilona's yard.

"Milord," she said. "I . . . I . . .. Thank you."

"Tell me his name and come home, Emely."

She stepped back in surprise before answering, "No."

He nodded and turned toward the manor house.

"Milord," Emely said drawing his attention back to her.

She walked to him and for the first time in her life wrapped her arms around his neck.

"Thank you," she said before releasing him.

He nodded again and turned back toward the manor house. She watched him go; his head hung in dejection. She turned back and returned to the hut. Inside she went to look at the bed again. Emely smiled, she and Wilona would rest easier this night. The bed included a stuffed mattress. When they added their covers, they would be warm.

"What will the villagers think?" Wilona lamented when Emely returned to the main room.

It made sense now, their distance. Lord Bryce thought he was doing something nice for her, but Emely knew his gift could be seen differently by the other villagers. She would have to work to regain their trust.

CHAPTER 14

Christmas came and the villagers went to mass. Father Bernard accepted their gifts for the baby Jesus and praised their generosity. The villagers set up tables in the church after mass and a celebration was held with music, dancing, and food. Beer and ale flowed, but Father Barnard kept a close watch to make sure no one over indulged. He knew spirits were being passed outside the church but would not admit it.

The New Year came and there was another celebration. Emely went about her daily routine, growing bigger each day it seemed. She and Wilona enjoyed the new bed and the ease with which they could get up each morning as the weak January sun came through their window. Emely had a cradle made and had made a small mattress for it from one of her tunics. One of the cotton surcoats had been transformed into a quilt she had hand sewn. Everything was ready for the child's arrival. January turned to February and winter swirled through the village bringing deep snow drifts making her daily walk to the baker harder. When she was over tired her child kicked deep within her, protesting. She reassured him she would rest soon, and he could once again settle in peace. Winter kept a cold grip on the manor. Emely was walking back to Wilona's hut one morning. Snow had fallen most of the night and continued making the day gray and bitter cold. Emely felt the tightening in her belly but ignored it then a second came several minutes later. the third would not be ignored. The pressure made her stop to catch her breath. She was almost back in the hut when the fourth tightening came, stronger than the last and longer. She stopped and waited for it to pass before going into the hut. the fifth as she put the bread on the table made her gasp. Wilona turned from the cooking pot to look at Emely. Her face went ashen.

"The child comes," she declared.

The tightness had passed but she knew Wilona was correct.

"Get the birthing woman," Emely requested.

"You sit and do not move until we return."

Emely just nodded knowing the last thing she wanted to do was move. She sat on the bench leaning against the table trying to take slow steady breaths and not panic. It seemed like hours before Wilona returned with the village birthing woman. The woman had Emely move to the bed so she could look at her and feel her belly.

"This one comes soon," Elga said. "Take your clothes off so they are not ruined with the blood when the child comes."

Emely did as she was told although every movement was more uncomfortable than the last. The tightness came at shorter intervals. It was hours later when Elga had Emely sit on the bench again and examined her closely.

"Tis close," the woman said.

Emely wished Christian was with her. He should share in the birth of their child. Emely almost said his name as the tightness came and encircled her, but she held it back letting out a cry of anguish more than pain. Then the squeezing stopped. Emely was at last able to breathe again, able to relax. She looked up at Elga smiling but the smile left Emely's face when she saw the uneasy expression of the birthing woman. The look on her face told Emely this was not right.

"You need to lie on the bed so I can get a better look," the woman said too quiet for Emely's comfort. Something was wrong.

Elga and Wilona poked and pushed Emely, The next squeeze that gripped Emely's body was harder and longer than all the others and the woman seemed satisfied.

"Sometimes the child stops moving, and the mother needs some help in pushing the child out."

Then another squeeze gripped Emely and she cried out.

"Help me get her to the bench," Elga said to Wilona.

The two women half carried, and half dragged Emely out into the main room and sat her on the bench. Elga had Wilona standing behind Emely and holding her at an angle so Emely could lean back. The next squeeze came and then another and then another. Emely wanted to cry out, but she knew if she did, she would say his name, so she held in her pain letting little pass her lips save a few moans.

"Now, push now," Elga ordered Emely. "It comes."

Emely pushed as she was told and took a quick rest before the next squeeze came. She pushed again and again when the squeezing came until the child was pushed from her body and into Elga's arms.

"Tis a boy," the woman said with some jubilation. She handed the baby to Emely as she finished her work. She had Wilona fetch a pot of water and wash the baby. She then wrapped the infant in the swaddling clothes before handing the tiny form back to his mother. Emely looked down at her son and cried happy tears.

"Rest, I will come back later." Elga said as she packed her things to leave.

As the woman left the hut Emely could see it was late as the sun had gone down and the village was lit by the light of the full moon shining off the new fallen snow. Wilona took the baby and put him in his cradle before helping Emely return to bed. Emely lay on her side so she could reach out and touch her now sleeping son. She smiled at his tiny form and wanted to take him in her arms and unwrap him so she could count his tiny fingers and toes. She fell asleep with her hand touching him as if to reassure herself he was real.

It was dark when a soft whimper woke Emely, and she realized it was coming from her son. Wilona lay beside her so Emely moved with hesitation to sit and lift her son into her arms. She guided his little mouth to her breast and felt a small tug as he latched on but nothing else. He still seemed not to be interested in feeding, so Emely just held him, smelling his new baby smell. It was hard to make out his features in the dim light, but she tried. She ran a single finger down his little face loving the feel of his soft new skin. When he had not taken any milk after several minutes and seemed content, she returned him to the cradle and went back to sleep. She remembered Elga's words, it was early yet. He, they, would do better with the sunrise.

Elga came a few minutes after sunrise and watched as Emely tried once again to feed her son. He still was not interested in taking her breast. Elga's face told the story of her concern. Emely questioned her.

"I have seen this before. It takes some longer than others to take the breast," Elga said trying to reassure Emely in her distress.

"How long?" Emely questioned.

"Every babe and mother are different."

Emely was not happy with the answer but as she looked down at her son she smiled.

"He will feed," she said more to reassure herself than the other two women.

Elga's expression did not change and Wilona, who had never given birth and knew nothing of babies smiled back at Emely and her son.

"I wish him to be baptized," Emely said. "Please ask Father Barnard to come."

"That . . . is a good decision," Elga said.

Emely looked up at the other woman and knew she had little hope for the baby's survival. When Father Barnard arrived, he was accompanied by Lord Bryce. Emely smiled to see the man who had been a second father to her present at this important moment in her life. The priest again asked Emely to name the father so he could be present for the baptism and again Emely refused. With a deep sigh the priest turned to Lord Bryce who gave a quick nod, and the priest began the short ceremony. He stopped at the place where the child was given his name and turned to Emely.

"David, his name is David, for he will have to conquer much in his life," she answered.

The priest studied her as if trying to remember who on the manor was named David, but none came to mind. She had reached back to the old scripture for a name. The priest continued the ceremony with Wilona and Lord Bryce standing as David's godparents. When the ceremony was done Lord Bryce gave Emely several swaddling clothes saying they were from the women of the manor house. Emely thanked him again surprised at the generosity since she had been so defiant. She held her son and when he whimpered, she put him again to her breast but again he took nothing. Lord Bryce and Father Barnard left. Elga made some suggestions on how to get the child to take nourishment. Some worked, most did not. at least Emely reasoned there was some progress. It would be difficult, but her child would live.

CHAPTER 15

Emely's life was now centered on her son. From the time she rose in the morning to the time she went to sleep at night her focus was taking care of her child. Looking into his green eyes and talking to him about his future. It would only be the two of them making their way through life. David's life filled with hope and promise but only if he took nourishment and grew into the fine man his mother envisioned him becoming.

First a week went by, then a second. Elga came every day to check on Emely and David. When she never referred to him by name Emely realized the other woman did not expect him to live. It seemed he grew weaker and lighter every day. David would stare at her with vacant eyes as she held him.

February changed to March, the days grew longer, and the snow stopped. The sun came up each day and began to melt the thick layer of white. Emely took walks in the village carrying David hoping the fresh air would stir some will to live. Father Barnard blessed David after mass each week, as if calling on God to save the boy. Nothing helped. Emely could feel her son slipping away from her more each day.

It was a bright sunny day. Emely decided it was a good day to be alive and planned to take David outside as she did daily for a walk and fresh air. She moved around the main room preparing wrappings to take him out before she got him from his cradle next to her bed. Wilona came back with the bread and Emely told the other woman her plan. Wilona smiled.

Wilona was no longer the distant and hostile woman of Emely's early days here in the village. She was friendlier now, not just to Emely but to the other villages who had stayed away from her in fear. The two women had formed a bond and the warmth of their bond had spread to others in the village. Their morning meal finished; Emely went to get David.

She lifted his little body, but he did not open his eyes as he had in the past. She spoke his name but still no response. She walked with hesitation into the main room fearful Wilona would confirm what Emely already knew but would not let herself accept. Wilona looked up from the pot she was stirring, smiling to see mother and child ready to leave the hut. Then Wilona's smile faded as she saw the pain and fear in Emely's face. She stood and went to them as Emely sat on the bench. What she saw made her draw back in unhappiness. Wilona left the hut, left Emely holding her son for one last time.

Emely was aware of nothing but the whiteness of David's face, the cool stiffness of his little body, the pain in her heart. She had prayed this day would never come, the day they would take him from her. She would never again see his sweet face, hear his soft whimpers, hold his little body. She sat rocking back and forth on the bench holding him close. They would not take him from her; she would not let him go. He was hers and she would keep him close to her heart until she too was cold and her skin white. They would go together; she would hold him in death as she had held him in life. She was unseeing of the shaft of light appearing and widening across the floor of the hut as the door was opened, unaware of Wilona going and then returning.

"Emely, give me the child" came a voice from a far off distance. It was too far to answer, and so Emely said nothing. She held David close to her heart.

"Emely, give me the child," came the voice again closer this time but not close enough to answer.

"Emely! Give me the child," came the voice again next to her.

Emely turned and saw Father Barnard standing next to her.

"No, he is mine."

"Emely, God has called him."

"God would not be so cruel."

"God is love. He calls those who have done him good service."

"God . . . God is nothing. What good service has David done? Why would your god call him?"

"God . . . knows it was the child's time. He will wait for you with the angels."

"David, his name is David!" Emely responded.

"God knows it was David's time."

"And mine."

"No, Emely, not yours."

"My work here is done," she stated.

"Emely, give me the . . . .. Give me David."

"No," she replied holding her son closer to her. They would have to pry her arms from around his tiny form. They would have to fight her to take her child and even then, they would have to force her not to follow and take him back into her loving embrace.

"Emely," the priest implored.

"No! Go away with your talk of God. A loving God would not have . . .," Emely stopped knowing she was about to admit what they were telling her was true.

"Emely," the priest said with loving concern one last time.

This time Emely refused to acknowledge him, focusing all her attention on the tiny body she held in her arms. She was again unaware of the shaft of light when the door opened. Unaware of Wilona, huddled in the corner of the hut watching her almost as if she was afraid. Emely was aware of nothing but the tiny body in her arms. She kept rocking back and forth as she spoke to David as if he could hear her. Her words were about her love for him and how much he meant to her, how he was the most important person or thing in her life. Nothing, nothing would ever separate them. She would keep him with her always. She did not notice when another shaft of light, weaker than the first, spread and then retracted across the hut floor.

"Emely," came a voice from far away. She had heard his voice most of her life, a voice she knew and trusted.

"Emely, give me the child," her father said.

"No," she replied. "You will put him in the cold hard ground."

"Emely, he is with the angels."

"No, he is here in my arms this is where he belongs."

"Emely, please, it is time to let him go to his rest."

"Do you love me?" she asked looking up at her father.

"How can you asked that?" her father responded, shocked she should ever question his love for her.

"Would you let anyone take me from you?"

"No."

"Then why would I let you take my son from me?"

"Emely," her father said with a catch in his voice. "He is already gone." He was in pain as was she. His beautiful loving daughter was hurting, and his first grandchild was dead. He could do nothing to help either one of them.

"No, he is here in my arms! I will never let him go."

"Emely," he started but then stopped knowing there was nothing he could say to change her mind. Perhaps her mother could get her to release the child. He left to bring his wife to his daughter.

Emely was aware of nothing but her son in her arms.

"Emely," came yet another male voice.

"Go away," she said. She had defied him repeatedly. She had left his house at his command. Why did he think she would do as he asked, ordered, now?

"Emely, I know what it is to lose a child," Lord Bryce said. "I held my first son as you are holding yours, his body cooling in my arms. I did not know if I could bear the pain. Lady Martha . . . she almost died. She did not know for days after. I was alone as you are alone."

Emely could hear the pain in his voice and looked up from her son's face. She saw the tears in the man's eyes. For the first time tears came to her eyes.

"How did you survive?" she whispered.

"I had no choice," he murmured. "People depended on me. Lady Martha, my knights, my serfs."

Emely felt the rawness in her throat. "He is so little," she said as the tears welled. "He will be so alone," she said as the first of the tears slipped down her cheeks.

"No, he will not be alone," Lord Bryce said. "He will be surrounded by those who have gone before, who will welcome him into God's holy place. He will have your love to warm him until you can join him many years from now.

"Not many years from now." she replied. "I will join him soon for I have nothing to live for any longer."

"Give me . . . David. I will take care of him as I took care of my own son."

Emely kissed her son's cool forehead one last time and then handed him to Lord Bryce. She knew she would never be able to tell him the child he carried away from her was of his blood. She could not cause him the pain of losing this first grandchild who he would have held precious. He would never know they shared this loss. The hut door closed behind him, and David was gone from her life. Emely stood and walked to the room where her bed was. She lay down and waited for death. Death, she hoped, would soon take her to her son.

CHAPTER 16

Christian – June 1095

Christian stood at the alter next to Arianna. He wanted to stop the wedding and take Emely and leave. He wanted to make her his wife, to have children with her, to sleep in her arms and wake to her smile. he knew it could not be. It would cause a war between his father and his father's oldest and best friend. His father could lose such a war. His father and brother dead, his mother and sister slaves at the mercy of Lord Rene's men. His father's serfs dead or enslaved. Even for his own happiness, even for Emely, he could not break his betrothal vow. So, he made the marriage vows. He did all he was supposed to do at the wedding feast until he could resist no longer and asked Emely to dance. He did not care what anyone thought, he had to touch her hand, gaze at her face one last time. Then he suggested she come with them. Emely was offended and he knew she was right to be. He watched her walk away and knew he could never have her even as a friend. He turned and saw the anger in Lord Rene's face. Sitting beside Arianna he tried to get her to talk to him, tried to find something in her they could build a marriage on. Finally, it was time for them to go to their marriage bed for the first time. He let the ladies prepare his bride but hated the thought of what he had to do to her. They were expected to produce heirs and there was only one way to do that. He was sure she was not prepared for what was to come. It had been different with Emely, they loved each other and wanted to be joined. The ladies left the bedroom one by one.

"Be gentle," Lady Gracen said.

"She is young," his mother said. "You will not mean to hurt her but the first time . . . is always difficult for a woman."

Christian hugged his mother feeling like he was going to his own execution rather than his wedding night.

Arianna was standing near the fireplace, eyes downcast when he entered.

"Arianna," he said. "What has your mother told you?"

"That . . .. you would . . . enter me and . . . leave your seed . . . and if God smiled on us I . . . I would be with child," she said, never taking her eyes from the floor.

Christian took a deep breath and took a step toward the girl. In fear of the unknown she took a step back. He stopped and took another deep breath.

"Arianna, please come to me so I can give you a hug," he said imploring her to accept him.

Fighting down her panic, at last she looked up at him. She had a childlike innocence about her, but she took a step, stopped, then another until she was a few inches from him, but her eyes were once again looking at the floor. He wrapped his arms around her and felt her stiffen. They stood, him holding her with only the slightest pressure until he felt her relax and she wrapped her arms around him.

"May I kiss you?" he asked with apprehension so she would not be any more frightened of him.

"I . . . I have never been kissed."

Christian pulled away from her a few inches, raised her face and smiled down at her before with great uncertainty he lowered his lips to hers using only the slightest pressure. She stood, eyes staring at him, lips unmoving, but she did not push him away.

"Now you have been kissed," Christian said smiling down at the girl.

"I . . . Will you kiss me again?"

"As much as you wish me to," Christian said smiling. "You must be getting cold in just your night tunic. Perhaps you should be in bed."

Her fear returned and she stiffened again but still did not push him away.

"If you wish milord," she said in a fearful little voice.

"Christian,' he murmured. "My name is Christian. I only wish you to be warm." He said releasing her.

He watched her walk with reluctance toward the big bed and then with uncertainty get under the covers. He disrobed and got in beside her.

"Come let me hold you," he said opening his arms.

When she came and lay close to him, he closed his eyes and imagined it was Emely. He kissed her forehead and then moved to her lips. Still no response, no softening and opening to him. He remembered; this was not Emely but a small shy girl. More important, she would be the mother of his children. So, he did what he had to do although with a lack of enthusiasm. She cried out at the moment of entry and then lay whimpering until he was done.

"I am sorry," Christian said when he rolled away from her.

She curled up in a tight ball protecting herself and sobbing. Christian touched her to try and comfort her, but she cried out as if burned. Christian lay staring at the ceiling listening to her sobbing slow and then end.

"God willing, we will be fertile, and a baby will come from this mating," he said praying he would not have to violate her again.

"If . . . not . . ., will you do that to me again?" she asked in a small voice indicating she was dreading the possibility.

"Yes," said Christian hating the thought of having to use her body. "Until you give birth to an heir. It is what your father requires of us."

"I will pray to the saints that your seed has found fertile ground, and a babe will grow in me," she sighed.

Christian hated Lord Rene for forcing Arianna into marriage. He hated his own father for forcing this on him. He hated himself for what he had done to this childlike girl and what he would have to keep doing until there was a babe. She fell into a fitful sleep hours later. Christian stayed awake. If she cried out and he touched her, she cringed away from him even in her sleep. He saw the first light of dawn and heard her stirring beside him. When they were up and dressed, he offered her his arm so they could go to the morning meal. She recoiled in fear, then with caution, slipped her hand around his arm. She still flinched away from him at his slightest touch at the morning meal and all through the day's activities.

They left Lord Rene's a few days later to go to their new home and still she flinched away from him. They spent little time together at their newly built home. He went to the village every day to check on the progress of creating a village where none had existed before. She spent her time in the little flower garden she created.

It was October and the first harvest was coming in, when Arianna told Christian she was with child. Christian stared at her before smiling and hugging her in happiness. She stiffened and then relaxed. It was over; he would not violate her again.

The months went by, and she grew great with the child. She was a tiny girl, and each day was harder than the last for her to do any task. Winter turned to spring. The snow melted and the first planning was done. Arianna was in her flower garden tending to it and the little shrine she had created there. April came, warm and promising a beautiful summer. Arianna was in the garden when the first discomfort came. She moved with concern into the cookhouse and let the cook know she might be ready for the birth of her child. The older women in the manor had told her what to expect. The birthing woman was sent for and arrived with Christian. He had already sent a rider to Lord Rene and his father. The birth was not easy. The baby, a beautiful girl, survived but Arianna did not. She was gone before her parents arrived. Christian held his beautiful daughter but did mourn the loss of his wife.

"Tell her how much I loved her," were Arianna's last words.

Lord Rene and Lady Gracen arrived the next day, but Arianna was already in the ground.

"You should have waited so we could have seen her one last time," Rene yelled at Christian.

"There was nothing to see."

"What did you do to her? Why did she die?"

"Women die in childbirth," Christian said.

"Better it was you who died. You killed her!"

"You want me dead! Who would care for our child?"

"We will! We will take her home with us and raise her as we raised Arianna."

"You are not taking my daughter anywhere!"

"I will destroy you," Rene yelled. "I will destroy this place, these people. Everything you have ever cared about. I will make war on you like you have never known."

"You want me dead! Kill me and the sin will be on your soul."

Rene looked at Christian, hatred consuming him then he knew what had to be done.

"No, I will not kill you, but you must do penance for killing my daughter. The pope has called for a crusade to the Holy Land. You go and I will not destroy this village. Survive and I might consider letting you live."

"What of my daughter? Do I leave her here?"

"No, we will take her home with us."

"NO!" Christian yelled. "You will pour your hate into her. No, I will take her to my father's. My mother will raise her."

Rene could not argue Bryce and Martha would not be good surrogate parents, so he agreed. Rene and Lady Gracen left the next day but left several knights to make sure Christian left his manor.

Two weeks later, Christian was ready to leave. He had chosen men to accompany him on the Crusade. The little caravan would include a cart for the wet nurse he had chosen from the village women and her children. Supplies for the trip to his father's manor were in a second cart. Christian mounted his horse and led the little procession from the village uncertain if he would ever see it again.

They arrived at his father's the next day. Villagers cheered as they passed through the village and into the manor house courtyard. His parents greeted him offering their condolences on Arianna's death. He went to the back of the cart to get his daughter, Gwyneth, and discovered a strange woman feeding the baby. When she spoke, he realized she was Emely. Emely holding his child just as he dreamed. Nothing was changed despite his joy at seeing the girl he loved holding his child as he had once dreamed. He would still have to leave, leave Gwyneth, and now leave Emely again.

CHAPTER 17

May 1096

She wandered the village. Her clothing was filthy and in rags. The tunic hung from her boney shoulders and touched nowhere on her emaciated body. Her once shiny hair was tangled and matted. Her blue eyes were vacant and empty. She saw nothing, heard nothing, felt nothing. Death had not come as she had prayed it would. For the first week without her son, Emely lay on her bed hoping to die. Then she had risen each morning and walked to the burial plot next to the village church. She would lay next to his grave, her arms lying over the little mound as when she had laid her arm over his little body in his cradle. She spoke to him as if he was still in her arms. She promised him she would soon join him, and they would be together forever. Her father and mother had come and laid flowers on the little plot but still she stayed and did not speak. Lord Bryce and Lady Martha had come and put a blanket over her and still she did not speak. Day after long day, she lived. Some nights she never left the little plot hoping the cold winter night would claim her, but it grew warmer, and the chill no longer cooled her skin even in the darkest hours. Day after day had passed, days had turned to weeks and weeks to months and still she lived. Wilona managed their hut and could on rare occasions get her to take a bite or two of food. When she passed other villagers, they would move away from her; little children would run frightened and crying to their mothers. No one spoke to her. Their sympathy and fear was lost on her. If she had come to live with Wilona because the other villagers thought the older woman crazy, now they thought worse of Emely.

The sun was high, the breeze was gentle, and the day was warm. The village hummed with activity, more than usual. Dust from passing carts rose and filled Emely's nose making her sneeze. For the first time in months, she became aware of something outside her pain and her wish to die. Traveling through the village was a small caravan moving toward the manor house. The villagers seemed to have stopped their work to watch it pass. Then Emely became aware of the sound, cheering. What she wondered, could cause the village to cheer. Had Lady Marilee had a child? The manor would welcome an heir for Lord Bryce. why the caravan? Were there visitors who came to welcome the new heir? Perhaps Christian and Arianna? Emely pulled herself from David's little grave and followed the caravan as the other villagers did. If it was Christian, she wanted to see him one last time before she died.

Not only were there carts but a group of serf men followed along. Emely recognized a few of these men. They were village serfs who had gone to live at Christian and Arianna's manor. So, he was here. why the carts? It did not make sense. She moved faster, pushing her way through the villagers until she was close to the leading cart. A baby's cry stopped her movement. The plaintive wail of a young baby could be heard. The carts stopped outside the gate to the manor courtyard and Emely was able to identify which cart the crying child lay. She reached it and pushed open the curtain at the back.

"No," said a woman's voice, "tis too bright."

Emely did not hesitate but climbed into the cart, closing the curtain behind her. In the dim light she could see a serf woman holding a noble baby. Its clothes were richly decorated in sharp contrast to the simple tunic the woman wore.

"Whose child is this?" Emely asked.

"Lady Arianna's."

"Where is she?" Emely asked not believing a mother even a noble woman would entrust so young a child to another.

"She died," the other woman said.

"Who are you?"

"The wet nurse. He chose me to take care of the child while he is away."

"Away?" Emely asked.

Before the woman could answer, the baby in her arms cried out again.

"The child is hungry," Emely stated the obvious.

"I am not making enough. I have a babe of my own."

Emely looked around the cart and saw the other children, a young boy, a younger girl, and another baby. She looked back at the woman. While the tunic she wore was clean and doubtless new this year, the woman herself as old beyond her years and had perhaps not eaten enough to feed both babies and still thrive herself.

"Give me the child," Emely said holding out her arms.

The other woman recoiled in fear. Emely looked down at her dirty hands and knew she could not hold this precious child as she was.

"Water, where is your water?" Emely asked. "And a cloth?"

The other woman pointed toward a bucket. Emely took the cloth from beside the bucket and put it into the water, and cleaned as best she could her hands, face and after tearing open the top of her tunic her breast.

"Give me the child," Emely requested.

The other woman hesitated but then complied because her own child was stirring.

Emely put the baby to her breast and felt for the first time the tug of a tiny mouth taking hold and drawing its nourishment from her body. Emely felt the pull of the baby sucking all through her body. Resting a little fist against Emely's breast, the baby opened its eyes to look at the source of its nourishment. Emely knew why she had been spared. Now she had a purpose, a reason for living again. If she could not be with her son, she would take care of Christian's child while he was away, wherever away was.

With a jolt the cart started moving again but only went a short distance until it stopped. Moments later the back curtain was flung open and bright sunlight filled the back of the cart, blinding Emely.

"What?" came a male voice Emely recognized from years of listening to his every word.

"She came, she . . .," began the other woman.

"Who are you to hold my child?" he demanded.

"Lord Christian," Emely muttered looking up from the child in her arms.

"Emi?"

"I did not know how to stop her?" wailed the other woman.

"No fear, Sarah. I know her. She will not harm the child,' he murmured after a few seconds of hesitation but never taking his eyes from Emely.

Emely could feel the tension leave the other woman. The baby at her breast stirred as if knowing the woman holding it was not giving it her full attention. Emely looked down at the baby and smiled. Her dream of holding and feeding her child was now as close as it ever would be. She was already in love with the small body in her arms. It would now be as hard to separate them as it had been to take David from her. Emely was a mother in need of a child, and this was a child in need of a mother.

"Follow me," Christian ordered and then turned to go.

"Wait," Emely called.

Christian stepped back so he could see back into the cart.

"Who should follow you?" Emely asked.

"You!"

"Not without . . . Sarah?" Emely asked looking at the woman across from her.

"I no longer need her, I have you to care for the child," he said as if it was obvious.

"You brought her here, you cannot abandon her," Emely said.

Christian started to say something but then stopped, looking at the frightened woman. He took a deep breath before agreeing she and her children could join Emely in following him. Emely handed the baby to Sarah and then climbed out of the cart. For the first time in months, she stood in the manor courtyard. Then she turned and took both babies from Sarah as she climbed out of the cart and helped her older children out. Emely handed Sarah's baby to her and turned to follow Christian. She heard a gasp come from Sarah and turned toward the other woman.

"Tis grand," Sarah said in awe of the manor house before them.

Emely turned and looked at the house she had grown up in. She had never thought of it as being grand. now seeing it through Sarah's eyes, she could see the beauty she had never appreciated before.

"Yes, it is," Emely said smiling before continuing toward the main door.

CHAPTER 18

"She may not enter," Lord Bryce said seeing Emely following Christian toward the door.

Christian stopped and looked toward the little group following him.

"Who may not enter and why?" Christian asked his father.

"Emely. She has been exiled to the village."

"Why?" asked Christian.

"She has not told you?"

"I have not seen her since Felise's wedding. I know nothing of what she has done. Why would you exile her?"

"Emely," Lord Bryce said turning to her. "You need to explain to us why you are not allowed in my house."

Emely took a deep breath and let out a sigh. Her answer was going to be hard and might cost her taking care of the baby she now held so dear. she had paid a price for her defiance before, and she would again if she must.

"I would not reveal the name of my child's father," she said loud enough so all could hear.

Christian's face showed his shock at this information. He had not been told of her situation.

"That is why . . .," he started. "She comes with me," he told his father.

"This is my house, and she is exiled."

"Then I will not enter. I will take my rest in the cart, and we will return to my manor on the morrow."

"Husband," Lady Martha implored Lord Bryce. "He will be gone so long, perhaps never to return from what will be a long journey. Let us have this time with our son."

Lord Bryce looked at his wife and then at his older son and then his younger. He could see in their eyes the shock at seeing Emely as she now was, dirty and unkempt. They had not seen the circumstances in which she had been living since her exile. Lady Martha had only seen the pathetic sorrowful woman who lay beside her child's grave. He seemed to consider with great apprehension what action he should take.

"Emely, will you tell me the man's name?"

"No milord," Emely answered. "I have chosen a path, and I will follow it for the rest of my life no matter what the cost, the punishment, or consequences," she continued in a way many would have found disrespectful.

Lord Bryce studied the woman before him. She had grown from the sweet compliant girl who he had known all her life to a woman strong and proud. She had the courage of her convictions and in this battle of wills he knew he would lose as he had already lost when he exiled her.

"She may enter," he said relenting.

"Sarah and her children come with me," Emely said indicating the woman and children behind her.

"Yes," Lord Bryce relented. "Welcome to my house" he said looking at Sarah. "Welcome home," he said looking at Emely with a slight smile. Then he turned and taking Lady Martha's hand went into the manor house.

"Thank you, milord," Emely said.

Christian entered the manor house door followed by Emely, Sarah, and the children. Inside Sarah continued to make sounds of wonder at the grand beauty of the manor house. In the entrance hall, Lady Martha turned to Emely.

"Lady Gwyneth, you, and the others may use the chamber next to Christian's. I am sure he will want to be close to his daughter."

Emely looked at the baby in her arms, a little girl, Gwyneth, was Christian's child, Christian and Arianna's, Emely corrected. Sweet, innocent Arianna who had died. Emely hoped the girl had had a chance to hold her child, to kiss her once, to tell her she loved her. Emely hoped Arianna was watching and would approve of her taking care of this precious child. Emely led Sarah and the children up to the chamber Lady Martha had indicated. It was like most of the bed chambers in the manor. One large window let the sun pour into the chamber. The large bed was designed for two adults. Emely knew she would not sleep in it. She would insist Sarah and her daughter take their rest there. She looked around for a place to put Gwyneth down so she could sleep but there was no cradle in the room. Emely knew the two babies needed somewhere safe to sleep. Sarah and her two older children stood in the chamber door staring at the room. Emely smiled, another new experience for them.

"Come in," she gestured to them into the chamber.

"We . . . we cannot stay here," Sarah breathed. "Tis too grand."

"Were you never in Lord Rene's manor house?"

"No, John, my husband, and I were only village serfs."

"You are with Gwyneth and me. You will not only stay here you will take your rest and regain your strength. You will help me with her. I have much to learn."

"You are a mother," Sarah said.

"My son . . . died," Emely answered.

"Oh, I am so sorry. God has blessed me," Sarah said looking with love at her children.

A knock at the door caused Sarah to react in fear. Emely opened the door realizing the other woman expected to be told to leave at any minute.

"Lady Martha said to bring these to you," said one of the male house serfs.

Emely looked at the three men following him, Two were each carrying a cradle. The third had a cloth bag. Emely smiled; Lady Martha had known what would be needed. Lord Bryce and Christian would never have thought of this.

"Thank her for us," Emely said opening the door wider and indicated where the two small pieces of furniture should be placed.

As the cradles were being placed the third put down the large cloth bag. Seeing Sarah's smile, Emely guessed it was clothing and bedding for the children. Once the cradles were in place, she thanked the men for bringing them. She opened the cloth bag and found bedding for the cradle and clothing for Gwyneth. She handed Gwyneth to Sarah and prepared one cradle for Gwyneth. When she was done, Emely put Gwyneth in the cradle and took Sarah's baby from her so she could prepare the other cradle. Once both babies were down and Sarah's children were on the bed taking a nap, Emely asked Sarah to watch the children while she went and got food for all of them. Leaving the chamber, Emely realized for the first time how filthy she was. She went to the kitchen and sought out the head cook.

"May I have a bucket of water and some cloths?" she asked. "I need to wash," she added with a half laugh.

The cook pointed toward a bucket and got her some cloths and a bar of soap. The cook also got Emely a clean tunic to replace the rag that gave little covering to her body after months of wear.

Emely took the bucket and clothes and went out into the yard outside the kitchen to the private area at the back where she and Felise had hidden as children when playing in the garden. She started with her face and worked down until the water was brownish gray and at least the first layer of dirt was off her body. She dumped the bucket and went to the well to get another. House serfs were there, but none spoke to her. They did not know she was no longer exiled. She took the bucket of water back to her hideaway and washed her hair the best she could. She put the tunic on and knew it would take a while but at least she looked presentable once more. She refilled the bucket, rinsed it out and then filled it again before returning it to the kitchen. Emely then sought out Christian. He was in the great hall with his family. They stopped talking as she entered. Emely moved to stand before him and gave her best curtsy.

"Milord, a favor, if I may?"

"What is it you wish?" Christian asked.

"A tub and water so Sarah and the children can wash the dust of travel from their bodies and a second smaller one so I may do the same for Lady Gwyneth."

"Granted," he said and gestured to one of the male serfs to take care of her requests.

"Thank you, milord," Emely said again curtsying before she turned to leave.

"She looks different," Emely heard Lord Benoit say.

Yes, Emely thought, I do look different. I am different. Exile has made me so.

"The child is gone the woman has emerged," Lady Marilee commented.

Emely ignored the comments. She was now a guest in this house and would do nothing to give them a reason to exile her again. Up in the chamber, the children were still sleeping, and Sarah was mending her daughter's tunic. Then she thought about Wilona. The other woman must be wondering where Emely was, although she had gotten used to Emely being gone for hours, sometimes days. Wilona knew where to find her and coaxed her to come back to the hut for some nourishment and rest. Sarah and the children washed and changed into clean clothes while Emely fed and changed a now awake Gwyneth. The baby studied Emely's face as she suckled. Emely found herself talking to the baby as she had talked to David. She found herself smiling for the first time since he had been born. It felt good to have a purpose and a warm cuddly baby in her arms. When Gwyneth was done feeding, she remained awake and watched Emely's every movement. The two were bonding so quickly. Emely rocked the baby for a long time, enjoying the sweet smell of her. Finally, Gwyneth went back to sleep and Emely was able to put her back in her cradle. She asked Sarah to stay with Gwyneth so she could go to the village.

CHAPTER 19

Emely slipped out of the manor house by the kitchen door as she had been doing since she was little. She was almost to the gate when Christian called to her.

"Where are you going? Where is the child?"

"I must go check on my friend in the village. Sarah is with Gwyneth. She is sleeping."

"It is late," Christian said. "You should not be walking through the village at this time."

"I have lived in the village for many months. No one will harm me."

"I will go with you."

"NO! I do not need your help."

The two stared at each other until Emely realized she could not stop him. She turned and walked out of the gate very aware Christian was following behind her. Emely found the other woman stirring a pot but looking pale and weary.

"Wilona, are you ill?"

"So, you came back at last," the other woman said. "I could not find you and I needed your help."

"I am sorry. Lord Christian is back and . . . he has a daughter who needs care."

"I am in need of care," the old woman whined.

"What can I do?"

"Fetch me some water and bread."

Emely turned to get the bucket they used for water and found Christian standing in the door of the hut. The look on his face showed the distaste he had for the little hut. She saw it through his eyes. She remembered how she felt the first time she had walked in. she had come to love and then hate these little rooms. They had surrounded her at the time of her greatest joy and greatest sorrow.

"I will get them," Christian said taking the bucket from Emely. "Stay with your friend. She needs you."

It was the first sign of change in him. Perhaps they had both grown over the last year. She turned back to Wilona and took the spoon from her hand.

"Go to bed. I will bring you your meal when it is ready," Emely told the older woman.

Wilona stood from the bench and with hesitancy made her way to the other room. Emely felt regret she had abandoned the woman even when she was here, she had been unaware of how much of a burden she had become. Emely vowed she would make up for her oblivious behavior. She could not be here all day, but she would come every day to see her and make sure one of the other villagers helped Wilona with the daily chores.

When Christian returned with the bread and water, Emely prepared a bowl for Wilona and took it into the other room. She helped the older woman sit up in the bed and made sure she was eating before she left the room. Emely then got another bowl and started to leave the hut.

"Where are you going?" Christian demanded.

"The goat needs to be milked. Can you do that?" Emely asked knowing the answer even as she ask the question.

Christian stared at her.

"It is only in the yard. You will hear me if I call," Emely said half laughing. The nobles living in the manor house knew so little of serf life.

Emely returned with the milk a short time later and gave a mug to Wilona. She stayed with the older woman until she fell asleep. Emely covered Wilona as she would a sleeping child and walked from the room. She signaled for Christian to follow her and left the little hut. She ask the woman in the next hut to look in on Wilona the next morning and told her she would return in the afternoon to check on her friend. Then she walked back toward the manor house, Christian still following her.

"They like you," Christian said.

"Who?' Emely asked without turning toward him.

"The old woman and the neighbor," he clarified.

"I like them. They are my friends," Emely said.

Christian looked at her but said nothing, so they walked the rest of the way back to the manor house in silence. Entering the manor house, she went up the stairs to check on Sarah and the children. The older children were up from their nap and playing in hushed tones with occasional bursts of laughter. Sarah was rocking her baby. Emely checked on Gwyneth and found she was awake but content to lay in her cradle. Emely picked her up and walked to sit beside Sarah. She knew so little about taking care of a baby, so she began to ask questions. Some made Sarah laugh. Emely's lack of knowledge was extensive. Sarah answered Emely's questions the best she could. Later, after they had once more put the babies to bed, a knock came on the door. Neither of the older children seemed to take notice and Sarah, while glancing at the door, did not get the panicked look she had earlier.

"The lord and lady call you to the evening meal," said one of the young messengers.

"Thank you. Come Sarah, children, we go to table," Emely said.

"They do not mean us also," Sarah protested.

"If I go to eat, you and the children go to eat." Emely answered. "Come children. The food here is wonderful. Lord Bryce's cook is the best in the kingdom."

The two older children scampered toward the door leaving their mother little choice but to follow. In the great hall, the Lord's family and household serfs were gathered for the evening meal. Emely took her place beside her parents and made sure Sarah and the children were seated near her. She wanted to make sure Sarah and the children ate. Emely's mother was so happy to see her daughter back in the manor house. Her father was a bit wearier as if waiting for something to happen which would send her back to the village in disgrace.

"I see we have some new guests this evening," Lord Benoit said looking at Sarah and her children.

Emely saw Sarah flinch and start to stand.

"Yes, milord," Emely said. "Lord Christian brought them from his manor to help care for Lady Gwyneth."

"You are doing that now are you not?"

"I have much to learn about caring for a baby, milord. Sarah is helping me."

"Does she have to come to table?"

Emely looked to Christian and Lord Bryce to stop this, but both were watching her to see how she would handle this challenge but saying nothing. "It has been your father's custom since I . . . we were children to welcome to his table all household serfs. Would you change this?"

"Not for our own."

"Sarah is Christian's household serf as am I now. Would you send me away from his table?"

"No," Lord Benoit said.

"No," Emely repeated. "Where I go Sarah goes. Where Sarah goes her children go. If I am called to table, she and they are called to table with me."

"You have been exiled once for defying my father, it can happen again," he sneered.

Emely stared at him. She had no idea where this hostility was coming from.

"Enough!" Christian said.

"You know what she is?" Benoit questioned his brother.

"Yes," Christian answered. "She is the wet nurse to my child and is under my protection. Sarah goes where Emely goes!"

"Her child . . .." Benoit started.

"Her child died because she was not protected by those who should have taken care of her. You included brother."

The brothers glared at each other for several more seconds before Lord Bryce spoke.

"We were all at fault," Lord Bryce said ending the intense exchange between his sons. "I gave Emely a choice. She chose a different path. It is possible we both regret our decisions, but we cannot change the past. We can only move forward. Now sit down both of you. This is my house and I wish her to stay. When she stays, Sarah and her children stay. Sit down!" Lord Bryce ordered.

"We will be hosting other nobles" he continued, "who are coming to travel with Christian to the Crusade. We will be united in support of each other with no sign of dissension. While we are protected from our immediate neighbors, others would be willing to make war on us to get our lands. You are my heir Benoit and will demonstrate your duty and respect for me as your father and lord by abiding by my rules and customs. Christian your manor will be in our keeping until you return. Lord Rene has agreed to respect your manor since Gwyneth is his only heir. She is as precious to him as his daughter was."

Both of the younger men sat down, and Lady Marilee was speaking in hushed tone to her husband. Emely watched them. Their marriage had not been a love match any more than Christian and Arianna's had been. Now they were faced with the child Arianna had conceived within a few months after her marriage to Christian while Benoit and Marilee remained childless. Emely could only guess Benoit's outburst at her had been his frustration. She had had a child, Christian had a child but Benoit, the oldest and the heir had not presented his father with the next generation of their family.

When dinner was over, Emely led Sarah and the children back up to their assigned chamber. She and Sarah fed the babies one last time before taking their rest for the night. Moonlight lit the chamber as

Emely lay on a mat on the floor next to Gwyneth's cradle. She thought of all she had to do the next day. Take care of Gwyneth, check on Wilona, asked one of Wilona's neighbors to make sure the old woman ate every day till she was able to care for herself, milk the goat and work her field so she would have vegetables at harvest time. She would also visit David's grave and tell him of her new responsibility of caring for a motherless baby. Her day planned, Emely went to sleep and rested better than she had since realizing she was with child; that seemed so long ago now.

CHAPTER 20

With the sun rise all were awake. The older children lingered in the big soft bed they had shared with their mother the night before. Emely asked Sarah to help her comb her hair. While cleaner than the day before it was still tangled. It took them an hour to clear the tangled mess but then Emely's hair fell like a waterfall down her back. Just as they were finishing there was a knock at the door. Sarah's son, Holt, went to answer. Flinging the door open in his excitement he turned white and took several steps back at who was standing outside the chamber. Then Christian entered.

"Good day," he said to no one in particular. "I thought I should check on . . . Gwyneth," he explained his presence.

"She is well. She slept through the night and is happy and alert this morning," Emely said smiling at the baby who was lying in her cradle making happy sounds. "Would you like to hold her?" Emely asked teasing, sure his answer would be 'no.' Babies she was sure were not something he would like or understand.

"May I?" he looked at her wondering if she trusted him enough to hold this precious child, his child.

Emely was surprised but regained her composure.

"Of course," she answered smiling as she went to pick up Gwyneth.

She walked back toward him seeing the confusion on his face. Was this the first time he had held his daughter, she wondered.

"Sit down," she ordered. "Put out your arms and fold them toward you," she instructed before placing Gwyneth in Christian's arms.

He looked down at his daughter's little face and studied the baby as intent as the baby seemed to be studying him. Then Christian smiled.

"She is . . . beautiful," he said. "I did not know I could . . . ." then he stopped and looked up at Emely.

She realized he was too much of a warrior to admit his love for this little child he and Arianna had created. Then she thought of the child they had created and knew Christian would have loved David just as she did.

"She is . . . so good. So trusting we who take care of her will always protect her and love her."

Christian said nothing, still intent looking at his daughter in his arms. He must have been holding her too tight because she began to wiggle and whimper.

"What is wrong?" he asked like any worried parent would. "Did I hurt her? Is she well?" he asked, looking a little panicked and indicating Emely should take the baby. He did not want to be holding her when she started crying.

"No, she is fine," Emely said smiling as she took Gwyneth.

"The morning meal is ready. Come to table," he said.

After they had eaten, Emely again left Gwyneth with Sarah while she went to the village to check on Wilona. Christian did not follow her this time for which she was grateful. It would allow her to also visit David's grave and lay a flower on it.

Wilona was still in bed, so Emely made her a morning meal, milked the goat, and tidied the hut. They talked for a short time and Emely let Wilona know all the arrangements she had made to ensure the older woman would be taken care of even if Emely was not here to help. Emely stayed until Wilona was sleeping again and then left to go to the graveyard next to the village church. She sat beside David's grave and told him about Gwyneth. While she sat there a shadow fell over her and the grave. Emely turned and looked up to see Christian standing over her.

"Your son?"

"Yes," she answered.

"Why did you not tell my father who the father was?"

"Because it would not have changed anything."

"You would not have been exiled."

"David is . . . was my son."

"Was he my son?"

Emely stared at the man she loved and decided he needed to find that answer on his own. "He was my son. that is all anyone needs to know," she said.

"But. . .."

"But nothing," she said standing to face him. "It would have changed nothing. The man was gone, married to another."

"But . . .."

"But nothing!" she yelled at him. Then she regained her composure. The shock on his face reminded her she was now in his employ, and he could take Gwyneth away from her. She would be left with nothing again and the pain of losing Gwyneth would be equal to losing David.

"I beg your forgiveness, milord;" she began "I should not have spoken to you in that manner. Please forgive me."

Christian looked at her and then the little grave behind her. He was sure David had been his son, their son. He should have been here to protect her, to celebrate his birth and comfort her when he died. Perhaps if he had been here David would not have died. They could have had the long and happy life they once dreamed of sharing.

"Did he live long?" he asked, a sadness she had never heard before in his voice.

"A fortnight. He was never strong."

He stood staring at the little grave for several more seconds.

"The midday meal is being prepared, and Gwyneth wants her . . . friend," he whispered then added gruffly, "Time to return to the manor house."

Emely smiled at Christian's embarrassment. Warriors were not trained to be fathers and expressed their emotions with rarity. She turned to walk out of the graveyard. When she got to the entrance, she realized he was not following her. She turned and saw he was still standing at the little grave, looking down at it.

"Christian," she called but got no response. "Lord Christian," she called again louder.

He turned then to face her and walked toward her with weariness. He had lost her, he had lost his son, and now he was going to lose his daughter. They walked in silence back to the manor house, each lost in their own thoughts of what could have been. She went to feed Gwyneth, and he went to the great hall. In their chamber, the babies were fed and then the women and children went down to the midday meal. Sarah and the children could eat with the family without question. Lord Benoit did not look at Emely. The meal was over, Emely led Sarah and the children out into the garden so the children could run around and get some fresh air. Lady Martha and Lady Marilee and their personal serfs including Emely's mother, came out a short time later with their sewing.

"May I hold her," Lady Martha asked Emely.

Emely handed Gwyneth to Lady Martha and the bond between grandmother and grandchild was formed.

"I remember when Felise and you were this small," Lady Martha said smiling. "The two of you were such happy babies. Your mother and I would talk for hours about how beautiful both of you were."

"I remember running around this garden and picking the flowers," Emely said laughing. "You were not happy with us."

"No not in front of you. You both had to learn to respect what belonged to others and to take care of the flowers. When you were not around, your mother and I would laugh at the silliness of children."

Emely looked at her mother who was also smiling, remembering happier days.

"How is Felise?" Emely asked, thinking of her childhood friend for the first time in months.

"She will be here later today. Lord Duran's younger brother is one of those going to the Crusade with Christian. Some have already arrived this morning more will be coming tomorrow."

"It will be a big group going to this . . . crusade?" Emely asked.

"Yes. The Pope has offered absolution to all who go to take the Holy land back from the infidels and those who die in God's services are assured a place in paradise," Lady Martha explained.

"Felise . . . is happy?"

Lady Martha looked at the woman who had been beside her daughter most of her life and knew she would soon see for herself. Her letters had revealed much, but nothing could be changed.

"She is . . . adjusting," Lady Martha said.

Emely saw the look Lady Marilee gave her mother-in-law and knew there was more than even what Lady Martha was hinting at. Minutes later Lord Bryce entered the garden.

"They are arriving," he said indicating the ladies should join him to welcome the next group. Lady Martha handed Gwyneth back to Emely as she stood.

"You should come," Lady Martha said to Emely, "Felise will want to see you."

Emely stood. Sarah and the children followed her. Emely smiled; she now had her own helpers. Lady Martha led the group through the manor house to the main door where they joined the rest of the household to greet the new arrivals. Emely had not been aware earlier of the number of people who were in the courtyard but there were tents at one side of the yard and extra horses at the stable. The main gate opened to welcome the new arrivals. Emely could see a tent city had sprung up just outside the manor house walls. The group entering the courtyard was led by Lord Duran and his younger brother, Michael. Following close behind them was a cart.

When they reached the steps to the manor house, Lord Duran and Michael stopped and got off their horses. Lord Duran went to the back of the cart and was helping someone get out. It was Felise and she was great with child. He helped her walk toward the steps and her smiling parents.

CHAPTER 21

"Welcome Lord Duran, Lord Michael," Lord Bryce said. "Please enter and take your ease."

"Thank you," Lord Duran said. "My brother, my wife, and I appreciate your hospitality."

Emely smiled. It was all so formal as if Felise had never been a member of this household before. Once the greetings were over, Felise moved with awkward haste to embrace her mother and then her father. Then she turned to Lord Benoit and Lady Marilee and last to Christian. It was after she had hugged her family when she saw Emely and made a sound of delight before she realized Emely was holding a baby.

"A child, you have a child?" she questioned.

"My daughter," said Christian.

"When?" Felise asked, shocked at this unexpected situation.

"The baby is Lady Arianna's," Emely said.

"Oh, then you can serve me."

"No, I take care of Lady Gwyneth," Emely stated.

"Why? Arianna can care for her own child," came the petulant whine.

Several seconds of silence followed as everyone thought how best to let her know Arianna had died so soon after giving birth.

"She died," Christian said at last. "Emely is my daughter's . . . guardian."

"Died!?" Felise said, the beginning of panic in her voice.

"Guardian?" Lord Bryce questioned.

"Yes, guardian," said Christian answering his father with a firmness not usual for a son to his father.

"What about Arianna? She died. How? When? Why?" Felise questioned, her panic rising.

"Does not happen to all," Emely said. "Many women give birth and live long lives. You have a loving husband and family who will care for you. Fear not and put your trust in God and those who love you."

"My mother and the other women of my father's house will help you," Lord Duran said to calm his vulnerable wife.

Emely smiled. He had learned how to deal with Felise's temperament; how to quiet her fears and panic. Lord Duran took Felise's arm. "Let us enter your father's house so you can rest," he said.

"You will use your chamber," said Lady Martha.

"I want Emely," Felise insisted.

"She is not available," Christian said.

"I want Emi!" Felise insisted again, this time shaking off Lord Duran's hand.

"I will come see you when I can," Emely said. "Lady Gwyneth is only a baby and must be attended to before all else."

"I . . .," began Felise before she was cut off by Christian.

"She will come when she can," he said in a tone that allowed no opposition.

Felise looked at her brother and knew she could not cajole him, and her whining would not move him. She turned and started into the house. The others followed her leaving Emely, Sarah, and the children on the steps. Christian was the last to follow, Lord Bryce and the others.

"She will not be happy," he said half smiling.

"Take no joy in her situation," Emely admonished him. "She could lose her life just as Lady Arianna did. Whatever small comforts we give will ease her way."

Christian stopped smiling. "Go to her when you can. remember Gwyneth is first in all you do."

"I will never put anything or anyone before Gwyneth. She is my life now!"

She left Christian standing in the entrance hall as she, Sarah and the children went to their assigned chamber. She had been harsh with him, and she knew it was unfair of her. She would have to apologize. he needed to know or perhaps be reassured Gwyneth was her life. The babies were fed and put down for naps before Emely went to Felise's room. The door opened in response to her gentle knock. Lord Duran looked exasperated, and Emely could hear Felise crying.

"May I suggest you go have a cup of wine with Lord Bryce" Emely asked smiling at the anxious man.

"Will you stay with her?"

"We need to talk she and I, women things," Emely said with a slight laugh, her smile widening.

"Thank you," he said as he moved past her and out the door.

"Emely," he said turning toward her once he was in the hall. "You have been missed . . . by both of us," he said.

"Thank you, milord." Emely said touched by his appreciation.

"Emely? Emely! I need you," Felise whined.

"What can I do for you, my lady?"

"My lady?" Felise asked. "You have never called me that before."

"You were my friend not a lady like your mother. It has been a year and we both have changed. You are a wife and about to become a mother. I am still a simple serf," Emely answered.

"You were never a simple serf," Felise said smiling for the first time since Emely had seen her leave the manor almost a year ago. They had both changed so much and their lives had moved in such different directions.

"Why can you not stay with me? With all the servants here, there must be someone else to take care of Christian's baby."

"He has chosen me, and I welcome the responsibility. Tis better than being a kitchen or village serf."

"What would you know of village serfs?" Felise scoffed.

"I have lived in the village since before Christmas. It was only yesterday when Lord Christian arrived, I was allowed to return to the manor house."

"What? Why? My father would never send you away . . . unless you did . . . something."

"I defied him. I would not tell him the name of my child's father."

"You have a child? Where?" Felise asked excited.

"My son died a few weeks after he was born."

"Who was the father? You can tell me."

Emely had been through this so many times before. Knowing Felise as she did, Emely had no doubt if asked, Felise would reveal the name without hesitation.

"I have kept this secret and will continue to keep it. It is of no importance now."

"Please, what secrets have we not shared all of our lives?"

"We were children. Now we are both women and there are some things we cannot share."

"tis me," Felise whined again.

"It is good you are home . . . here," Emely said standing to leave.

"Stay, I promise not to ask again," Felise cajoled.

"Gwyneth will be waking from her nap and will need my attention."

"Emely?"

"I will see you at evening meal," Emely said smiling at her friend as she took her leave.

The rest of the afternoon passed. Lord Bryce's extended family and one other group of nobles shared the evening meal. One more group would be arriving the next day and after a day of rest they would all begin their journey toward the Holy Land. The talk at the nobles table was about how the infidels in the Holy land were harassing and cheating Christian pilgrims. The Pope had called for a Holy crusade to take back the sacred places.

Felise seemed to be in a better mood. Especially since one of the other men, Piers, was another younger son and about Felise's age. He was very different from Lord Duran and flattered and flirted with Felise. Felise flirted back blushing and giggling when he spoke to her in whispers only, she could hear. Emely watched her friend and worried. She also watched Lord Duran and Felise's parents who were also observing her inappropriate behavior. It became obvious Lord Bryce intended to speak to either Piers, Felise or perhaps both of them. Lord Duran spoke to Lord Bryce. The two exchanged quiet words and Lord Bryce remained in his chair; a less than happy look on his face.

CHAPTER 22

The next morning was a repeat of the day before with Emely going to check on Wilona. Walking toward Wilona's hut, she noticed the large tent encampment of the serfs who were traveling with the other nobles. Not only men but also women and children occupied the tents. The wives, and children of some of the serfs. They would continue to travel with the group all the way to the Holy Land because they could not work their holding at their own manors. Emely saw the hard life they were leading and knew it was far worse than anything she had experienced in the village. She was also aware of the number of men who had no women with them. She was aware of their eyes following her as she walked through the encampment.

At Wilona's she found the other woman still ill and began to become more concerned. She checked the neighbor to make sure Wilona was taken care of and was eating and resting. The neighbor assured Emely she looked in on Wilona at least three times each day and even had her oldest daughter stay with Wilona and make sure she ate and rested. Emely tidied up the hut and made sure there was plenty of firewood. She sat and talked with Wilona for a time, but the older woman kept drifting in and out of sleep and after a time Emely left to let the older woman get the rest she needed. Passing through the village, she was greeted by the friends she had made during her time there. It felt good to once more be accepted by these people she had come to love and respect.

She was not aware of the three men following her as she passed through the tent village. as they drew closer, they began to speak to her, offering to show her their tent and more. Because she ignored them, they got bolder, beginning to state their intentions with regard to her. Emely walked a little faster hoping to reach the protection of the manor house gates before they got bold enough to touch her. She did not make it. Passing a tent, an arm came from behind her and pulled her against the hard body of one of the men. A hand was put over her mouth and nose so she could not yell or even breathe. Emely wiggled to try to break loose but the arm around her only tightened. She felt herself being dragged backward. She tried kicking backward at the man holding her and was rewarded by a grunt of pain. More hands tried to grab her thrashing legs. Emely took advantage of being able to see him. Before he could grab her legs, she kicked out. She knew she had hit him when he crumpled to the ground with a howl of pain. The third man bent over the first and then turned toward Emely with a menacing look on his face.

"You bitch," he said lifting his hand to strike her.

Emely again took advantage and lifted both her feet off the ground and kicked him also. Her foot connected with his chin, and he too went down. The man holding Emely was caught off guard by having to hold her full weight and collapsed to the ground taking Emely with him. Hitting the ground Emely felt him exhale as breath was knocked out of him. Stunned, he released her, and she scrambled to her feet. She turned and was going to run but slammed into a wall of male chest. Without knowing she raised her hand to slap whoever it was. before her hand could connect, a larger hand grabbed her wrist.

"Emi!" Christian said.

She stopped and looked up at him, all fight and flight leaving her.

"The bitch near killed us," said the second man as he was rising from the ground.

"Unfortunate she did not, for now your masters' will have to deal with you. Who do you belong to?" Christian asked as the other two men began to stand.

"Lord Michael," said one.

"Lord Piers," said the second.

"You have no need to tell me," Christian said to the third. "I will deal with you later. Now all of you leave before I run you through right here."

Emely watched as the three men scurried away.

"You will have a guard with you whenever you go to the village until we are gone," he said in gentle tones so he would not frighten her. Emely had no doubt she would not be allowed to walk anywhere outside the manor house gates without a trusted warrior with her.

"I can take care of myself but thank you," she muttered.

They walked back to the manor house in silence and parted in the entrance hall. She walked up the stairs and down the hall toward their assigned chamber with an outward calm that belied her inner turmoil. Once at the chamber door, she took a moment to rest against the wall. She could not go into the chamber as upset as she was. Even if Sarah and the children did not notice, Gwyneth would. The little girl had become sensitive to Emely's moods and responded in the same way; happy when Emely was happy and upset when Emely was upset. Once she had calmed herself, she entered the chamber and she smiled at the sight before her. The children were playing, and the two babies were on a fur on the floor wiggling and smiling with joy at being outside the confines of their cradles. The peace and happiness in this chamber wiped away all fear. In the garden, after the babies were fed and the midday meal eaten, the children ran chasing butterflies. Lady Martha and the others joined them, and the women enjoyed several hours of pleasant conversation.

Emely, Sarah, and the children were leaving their chamber when Lord Michael and Lord Duran approached Emely.

"Emely?" Lord Michael asked.

"Milord," Emely responded curtseying.

"Lord Christian told me one of my men attacked you in the village today. I am so sorry. The man has been spoken to and as a punishment he will only receive half ration for the next week. He has also had to give a confession and receive absolution from your manor priest. I was clear to the priest it should be more than just a few prayers. He was also told he had to come to you direct and ask your forgiveness. My brother and sister-in-law have always spoken very highly of you. I am so sorry."

"I thank you milord."

He nodded to her and turned to leave.

"He is a good man," Lord Duran said watching his younger brother walk away. "He wanted to be much harsher, but the man will need his strength during their journey."

"Twill be hard watching the people we love go away. Wondering if they will ever return to us," Emely said.

Lord Duran said nothing but smiled down at her. Then he too walked away to go down to the evening meal. Emely followed. One more day was all they had and then the lords and their followers would be gone. Once everyone was seated and was partaking in their evening meal Lord Piers stood.

"Emely," he called across the hall bringing it to silence.

"I have been told you had an unfortunate experience with one of my men today. He has been dealt with," he finished and sat down.

"Thank you, milord," Emely said.

"Dealt with how?" Christian asked so all could hear.

"Dealt with," was Piers curt answer.

"How?!" Christian pressed.

"Since he is my man how I deal with him is none of your concern. I understand one of your own men was involved. Did you deal with him?"

"Yes," answered Christian.

"How?" Lord Piers asked.

Christian leaned back in his chair and gave Piers a look intended to frighten the man and it did. Piers had the good sense to look humbled and dropped his eyes, so he did not have to look Christian in the face.

"I gave him twenty lashes," came Christian's response after several seconds.

A gasp came from those present. Lord Piers went white.

"He will deliberate with care before he ever attacks another girl," Christian added.

The hall remained silent for several more seconds, then Lord Bryce spoke.

"I have ordered no one from the manor house go unaccompanied into the village."

Several sets of eyes turned to look at Emely. She was the only one from the manor house who went to the village. She finished her meal in uncomfortable silence and went to their chamber.

"My lady," Sarah said.

"I am not a lady," Emely corrected her, surprised the other woman would misuse the title so easily.

"I . . . I want to go to the tent village," Sarah continued.

"Why?"

"My husband is there."

"What? Why did you not tell me before?"

"I . . . did not know how long we would be here."

Emely smiled at Sarah. It was clear she loved her husband very much. He would be gone they knew not how long. They wanted, needed this one last time together.

"I will talk to Lord Christian. I am sure it can be arranged. The children can stay with Gwyneth and I tonight," Emely added smiling.

"My lady."

"I am not a lady," Emely said again but from the smile on Sarah's face Emely knew it would do no good to change her mind.

Emely went and found Christian still in the great hall and explained what Sarah wanted. He smiled and told Emely to send Sarah to him and he would take care of her request.

"Emely," he said as she turned to leave.

"Milord?"

"What would you like? You must have some request."

"I . . . I would . . .. Nothing except to care for Gwyneth."

Christian studied her for several moments.

"If you could do that without . . . guidance . . . assistance . . ., would you? Could you?"

Now she studied him. "I . . . Yes."

"Today when those men grabbed you, what would you have done if I had not been there?"

"What I did! Fight."

"Fight," he said with a smile. "Fight you did. Who would you fight? Anyone, everyone? Would you fight to protect Gwyneth? Would you fight to protect what is not yours? Something or someone in your keeping but not yours to keep?"

Emely stared at him. What test was this? Was he trying to tease her as he had before?

"I would do whatever it took to protect Gwyneth and anything or anyone I was given responsibility for."

Christian smiled. "Good. Please, send Sarah to me."

Emely stared at him a moment more before going back to the chamber and sending Sarah on her way. She and the older children played a game, and she told them a story as they lay on the big bed and went to sleep. She smiled at their innocence. If Christian had been suggesting Sarah and her children would be sent back to his manor, she would fight him. Sarah and her children needed protection and Emely was determined she would be the one to provide it.

Christian watched her go and knew what he was planning was risky, but he wanted to protect his manor and the people he had left there. She had stood up to his father and himself. He believed she would stand up to Rene. He went to talk to his father.

"Father," he said, finding him in the little room where he kept the manor accounts. "I am not leaving for the Crusade tomorrow. I am taking Gwyneth home." He hesitated, unsure of how his father would react, to what he was planning to do. "I am also taking Emely to be my . . . overseer."

"Christian, she is a serf, well-educated and capable but a serf. She will be vulnerable."

"Only to Rene," Christian said. "You would not attack my manor which gives it protection on three sides. Only Rene would try to take back what he gave me through Arianna."

"She is young and a woman!"

"She is strong, she has been tested and toughened. She is no longer the child she was a year ago. She has defied you; she has stood up to me, she was successful fighting her attackers. She even stood up to Benoit. Gwyneth needs to be home. She needs to be as near Rene and Gracen as she is to you and mother. The people in the village need someone to guide them, keep them productive, to bring justice to the village in my absence."

"You are asking a lot of a young girl."

"She is not a girl anymore. She is a woman, matured beyond her years."

"Christian," Bryce asked, "were you the father of her child?"

"I think it is possible. We were . . . together the day you announced my betrothal. I was her first."

"That is why she would not tell who the father was," Bryce said aware he had exiled the mother of his first grandchild.

"Will she agree to your plan?" Bryce asked.

"Yes, I think she will. She loves Gwyneth deeply. It means however that I am abandoning her again. How do I protect my manor, Gwyneth's birthright, and Emely?"

"You could ask Benoit to go."

"He would not have her gentle way. She has lived in a village, knows the ways of the serfs. He would rule with . . . retribution and cold hardness. The village is too new, the people are just starting to come together. They need . . . kindness. Emely has always been kind."

"Will you ask her? Or tell her?" Bryce asked, knowing his son's warrior way.

"I will ask her," Christian said smiling knowing his father's thinking.

"She will say yes to please you even if she is unsure if she can do it."

"She can do it." Christian said, sure of Emely's love for Gwyneth, sure of her love for him, sure of her strength and maturity. "She can do it," he repeated confident in the woman he loved.

CHAPTER 23

When Sarah returned in the morning her hair was mussed and her clothes looked like they had been tossed in a pile all night. Emely said nothing but smiled and handed Sarah a clean tunic and a brush which she accepted blushing. They went down to the morning meal where the mood was somber as the lords and their warriors would be leaving this day. Farewells were to be said, last kisses and hugs shared, last looks and then the long march or the long wait would begin. The morning meal was over, everyone went out into the courtyard where horses in battle gear were gathered. The sounds of orders being given and the dust of men hurrying to obey filled the courtyard.

Emely looked at the assortment of men and animals in front of the manor house door, she sensed something was not right, something seemed to be missing. Then she realized Christian's horse was not there, Mighty Gray, was not among the mounts ready to leave. 'Had he changed his mind,' she wondered. Then another sight distracted her. Lord Piers entered the courtyard from the garden with a large bouquet of flowers in his hand and a troupe of musicians behind him. He walked to Felise and presented her the flowers and announced to all he had commissioned a special song in her honor. The musicians surrounded them and played and sang about a fair knight going to war and his love for the lady fair he left behind and how he dreamed of returning to her.

It was embarrassing to everyone since she was married to another and great with child. Emely looked at Lord Duran who, as usual, showed nothing on his expression until the song had ended.

"Lord Piers," he said moving to Felise's side as if to protect her from the scorn this inappropriate display could provoke. "You honor us with your wonderful words of love. I am sure all who are being separated today from their loved ones appreciate this gift. Thank you."

Emely was amazed at Lord Duran's calm and how he had turned what was meant to be a love song to a chosen woman into something they all could share. Lord Duran then put his arm around Felise's shoulders as she wept. With a forgiving smile at the younger man, Lord Duran took his wife into the manor house.

"Milords," Christian spoke in a loud clear voice. "I have chosen to take my daughter back to my manor and so will not be leaving with you today. My people are given into the care of Lord Michael until I rejoin you in a few days. Follow his command as you would my own."

A murmur of surprise went through the gathering. Emely looked at Lord Bryce and could see he was not surprised by Christian's announcement. then her attention was drawn back to the lords as they mounted their horses and the procession of their leaving the manor courtyard began.

"Sarah, will you take Gwyneth and the children to the garden? I need to go to the village."

Sarah was brought out of her wistful state by Emely's words. She reached out and took Gwyneth from Emely and called the children to come with her. Emely began to walk toward the village.

"Where is your escort?" Christian asked.

"Now the men are gone do I still need one?"

"No. but do not take long. We need to talk."

"Milord," Emely said curtsying. She did not like the sound of his voice. It was on the edge of his teasing voice and yet still serious.

Emely went to Wilona's hut but found it silent. The fire was low, and the pot empty. In the second room Emely found Wilona on the bed looking as if she was sleeping. It was not until she got closer Emely realized Wilona was dead. She had slipped away in the night. Emely sat by the bed and cried for her lost friend. She felt remorse at having abandoned the older woman who had been so kind to her. Someone entered the hut and moved about in the first room. She stood, wiped away her tears and went out. The woman from the next hut was building up the fire and had brought a chuck of meat and a basket of vegetables with her to make the day's meals.

"You need not do that," Emely murmured so she did not startle the other woman.

"I did not know you were here," said the neighbor smiling. "I am late today. With all the lords going . . .." Then she stopped as Emely's words took effect.

"She . . ..?"

"During the night."

"God rest her soul," the woman said crossing herself.

"Would you please get Father Bernard? Arrangements must be made."

With a quick nod the woman was out the door. Minutes later Father Bernard came and gave Wilona the final blessing. He and Emely arranged to have a service the next day with burial in the village cemetery. Wilona would lie next to her parents. Then Father Bernard left, and the village carpenter came. Emely paid him to make Wilona a coffin. They left the hut together.

Emely then went to David's little grave. She told him of the day's events. Standing, she found Christian was once again standing looking at the little grave.

Emely said nothing as she started to walk toward the manor house.

"I am taking Gwyneth back to my manor," he said.

Emely said nothing and waited.

"I am putting you in charge of my manor, my house and my daughter,"

"What?" Emely said stopping in the middle of the road and drawing looks from the passing villages.

"My people and manor are vulnerable without me there. I need someone to protect them."

"Me?"

"Yes, you," he said. "I have seen you protect Gwyneth, Sarah, Wilona, and yourself. You can do this! Twill not be easy. Lord Rene may pounce on you. You can handle him. Rand, the reeve, will help you. He is not John, but he will be good. On my command, he will do as you tell him to do."

"Lord Rene?"

"He might come."

"Why?"

"We did not part on the best of terms."

"Why?"

"Emely," he said in exasperation. "You will be in charge. You will have Gwyneth in your care. You will be . . . your own mistress! Felise, Marilee even my mother could not wish for more."

She stared at him for several more seconds before turning and walking toward the manor house. Then she stopped and turned on him.

"Who knew you were planning this?"

"I spoke to my father last night. I can give you nothing to make up for what I did to you."

She stared at him in shock. "You Did Nothing To Me!" she said emphasizing each word.

"Emely . . . "

"Not another word," she said cutting him off. "We will never speak of that day again, never!" She turned then and marched back to the manor house.

He had little choice but to follow her. In the main hall he watched her climb the stairs, his heart and his love going with her. Christian knew he was giving her a challenge and Rene would not make it easy but if anyone could protect and defend his small manor and keep his daughter safe in her own home it was Emely.

In their chamber Sarah was feeding her baby. Emely went to get Gwyneth and did the same. When they went down to the midday meal, there was tenseness in the room. Emely was sure it was due to Christian's announcement earlier. Lord Bryce approached Emely after the meal.

"I wish to speak to you," he said. "Alone," he emphasized when Christian moved to join them.

"Milord," Emely curtsied and then followed him to a small room furnished only with a table and two benches. Pieces of parchment sat on the table.

"Christian is taking you with him back to his manor."

"He has asked me to go, yes."

"You agree? I will not have you go if it is against your wish. I can force him to leave Gwyneth and you here."

"It will be good to be some place new," she answered after a moment of thought. "I . . . I look forward to the challenge. It is what I have been trained to do." She smiled at his reaction. "I sat beside Felise every day while she learned, I learned thanks to Lady Martha's kindness," she added smiling.

He smiled. "You have grown up too fast," he added.

"I grew up. I could not have asked for more. I knew every day I was loved by my parents, by you and Lady Martha, by Felise. It was a happy childhood."

"Has it been a happy adulthood?"

Emely hesitated then answered. "It is getting better. This . . . opportunity . . . will make it better. I think I will be happy. I will give Gwyneth all the love and care I would have given David. She does not replace him but fills a little of the emptiness."

"Have you let Wilona know?"

"Oh, you know not. Wilona died during the night. Father Bernard will bury her on the morrow."

"Does Christian know? He is planning on leaving soon."

"No. I will tell him. I cannot . . . will not go until I see her at rest."

"I will take care of telling him. Please let me know what time so Lady Martha and I can attend."

"Yes, milord," Emely said standing knowing their talk was over. She started to leave but then turned back and hugged him. "Thank you," she said tears starting to gather. "You have shown me such love and kindness. You and my father are the kind of men I wanted David to grew up to be. I love you so much."

The midday and evening meals were quiet with all the others gone. Emely was awake when the first light of dawn came through the window. It would be a long day. Once everyone was up and the children fed, Emely left to go to the village church. In the entrance hall Lord Bryce, Lady Martha, and Christian joined her. Several villagers also joined them for the ceremony. They carried the wooden coffin to the graveyard next to the church and watched as it was lowered into the ground. Father Bernard said a few prayers and the others drifted away one by one. The villagers began to shovel dirt onto the coffin. The sound was like a dull thud. Emely stood until the grave was filled before she went to the grave of her son to say her goodbyes. She promised he would always be in her heart. When she stood Christian was again standing behind her. His expression was one of extreme sorrow and loss. She turned and headed back to the manor house. He fell in behind her saying nothing until they reached the courtyard where two carts were waiting. His horse was also there ready to be ridden.

Sarah was overseeing the loading of the cart the women and children would be riding in, as the older children ran around the courtyard weaving around the men loading the other cart with the two cradles and supplies. Emely hugged her parents and was surprised when Lady Martha hugged her.

"Take care of my granddaughter," Lady Martha said. "And yourself. You are as precious to me as my children."

"I would die before letting anything hurt Gwyneth. She is my whole life."

"And yourself. Take care of yourself," Lady Martha said again. "Be happy."

"Watching Gwyneth grow will make me happy."

Lady Martha hugged Emely again and then Emely climbed into the cart. Christian mounted his horse, and they started moving out of the courtyard. Emely watched as the people she loved seemed to grow smaller and then were lost behind the manor house wall as they passed through the village. Then it was gone as they moved into the forest.

CHAPTER 24

They traveled under a canopy of green spring leaves. The sounds of birds chirping and the soft breeze dancing through the trees accompanied the plop of horses' hooves. The cart swayed back and forth rocking the babies and children to sleep. Several hours later, Christian called a halt so everyone could get out and walk a bit and they could eat a brief meal. Then it was back in the cart and continuing traveling until they stopped for the night. From her place in the cart Emely could watch Christian as he sat by the fire. He was lost in his own thoughts it seemed. Once he looked up to see she was watching him. He did not look happy, but Emely knew he did not regret his decision to leave her in charge of his manor. She closed her eyes and went to sleep. The next day would be almost as long as this one had been.

They were up at first light, ate quick and were back traveling. It was sometime after the midday meal when they entered a clearing and then the village. Emely could see serfs stopping their work to watch the group pass. They were through a rough wooden gate and into a small courtyard before they stopped. Christian came to the back of the cart and helped Emely and Sarah get out. Emely looked up at the manor house before her. It was wood and had been hastily constructed. There were gaps between the wooden boards that were the walls of the house. The few window openings were small and open to the spring air. The house itself was much smaller than Lord Bryce's but it was raised with five steps leading up to a door. Emely presumed this was the main door into the manor house. Christian indicated she should follow him into the house. Emely started up the stairs but stopped and turned to find Sarah walking toward the village.

"Sarah? Where are you going?"

"Back to our hut," the other woman replied disconsolate.

"No," Emely said smiling. "You are my . . . helper. You go where I go. Now come along. We have work to do."

Sarah smiled, her happiness at this continued friendship and support evident. She led the children back toward the house and up the stairs. Just inside the door there was a set of stairs leading to the upper floor but the whole main floor was one large room with a great fire pit in the center made of stone. Here the walls were also wood but across rather than up and down like the boards on the outside, so the gaps were somewhat covered. Four tables were pushed against the walls and benches were next to the tables. Torches placed along the walls would provide light once darkness fell. Otherwise, the room was bare. Emely then noticed there was a dais at the far end of the room and two great chairs. Christian stood in the middle of the room as if seeing it for the first time.

"Not my father's house," he said turning to Emely. "but it is mine." He said with a sound of satisfaction. "Sarah will show you to Gwyneth's chamber," he said and in doing so dismissed Emely.

Emely turned to Sarah who indicated they needed to go to the upper floor. A landing and hall ran the length of the available area. Six doors were all the hall contained. The light came through a row of windows in the wall over the stairway. Sarah led Emely to the second door. When Emely walked in, it was clear this had been Arianna's room. The walls were adorned with small tapestries of flowers. The large bed filling most of the space was covered with soft yellow draping. Two windows let light into the chamber.

Two men brought in the two cradles and the bundles of Gwyneth's clothing. Emely put the clothing away in a cupboard with shelves. One of which seemed uneven, but she thought nothing of it.

"My lady," Sarah said, "I would like to return to our hut. May I?"

"I am not a lady," Emely reminded the other woman one more time. "How will you live if you go there? How will I take care of Gwyneth without you to help me?"

"I will come every day," Sarah said with a smile, feeling good she was wanted. "the children and I will sleep better in our own hut."

"You will come for the morning meal and bring the children and stay until after the evening meal."

"Agreed," said Sarah smiling.

Another knock on the door announced the evening meal. One table had been pulled from the wall and benches placed on each side. The table held several wooden bowls containing bread, vegetables, cooked apples, and some chunks of pork. Father Francis the village priest and Rand, the village reeve joined them at dinner. The priest gave his blessing on the food then they ate.

"Father Francis, I wish to hold a fidelity ceremony tomorrow night after the evening meal. Please help Rand make sure all the villagers come as they should all renew their oaths to me."

"We all swore our loyalty to you when you came last year."

"Things have changed," Christian said. "The villagers need to understand Emely's position here."

"And what is it, milord?" asked Rand.

"She will be in charge," Christian said but making it clear to him and the others there would be no further discussion.

They finished their meal in silence and then Emely asked Rand to make sure Sarah and her children got safely to their hut. She also ask him to take one of the cradles with them for Sarah's baby. Emely walked around the room looking at the walls after they had left.

"What are you looking for?" Christian asked.

"May I do some wall hangings?"

"Wall hangings?"

"They will make the room warmer and more comfortable."

"Do whatever you wish. It will be your home."

Emely planned to make hangings but until they could be finished, she would send to get some from Lady Martha. Emely planned the first hanging made here and smiled to herself. She would make this a warm home for Gwyneth which would show the love Emely was sure Arianna and Christian had for their daughter. Working on these hangings would help fill the long winter days. They would be good projects and she would get help from some of the village women.

"You are smiling," Christian said. "I had forgotten . . .."

The smile left Emely face. She had forgotten he was in the room. The room seemed to close in on them. She felt herself drawn to him and knew she could melt into his arms if he approached her.

"Tis late milord. I need to be abed," she murmured.

He said nothing but nodded his agreement. He made no move to follow her as she walked toward the stairs. She slipped into Gwyneth's chamber and looked to make sure the baby was sleeping. Emely prepared a mat on the floor next to the cradle. She smiled. How many years had she slept like this next to Felise's bed?

Morning came and Emely was up early. She fed Gwyneth and put her back down to sleep more. Passing through the main room she found the other door leading out to the cookhouse and a small vegetable garden area at the back of the manor house. In the cookhouse one woman worked preparing the day's meals. Emely introduced herself and asked if she could help. The woman assigned her the task of cutting up vegetables and adding them to the pot. When the morning meal of cooked grain and fruit was ready Emely put it in bowls and helped the other woman carry them back into the main room. Sarah arrived a short time later and then Christian came down. Emely and Sarah discussed what they would do as they sat and ate. It was obvious in the daylight the room had been neglected not just since Christian had been at his parents but perhaps for several weeks if not months. The plan for the day was a good cleaning. When they were done eating Christian announced he had to go deal with matters in the village. He asked Emely to accompany him. Some petty crimes had happened while he was gone, and the thieves had to be punished.

"Why me?" Emely asked.

"Because when I am gone this will be your responsibility. Rand has only to catch offenders. It will be your responsibility to hear the witnesses and evidence against them and to decide if they are guilty or not and if they are guilty to pronounce their punishment."

Emely realized and was for a moment overwhelmed at how much more than just taking care of Gwyneth and the manor house she would be responsible for. She would be in essence both mistress and master of the manor. Taking a deep breath, she followed him after making sure Sarah would take care of Gwyneth. In the village church several people were gathered and parted as Christian and Emely walked in and to the alter.

"Our lord Christian has come to hear witnesses against Grandy accused by Jerod of stealing two chickens. If you wish to be heard, come forward," announced Rand.

Three people moved to the front of the crowd.

"Grandy," Rand said, "tell us your tale."

They listened as Grandy explained he thought the chickens were his because they had the same markings. Then Jerod explained the chickens were his because he had raised them since they were chicks. Both were good layers and thus provided his family with eggs. Christian ask some questions about the distinctive markings on the chickens. The two chickens were brought forward so Grandy could show the markings. Except the markings were so slight it appeared they may have been put there with ash. It was clear while there had been markings, they were not natural.

"Grandy either someone put the markings on these birds to cause you trouble or you did it yourself. Either way the chickens are not yours. They are returned to Jerod. Since there have been no other claims against you, I believe this was a mistake on your part and thus no punishment will be assigned. However, if another such incident occurs, you will be dealt with appropriately."

Rand then called the next case and the process of hearing evidence and Christian making a judgement was repeated once more. On the way back to the manor house Christian explained this was why he needed someone in charge at the manor. Since she knew nothing of the people of the village, she would be able to be objective in her decisions. After the midday meal he again ask her to accompany him as he met with various people on the manor, the smith, the baker, the tanner, and the miller. Christian had each man explain what he did. Emely had no idea what it took to run a manor. She did not ask questions except to ask if she could do some of the work they did. Her request was met with a look of skepticism but all relented when Christian made it clear she had his support. While she was not as expert as they were, she was capable of doing a little work at each site and hoped to earn the respect of the men. Walking back to the manor house Christian explained everyone had to work together to keep the manor running smoothly. Emely wondered if she was up to the task he was giving her.

"You can do this," Christian reassured her almost as if he could read her thoughts.

"There is so much," she said still unsure of her ability.

Christian stopped and drew her attention to him.

"You can do this!" he said again emphasizing every word. "I need you to do this. Hold my lands, my house, and my daughter until I return."

After a deep breath she agreed. Once they returned to the manor house Gwyneth was fed and then they had their evening meal. Bowls were being cleared when there was a knock on the door and Sarah opened it to admit the villagers.

"Milord, we your serfs come here to once again swear our loyalty to you," Rand announced.

"My people," Christian said as he took his place on the dais, "I leave on the morrow to go to the Holy Crusade as Pope Leo has requested. I ask you to give me your loyalty because I know not how long I will be gone. Rand."

Rand stepped forward. He was bareheaded and without any weapon. Emely had seen this ceremony many times before, but this one felt different for the oaths were being made to Christian rather than his father. Rand knelt before Christian and clasped his hands as if in prayer and stretched them toward Christian.

"I promise on my faith I will in the future be faithful to my Lord Christian, may I never cause him harm. I will observe my homage to him against all persons in good faith and without deceit. I swear this before my Lord Christian, this company, our lord Christ's priest, Father Francis, and God almighty."

"I accept your promise and thank you for your loyalty," Christian said taking Rand's hands between his own.

Father Francis then blessed Rand and Christian pulled the man to his feet. Rand then stepped to Christian's left side.

Man after man came forward to make the same promise. Finally, Father Francis stepped forward and made the same promise. When everyone from the village had made their promise, they expected to be given their leave.

"Is there anyone among you who has not made their oath?" Christian asked.

A murmur ran through the villagers as they looked at each other.

"Anyone?" Christian asked again. still, no one stepped forward. Emely looked at the villagers in front of her and was sure everyone had come forward.

"Anyone?" Christian asked again turning to Emely.

Their eyes met and she realized he expected her to take the same oath.

"Milord," she said stepping forward and kneeling before him, she made the promise.

"I accept your promise and thank you for your loyalty," Christian said taking Emely's hands between his own.

Father Francis then blessed Emely and Christian as he pulled her to her feet. He moved forward to kiss her, and Emely saw the look of desire in his eyes. Rather than kiss her on the cheek he took her face between his hands and lowered his lips to hers. It started out as a soft kiss but then she could feel the change as his desire for her took over and the kiss deepened. She was too stunned to do anything at first but then her love for him came over her and she kissed him back, deep and wanting. The collective gasp of the villagers brought both of them back to the place and company around them. He stepped back from her, but desire was still in his eyes.

Taking a deep breath, he turned to face the villagers before them.

"This is Emely. She has been my sister's companion and friend since childhood. She has been well trained in the running of a manor house and with your help she will learn quickly I am sure to run this manor," he said turning to glance at her.

"Her commands are to be followed as if they were my commands. Your loyalty to me is also your loyalty to her. She will protect you, but you are now required to protect her from any who would do her harm or try to take her or Lady Gwyneth from this place. You have sworn before God and if you fail in your loyalty your souls will be damned for all time."

A murmur ran through the villagers but was stopped short by Rand.

"To our lord Christian and to Emely, the guardian of our lives, our village, our manor, and our Lady Gwyneth."

"To our lord Christian and our guardian, Emely," responded the villagers in unison.

The villagers began to leave the manor house until only Father Francis, Christian and Emely were left.

"You may leave good father," Christian said knowing the priest would seek to protect Emely from him. Christian needed no lecture or scolding from the priest. What did a man of God know of the love a man and woman could share? Christian looked up and became even more angry that the priest had not left.

"As God's representative in this village I cannot in good conscience leave this place without being assured there will be no sinful behavior this night," the priest answered.

"What happens this night will have nothing to do with you, good Father."

"Emely, you should not stay in this house tonight. I fear for your soul."

"You have nothing to fear, good father. I . . . I know Lord Christian will do nothing to jeopardize me or my soul. We have known each other too long and too well for him to ever hurt me." She wanted to add 'again' but knew an explanation would be required.

"Emely . . ." the priest started.

"She told you she would be safe. Go now before I throw you out," snapped Christian.

He had shocked both the priest and Emely. She turned to the priest and indicated he should leave. He spoke one last time as he reached the door.

"If you need refuge come to the church," he offered.

"Thank you, Father, but I will be safe here. Gwyneth may need me during the night. Good morrow father." She said, opening the door so he could leave.

He took one last look at Christian and then Emely and walked out the door with great unwillingness.

"Pest," Christian said filling his cup with wine.

"What did you expect their reaction to be?" Emely questioned him.

"This is my house . . .. "

"I have to live here while you are gone!"

"They are nothing. You will be mistress here."

"I have to live here among them. I have to rule them. How do you expect me to do that if they think I am an easy woman? Why should they obey me?"

"They will obey you because I have told them they must!"

"You will not be here!"

"Emely," he said in a cajoling voice. "It is late, I am tired. Let us not fight."

She sighed. "I am going to bed. I will see you on the morrow."

"No, I will be gone at dawn. We will not see each other again until I return. If I return."

She stared at him for the first time, realizing he was not sure he would survive the ordeal ahead of him.

"Christian," she whispered wanting to go to him, be with him, comfort and love him with her heart, soul, and body.

He looked up at her hope in his expression. With tears in her eyes, she turned from him and climbed the stairs. In Gwyneth's chamber Emely pushed the bolt preventing anyone from entering. She lay on the mat next to Gwyneth and let her tears fall until she had none left.

CHAPTER 25

Emely was up before dawn and down in the kitchen hut. She packed extra provisions in a cloth bag and put together a morning meal. She took both to the main room and waited. Christian came down the stairs and started out the door.

"Milord," she called. "Come break the fast," she offered, indicating the meal she had prepared for him.

"My horse . . .. "

"He is getting an extra portion of grain in the stable so you both will leave this place well fed."

He smiled and walked to the table. He sat and she handed him each bowl in turn so he could take his fill. Then she sat beside him making sure he ate. They did not speak because there was nothing to say. She watched him hoping to memorize each feature of his face, all the wrinkles acquired during this last long year, wrinkles he had never had before. He had aged this year; the boyish looks were gone. Now he was a man made hard by the loss of his wife and the burden of fatherhood. Now before he even got to know her, he would be gone from Gwyneth's life, perhaps never to return.

When he was done, he stared at the bowls in front of him as if trying to memorize all the comfort he was leaving behind. Then he stood and walked toward the door like a man about to face his execution. Emely followed with the additional bag she had prepared. They walked to the bottom of the stairs where his horse was waiting. He thanked the boy who handed him the reins and then turned back to look at the manor house one last time, then to Emely.

"Emely," he said, tenderness in his voice.

"I will be here protecting your daughter, your people, and your land until your return," she promised.

"Emely," he said again as if there were so many other words he wanted to say.

She put her hands on either side of his face and raised on tiptoes to put her lips to his. He made no move, but a soft moan escaped him.

"I will be here," she whispered. "Waiting for you."

He turned and mounted his horse and turned it toward the gate. He stopped one last time to look back at her. Then he turned and rode through the village and into the wood beyond. Emely stood watching him go. Even after he was gone her tear-filled eyes looked at the road into the wood. She looked to the sky and prayed God would keep him safe and bring him back to them.

In the cookhouse, she asked the cook to join her and Sarah as they broke the fast. The woman seemed surprised but agreed. Emely then went to check on Gwyneth who was awake and wanting to be fed. After Gwyneth was taken care of, Emely returned to the main room where Sarah and the children were arriving. Emely asked Nelda if she could work in the cookhouse for a few days. Sarah and Nelda both stopped eating to stare at her.

"Someone as grand as you should not be working with the likes of me," Nelda said not believing this slip of a girl had ever done a hard day's work.

"I am a serf just as you are," Emely said. "If I am to indeed be the guardian of this manor, I need to know how everything, and everyone works. I have worked in the kitchen at Lord Bryce's manor. I want to learn your ways."

Sarah and Nelda looked at each other before Sarah spoke.

"Lady Emely is sincere Nelda. She knew nothing about caring for babies when we met but has learned so much so quickly. She will follow your teaching."

Nelda was surprised at the title Sarah gave Emely but then considered the girl before her. Then she smiled. If the girl wanted to work in the cookhouse, work she would.

"When do you wish to start?" Nelda asked.

"Today if I can," Emely replied. "I have much to learn."

"I can use the help. Planting has finished but there are still people to be fed."

"Sarah, will you take care of Gwyneth and come and get me when she needs me?"

"As you wish my lady," Sarah answered.

After reminding Sarah again she was not a lady, Emely gave Sarah a list of tasks she wanted done in the manor house. It had been neglected. Now it must be cared for. When they were done with the morning meal Emely followed Nelda to the cookhouse and asked questions as she worked at whatever she was told to do. Following the midday meal and Gwyneth was taken care of, Emely continued working in the cookhouse and Nelda seemed pleased despite the mistakes Emely made on occasion. Emely asked Nelda at the evening meal if she could return the next day and do more. The cook was again surprised but agreed. She wanted to see if the girl would continue to be amenable to the demanding work of preparing the day's meals.

When she was not in the cookhouse Emely spent as much time as she could with Gwyneth. The little girl's smiles came with ease and often. She could be demanding and was not happy if she was not fed when she was ready. Emely had learned to anticipate Gwyneth's moods and knew how to calm her. Emely worked in the cookhouse every day for a week after she had given Sarah her tasks for the day. The only real break Emely got was on Sunday morning when she attended mass with the other villagers.

She caused a stir when she walked into the little church carrying Gwyneth. The villagers parted row by row as they became aware of her presence to let her pass to the front of the church. Once there she was given a place of honor. She knew all the proper responses but as she listened, she realized most of the villagers had no idea what was happening during the service. She stayed behind after the service to speak to Father Francis.

"They know not the service," Emely said to the priest.

"They are humble serfs. There is no need for them to know."

"They are children of God and should know how to worship him."

"They have not been taught."

"Can you teach them?" Emely asked.

"I . . . I can," replied the priest.

Emely smiled. "Then you shall start lessons. If you need my help, I will be available at your wish."

Emely then went back to the cookhouse and began her day's work. She knew what Nelda wanted and expected of her and went about the tasks without direction. Emely asked Nelda if she still needed her in the cookhouse as they sat eating the evening meal. The cook laughed and said no, she had only agreed because she wanted to see what Emely would do. Emely smiled and thanked the woman for her patience but added she should continue to take her meals in the manor house.

"Nelda, when Lady Arianna was here who took care of the manor house?" Emely asked.

"No one," came the answer. "Neither she nor Lord Christian hired anyone from the village. She spent her days praying or in her garden."

Emely asked Sarah to bring a girl or two from the village to help them clean the manor house. The next day when Sarah arrived, she had two girls with her. Emely had them eat the morning meal with them and then they all set to work cleaning the house from ceiling to floor.

In her cleaning, Emely made it her personal project to clean Arianna's chamber. While this was now Gwyneth's chamber Emely had not looked through the cupboard thoroughly or at the bed but now, she did. She found a small book on the shelf she had thought uneven. She was surprised when she discovered it was Arianna's writing inside. She closed it as if it was aflame, not wanting to read the other girl's innermost thoughts. Emely put it back in the cupboard and cleaned the chamber, The whole time the little book called to her. She knew so little about Arianna and her life with Christian. Emely went to the cupboard often and lifted the little book from the shelf but always put it back without opening it.

Christian's chamber was the last to be cleaned. It was as empty of decoration as the main room reflecting his warrior training. Emely cleaned the chamber and when she was done, she looked around and felt its emptiness. Nothing here indicated he had ever been here. No sign of the man she knew. She decided she would change the room so when he came home, he would have a sense of belonging here.

Once she was done with Christian's chamber, Emely turned her attention to the other four chambers on the upper floor. They would be needed when Lord Bryce or Lord Rene came to visit. She had no doubt each would be coming. Lord Bryce to make sure she was doing well. Lord Rene was a question. She was not sure what he would think of Christian's decision to put her in charge of the manor. She would deal with him when he came.

CHAPTER 26

Once the house was cleaned Emely turned her attention to the rest of the manor. She went and helped in all of the village services, so she knew how everything worked. Her main focus was Gwyneth who stayed awake longer and was more alert each day. She wanted to be held and played with. She was a happy baby and responded to smiles and tickles with delight. Her big green eyes watched Emely with complete trust. The village was her second focus. Emely talked daily with Rand about any problems. She had to sit in judgement in only one case. Two of the village women argued over who got a loaf of bread first. Emely gave Rand a questioning look when he made her aware of the case. He shrugged.

"So how do I judge this? What difference does it make?"

"Well, the older woman, Mita, has done this before. Each new bride has had it happen to her," he said with a smile.

"So, they are being tested by . . . Mita?"

"She pushes in and takes what is someone else's?"

"That is what has happened in the past."

"What has Lord Christian done about it?"

"He ordered she get no bread that day."

"She however keeps trying," Emely said, a question forming.

At the hearing in the church Emely listened as the two women detailed or tried to detail how they knew they were first. Emely did not believe the younger woman. She was vague about the time and who was at the baker's when she arrived. Emely had not expected this outcome. She presumed the younger woman had been told about what Mita had done in the past. This was her way to cover up she had been slow getting to her chores that morning. Emely made her ruling on the detailed description both women gave her and ruled in favor of Mita. She ruled the younger woman was to get no bread that day or the next. The villagers, gathered in the church, murmured at the decision. Emely reminded them they were in the house of God and to bear false witness was a sin and to conspire against one of their neighbors was not acceptable behavior. With her judgement the villagers seemed to accept Emely's authority. They began to give her the respect her position deserved. It seemed it had been a test.

Having lived in the village at Lord Bryce's, Emely knew what it took to run a village household, but she decided to spend a few days living in Sarah's hut. Doing all the things the village women did to maintain their families. It also gave her a chance to get to know the other villagers. It took a few days before they accepted her presence in the village but then they would talk to her and gossip around her as if she was one of them. Emely learned so much during these times at the well and getting Sarah's bread.

It was August before Lord Bryce and Lady Martha came for a visit. They had never been to Christian's manor before, so they were surprised by the simpleness of the walls and the house. They were also surprised Emely was still wearing the serf's tunic she had been wearing when she left their manor. Lady Martha promised she would send some clothes to Emely. What they were impressed with was how happy Gwyneth was. Lady Martha complimented the cook on the quality of the food at the evening meal. It was a good start to their visit. They spent a week with Gwyneth and Emely. Lord Bryce went around the manor with Rand and Emely. He inspected all the service areas and made a few small suggestions on how to improve some things. He told Emely on their last night at the manor everything was going very well, better than he had expected. Emely smiled and gave credit to Rand and the others because it was they who did the work.

"No, Emely," Lord Bryce said, "You are in charge. They follow your lead. You set a high standard and they work harder to live up to it. They told me how you have come to work in all of their areas. Neither Christian nor Arianna did that. They like that you have taken an interest in what they do. It shows you care, and they like that also."

Emely was touched, the villagers had been so generous in their praise of her. She worried every day if she was doing enough, this seemed to confirm she was.

Lord Bryce and Lady Martha left the next day and the village and manor house slipped back into a routine. Two weeks later clothes arrived including a fur lined cape. Lady Martha was thinking ahead to the coming winter. Included was a note; Felise had had her baby, a boy. Emely smiled. Felise would be a good mother as she was by nature a loving person. She would have a lot of help from Lord Duran's mother and sister.

Emely's routine was simple but satisfying. She got up every morning, took care of Gwyneth and then went down to the morning meal with Sarah, Nelda, Rand, Father Francis, and the two helper girls from the village. Then she conferred with the cook about the meals for the rest of the day. Rand discussed any problems in the village needing her attention. Father Francis let her know of any births, deaths, or upcoming marriages so she could visit the families. She then gave Sarah and the girls their tasks for the day before she went to the village to visit the sick. She always checked with all the crafts people. Sarah and the girls would work on the tapestries Emely planned for the walls of the main room each afternoon. Emely carried Gwyneth in a sling over her shoulder, so the baby was close to her heart.

Emely had asked the smith to make a shield, a helmet, and two broad swords as decorations for Christian's room as well as some metal tankards. She had asked the tanner to prepare hides for two jerkins. She also had the wood wright making up two wooden shields. One would have Lord Bryce's coat of arms, the other Christian's. When he returned, this manor house would be welcoming and clearly his home.

By late September there was a nip in the morning air and crops were ready to be harvested. The whole village worked in the fields and orchards. Emely, Sarah, and the children went every day to help wherever they could. Two weeks later the granary was full, pigs had been slaughtered and the meat salted and prepared, fruits and root vegetables were in the storehouse. They were ready for the winter.

On the last day of the harvest the whole village gathered together to hold the annual harvest celebration. The tables set up on the green were loaded with food, villagers got out their crude musical instruments, and beer, ale, and mead were flowing like waterfalls. Emely and Gwyneth were part of the good talk and lots of laughter. Gwyneth was a curious six month old who wanted to see everything. Emely, with Gwyneth in the sling over her shoulder, was a familiar sight to the villagers and they were accepted as part of the village family. Within a few months they all referred to Emely as Lady Emely. She had given up correcting them. The whole village was happy, healthy, and a haven of peace and prosperity.

The arrival of Lord Rene and Lady Gracen brought a bit of seriousness to the village. Lord Rene took in the scene of happy villagers and looked none too happy. The growing silence made Emely turn from the group of women she was talking and laughing with to come face-to-face with Lord Rene.

"This is how you frolic when your lord is away?" asked Lord Rene angry at the apparent carousing.

"Milord," Emely said walking toward him. Once she reached him, she gave him a deep curtsy. "We are celebrating a good harvest. The village has worked very hard this year, and they will not face starvation. It is a good time to be alive."

"And where is my daughter's daughter?"

"Here, milord," Emely said indicating the sling over her shoulder and showing him Gwyneth's little smiling face.

"This is how you treat a lady?" he asked even angrier than he had been before.

"There is work to be done but Gwyneth had to be cared for first and foremost. So, where I went Gwyneth went."

"Lady Gwyneth," he said ice in his voice.

"Lady Gwyneth," Emely repeated after a deep sigh.

"We have been traveling for two days. Lady Gracen would like to rest properly. Where is the manor house?"

"This way milord," Emely indicated and turned toward the manor house but then turned back toward the villagers.

"You have all worked very hard this year, please continue your celebration," Emely said smiling at her friends.

"Milord." She said again indicating Lord Rene and his party should follow her.

They walked side by side to the manor house, neither speaking. Emely could see Lord Rene looking at everything, assessing its condition but still he said nothing. In the manor house, the late afternoon sun still gave light to the main room.

"Lady Gracen, may I show you to a chamber?" Emely asked concerned as the other woman look distressed and tired.

"Can I hold her first?"

"Of course," Emely said smiling. "Here, be seated," she offered a bench to the older woman.

Once Lady Gracen was seated, Emely put Gwyneth into her arms and stepped back still smiling.

"She is so small," Lady Gracen said.

"She has grown in the six months we have been home."

"She has Arianna's dark hair."

"Yes, and Lord Christian's green eyes."

"Yes, Christian," Lady Gracen said.

"They were not happy?"

"No," said Lady Gracen. "She wrote from the beginning of their time here. He was . . .. marriage was not . . .. She was a child. I am . . . was her mother. I should have . . .."

"You could have done nothing. Once she was betrothed, their future was set," Emely said consoling the older woman.

"What do you care?" Lord Rene said angry at the presumption of this mere serf as he entered the room.

"I have known Lord Christian all my life. Lady Arianna . . . seemed so young when we were at your manor for the wedding. Too young to know anything of life."

"What do you know of . . . life?" he said a nasty tone in his voice.

"I know it is hard. I know things happen to change you . . . a person forever. I know loss."

Lord Rene studied her. His memory of her increasing his anger at Christian. How dare he let his infatuation take care of Gwyneth?

"Why are you here?" he demanded.

"I care for Lady Gwyneth and Lord Christian's manor while he is gone."

"Not well, from the carousing the villagers were doing when we arrived."

Emely decided it would be better not to respond so she changed the subject of their conversation.

"How long will you be with us, milord?" she asked. She had no concern they would not be fed and housed well.

"As long as I wish," he snapped.

"Rene please let us just enjoy being with Gwyneth?" Lady Gracen said to her husband.

He looked at his wife holding their granddaughter and then at Emely.

"We will continue this later." He then turned his attention to Gwyneth.

"She has Arianna's hair," he said. For the first time Emely saw the softer side of Lord Rene.

Minutes later Nelda, the cook, entered followed by the two girls who helped. Each of the girls was carrying two large bowls filled with food. Nelda was carrying a tankard of wine and three mugs. They put the food and wine on the table and left as Emely thanked them.

Lord Rene took a small piece of meat and from the look of surprise on his face, Emely could tell he was impressed by the quality of the cooking. She had come to trust Nelda. She brought out flavors in food as good as any Emely had ever had at either Lord Bryce's or Lord Rene's. Gwyneth was getting fussy in Lady Gracen's arms and Emely knew it was time for the baby to be fed.

"Please have something to eat while I feed Gwyneth," Emely offered.

Lady Gracen released the baby with some reluctance. Emely took Gwyneth up to her chamber. Emely put Gwyneth her down for a nap after she was fed and returned to the main room. Lord Rene was no longer there but Lady Gracen was. She was looking at the tapestry Emely and the others were working on.

"It will be lovely," Lady Gracen said.

"I tried to draw her as I remembered her," Emely said standing beside the older woman as she looked at the beginning of her daughter's face.

"She is smiling," Lady Gracen said sadness in her voice.

"I thought she was happy to be with child."

"She was. It was the only thing she was happy about."

"I remember seeing Felise the morning after her marriage. She had the same . . . sad look as Lady Arianna had. Men . . . I do not think they mean to hurt us . . . . "

"You have been . . . taken?" Lady Gracen asked.

Emely said nothing. She did not need to. Lady Gracen knew Emely was Gwyneth's wet nurse and must have given birth.

"Your child?" Lady Gracen asked.

"Died," said Emely. The pain was still too deep.

"We wanted a son, but all died within their first year."

"You had Arianna," Emely said with a smile and was pleased to see Lady Gracen smile also.

"Yes, we had Arianna and now we have Gwyneth."

"Would you like to rest now? Traveling can be exhausting."

"Yes," Lady Gracen said taking one last look at the tapestry before following Emely up to a chamber on the upper floor. It was a simple unadorned chamber, but the bed had fresh bed clothes, and the room had recently been cleaned. Lady Gracen looked around the room but said nothing. Emely left the older woman there and checked on Gwyneth who was still sleeping peacefully. Down in the main room she picked up the half empty bowls and the tankard and took them back to the cookhouse. She again thanked Nelda for bringing the food. They talked for a moment about meals for the next couple of days since Lord Rene had not given any indication of how long he intended to stay, Emely wanted to make sure they were prepared for an extended visit. Emely checked on Gwyneth again who was now awake and ready to be played with. Emely smiled. The baby never questioned or judged her. She was always happy to see Emely and was easy to please: feed her, change her, and play with her and she was happy. Down in the main room Emely went to work on the tapestry. It was just getting dark when Lord Rene, Rand, and Father Francis came into the manor house. It was obvious Lord Rene had been inspecting the manor and from the look of Rand he had asked a lot of questions. Whether he was satisfied with the answers was unclear. Minutes later Nelda came in with the evening meal. When Emely asked Rand where Sarah was, he said she and her children were staying in the village. Emely guessed Sarah did not want to have to face Lord Rene. Emely had seen the expressions of all the villagers change when he had arrived.

"Did you find everything to your liking?" Emely asked Lord Rene as they ate.

"It looked . . . acceptable. I will decide after further inspection."

Emely smiled. She knew he would find everything running to perfection. The villagers worked hard, and they had had a good year. The skilled craftsmen were always prepared for emergencies with extra supplies. The house was not as grand as Lord Rene's, but it was warm and welcoming.

For the next several days Lord Rene was up early each day but not before Emely. She greeted him each morning with a meal and a warm smile. If he was going to find something to criticize it would not be their hospitality. Once he left, she took the bowls back to the cookhouse and then went to take care of Gwyneth. Sarah and the children arrived, and they had their morning meal before getting to work on whatever tasks Emely had planned for the day. They had come to follow a routine and fell into it easily. Sarah's son went to get Lady Gracen a bowl of food when she came down. On the third day of their stay the wood wright brought the new larger cradle Emely had asked him to build for Gwyneth. She was starting to try to sit up by herself and she had two teeth. On this day she was more difficult than usual and would not let anyone, but Emely hold her. Lady Gracen looked on worried when Emely had to take Gwyneth back. Emely knew what was happening and smiled.

"She is going through a growth spurt," Emely explained.

"How long will it last?"

"A few days, then she will settle down again."

"A few days," the older woman said disappointed at not being able to hold her granddaughter.

Lady Gracen turned to the tapestry and asked if she could work on it. Emely welcomed an extra pair of hands. The women sat and talked about babies, the fine weather, the coming holidays, and many other topics, an easiness growing between them. The sun was setting when Lord Rene, Rand, and Father Francis entered the house. The women were laughing. Lord Rene looked at his wife and the other women and looked none too happy that Lady Gracen was so content with Emely. He wanted his wife's full support in his decision to take Gwyneth home with them, away from Christian's paramour. He said nothing but was not happy with the growing friendliness between the two women.

Two more days passed before he asked to speak with Emely. She knew it was not going to be good from the frosty tone of his voice. Sarah, her children, Rand, and Father Francis left as soon as they were done eating.

"We are leaving tomorrow," Lord Rene told Emely.

"I will have Nelda prepare a packet for you," Emely said relieved he would soon be gone.

"Thank you. Gwyneth is coming with us," he said with disdainful authority.

"Where Gwyneth goes, I go," Emely said in a tone that refused to accept his power over her. "And we are not leaving."

"You do not have a choice. Gwyneth is our daughter's child, and we are taking her home so she can be cared for as a lady of her station requires and not by Christian's woman of . . . enjoyment."

"She is properly cared for and this is her home. Her father left me in charge of his manor, his people, and his daughter. We are staying."

"How dare you defy me. I am a noble and you are . . . what? Serf, easy woman, his paramour?"

Emely felt as if she had been struck as she stared at the man but then regained her composure.

"I am the person Lord Christian put in charge. I am not leaving, and Lady Gwyneth is not leaving. Do you plan to rip her from my arms? Do you plan on dragging me by my hair out of this house? Do you plan to abandon these people? You cannot and will not take Gwyneth away from her home nor can you take me away from Lord Christian's manor!"

"I . . .." Lord Rene started to speak but Rand, Father Francis and several of the village men came into the main room.

"Do you need assistance, my lady?" Rand asked.

"No, thank you, Rand. I believe Lord Rene and I understand each other."

Lord Rene and Emely stared at each other in a battle of wills. When Lord Rene dropped his eyes conceding defeat, Emely took no pleasure in his shame.

"You loved Lady Arianna, and you love Gwyneth. You are welcome to come and visit her anytime you wish. "This is her home," Emely emphasized but with a gentle tone.

"I only want what is best for her," he lamented.

"She is happy, healthy, and loved more than you will ever know. She is my life."

"And him? What is he to you?"

"Lord Christian is the lord of the manor where I live just as Lord Bryce was lord of the manor where I grew up."

He looked at her, the questions he wanted to ask reflected on his face but said nothing more.

"We are still leaving in the morning," he said.

"You will be missed," she smiled at him. "Gwyneth needs her grandparents." Emely said and then turning toward the villagers thanked them for coming but assured them she did not need their help.

They looked at Lord Rene one last time and then most of them left. Rand and Father Francis stayed. Emely looked at her two friends and smiled.

"You need to be in bed. It is late," she said dismissing the men.

Father Francis and Rand looked at each other and then said their 'good morrows' and left. Emely took Gwyneth from Lady Gracen and said her good morrows. Up in Gwyneth's chamber after she put Gwyneth down for the night, Emely took a deep breath and sat on the bed. She knew what he had said, many others would think; she was easy. It would be her lifelong penance for the pleasure they had shared. She laid down to sleep knowing she would never marry, never have more children, never have a home of her own. She knew when he came back, she would have to leave because she could not, would not, watch him marry another. He would marry. He would need heirs if only to protect Gwyneth from men who would only want her lands and wealth. It was a long night filled with fitful dreams. She was up early and down in the cookhouse helping prepare the morning meal and the food for Lord Rene and Lady Gracen to take with them.

CHAPTER 27

Christian May 1096

Christian carried with him the memory of Emely standing in front of his manor house. He spent hours in the saddle. It had taken him three days to join the others. Then over a week from London to Dover to board boats to Calis across the channel in France. Christian walked through the camp every night to check on his men and found them well provisioned, well behaved, and in good spirits. The same could not be said for some of the others, particularly Lord Piers' men. Christian knew they would cause trouble. They crossed the channel to France, leading the small army through the French countryside. The nights and rest periods were never long enough but this is what he and the other knights had been trained for, to be warriors. Christian liked young Lord Michael. He was respectful of everyone, knight, or serf. He checked on his men each night also. Christian and Michael often walked together through the camp.

Passing through the French countryside, they sometimes came to villages. Christian and Michael often bought extra food for their men. Much to Christian's displeasure, Piers' men often harassed the women in these villages and tried to steal food and drink. Christian put a quick stop to it by making Piers responsible for paying for what was stolen and punishing the men who harassed the women. Christian as the oldest of the three was the recognizable leader. Piers resented the control Christian exerted. Piers would grumble as he walked away after Christian reprimanded him. It was never loud enough so Christian could hear the complaint, but he knew Piers was unhappy at the boundaries placed on all the men.

Two long months after leaving home, they reached Venice where they would board ships to sail to Constantinople, capital of the Byzantine Empire, the last Christian stronghold in the east.

Their last night there, Christian sat and wrote to Emely. It was short, he told her of crossing the channel and then France and northern Italy. He told her about how much he liked Lord Michael, hoping she would share the information with Duran and thus reassure Michael's parents he was well. He also let her know John, Sarah's husband, was well and proving a good second in command of their men. He wasted no space on Piers. They had both seen his behavior at Lord Bryce's and Emely would know things were not well between the two men. Then he hesitated. Did he write of his love for her? Did he ask her to wait for him? He decided not to express his love and need for her warmth. She needed to find someone to love her as she deserved and there was no guarantee he would return. He sealed the letter and found a merchant caravan traveling to France and paid the man to take the letter and gave him enough additional to make sure it was carried to England and home.

In the morning, they boarded ships for Constantinople where they would be the guests of the Emperor. The rift between the eastern and western churches put aside to deal with the infidels control of the Holy land. The Mediterranean was not kind to men who had never seen so much water before. The men who did not spend their days emptying their stomachs over the side of the ship, lay prostrate wherever they could find space. Their occasional port calls helped replenish their food and fresh water and gave the men a short time on dry land.

After four long months they sailed into the capital of the Eastern Empire. Constantinople was a wonder, a city larger than any the Crusaders had ever seen. London was a mere village compared to the glorious Constantinople with its tall gleaming buildings, people dressed in every color of the rainbow, streets filled with exotic smells of spices westerners could not get enough of. If the food was tempting, the women were more so to men who had been too long without female companionship. The women dressed in more fitted, translucent material that was no less revealing than western dress, but softer and more flowing, gentle curves were not hidden under thick wool tunics.

Christian wrote Emely of his sea voyage, the beauty of the eastern capital, floors made of polished stones and windows to let in sun light in even the humblest buildings and homes. He told her about the exotic foods and drinks, the lush greenery and the variety of arts, crafts, fabrics, and decorations in the marketplace. The churches with artwork embellished with jewels and trimmed in gold. He also shared John and Michael were still doing well and had earned his trust and respect.

The emperor invited the leaders to stay on his palace grounds but insisted the common men camp outside the city walls. They were allowed into the city to get food and drink but were required to be out by nightfall or find some accommodation within the city for the night. The message was clear: common soldiers were not to be roaming the city after dark. Men who wished, did find places of gratification to spend the night with what little money they had. Still, some were not satisfied. Many walked the streets during the day, harassing and abusing the women of the city, young and old. The lords received daily reports and had to deal with their men. Christian and Michael were swift in punishing such transgressions and soon their men were staying out of trouble. Piers seemed to take pleasure in hearing the conquests of his men and often joined them.

A few days after Christian and the others, another group arrived. Lord Drake was known to Christian but not well. They had met at tourneys over the years of their training. Christian was not inclined to like Drake, but they were here to fight and the more warriors the faster they could all go home. Piers became Drake's follower, and the two men drank and womanized together with their men. They drew the displeasure of the Emperor often but ignored and laughed at his angry reprimands.

A month later, having overstayed their welcome the knights and their men were ordered to leave the city for Jerusalem. Christian had seen enough of the city and how the westerners had abused the hospitality they had been given. He was happy to leave, to go to war. The men needed to be busy with something other than eating and taking their ease wherever they could, even within the palace walls. The emperor provided the crusaders with as much food as he could spare to help hurry them on their way.

CHAPTER 28

It was not long after sunrise they were gathered in the courtyard. Lord Rene's horse was saddled, and the cart for Lady Gracen was ready. Some of the villagers had come to say their farewells and, Emely thought, also to make sure Lord Rene did not try to take either Gwyneth or both girls from Christian's manor. Emely smiled at how protective they had become of her and Gwyneth.

"Come again," Emely said to Lady Gracen, "Gwyneth needs to know you."

Lady Gracen looked at the very alert baby in Emely's arms and smiled.

"We trust you to care for her as Arianna would have," Lady Gracen said and then unexpectedly, hugged Emely.

"We will be back in the spring," Lord Rene said after helping his wife into her cart.

"Perhaps Gwyneth and I can come visit you," Emely offered.

"You would do that?"

"Gwyneth should know her mother's home. Now we, you, and I, understand each other, Gwyneth and I will come as often as we can."

He smiled. He was a warrior, but he did not make war on women or serfs except in battle. He then also hugged her but stepped away as if embarrassed at his display of admiration and growing affection. Emely smiled as he climbed on his horse. She watched as the little procession moved out of the courtyard and through the village.

Once they were in the wood and out of sight, Emely released the breath she had been holding. The manor and she could return to their comfortable familiar routine and the work to be done. The harvest was in but there was still the repair of farm tools, preparing wool for weaving, salting meat and much more to be done before winter surrounded them.

The lack of constant work resulted in an increase in petty crimes, and she had to deal with those. Emely tried to spend time a few days a week at the school Father Francis was holding in the church. She even helped with some of the lessons when she could. Gwyneth was crawling and wanted to explore everything, which meant Emely had to be extra vigilant. It was, however, fun to watch the baby explore and touch everything Emely would let her.

It was the second week of October when a rider approached the village and sought Emely with a letter from Christian. Emely ordered food and a bed for the messenger and made sure he was given their full hospitality. Emely waited until Gwyneth was in bed and Sarah and the children had gone home before she read it. She savored every word, reading and rereading it before placing it in a safe place. She talked to Sarah in the morning and let her know John was doing well and sent a message to Michael's family. Since there was nothing of Piers, she hoped he would keep his own family informed of their progress.

Emely sat that night and took parchment and pen to write back. She told him of Gwyneth's progress and how smart and happy the child was. She let him know Sarah and the children were well. She also told him of Lord Rene's visit and their understanding. Then she hesitated. Did she tell him she missed him, and she loved him? She was waiting for him. He had offered no words of love and longing, so she ended her letter. She sent it off the next morning by courier.

Autum turned to winter and Christmas came. Gwyneth and Emely gave small presents to all the villagers at the celebration in the village. The manor house was decorated, and laughter and music filled the air.

Then came the first snow and the village children frolicked. Emely smiled remembering her happy childhood at Lord Bryce's. Only one person was missing. She wondered where Christian was and if he was safe and warm in whatever far away land, he found himself.

CHAPTER 29

Spring 1097

Gwyneth had her first birthday and was walking, slow and hesitant but walking. Spring planting was done, and everyone was happy to be able to enjoy the outside. Petty crimes stopped enough Emely thought it was a good time to visit Lord Bryce and Lady Martha. Emely was excited to share Gwyneth's progress with her grandparents. She was not only walking but was starting to talk although most people who were not with her every day could not make out the words she was saying. It had been one of Emely's greatest joys and sorrows when Gwyneth had said 'mama' the first time.

"Emely," she corrected.

"Mama." Repeating what she heard Sarah's children call her.

"Emely!"

"Emi?" Gwyneth said smiling. Gwyneth's use of Emely's childhood nick name brought back happy memories. Felise could not manage Emely's full name when they were Gwyneth's age either. Emely smiled back at Gwyneth and accepted the nickname once again.

Now Gwyneth was putting words together and 'talking' with Sarah's baby, Eden. Sarah and Emely tried to understand what the two children were saying to each other, but it did not make much sense.

Emely arranged everything for the short trip. Rather than taking a cart that would slow them down, she would ride with Gwyneth in front of her on the horse. She would take two male villagers with her for protection. She sent ahead to let Lord Bryce know they were coming. If they traveled without stopping, they could be at Lord Bryce's manor by night fall.

Just before sunrise with a still sleeping Gwyneth in her arms, Emely and the others set out. They made the good progress she had hoped for and arrived just after sunset. It had been a long day in the saddle and Gwyneth was ready for bed, but it was worth it. Lord Bryce, Lady Martha, and her parents welcomed Emely with great joy. Once Gwyneth was settled in Christian's old room the adults sat and had a cup of wine and talked. Lord Benoit and Lady Marilee were there but said little. The next day Lady Martha wanted to hold Gwyneth all the time, but Gwyneth had other ideas. She wiggled until she was put down and could go exploring although she often looked back to make sure she could still see Emely. The third day of their visit while Gwyneth was taking her nap Emely went to the village graveyard to put spring flowers on David's grave. She noticed it was well kept and there were flowers already there. She was glad someone was caring for her son's spot. She went to Wilona's grave and left flowers there also. Leaving she met Father Bernard coming out of the village church. They greeted each other and Emely thanked him for looking after David's grave.

"Not me," he answered. "Your mother and Lady Martha, one or the other comes at least once a week."

Her mother, Emely, understood. David was her grandchild but Lady Martha? Emely wondered if she had figured out who David's father was. Walking slowly back to the manor house Emely wondered and hoped the older woman had not figured it out. Lady Martha would be sad she had never held her first grandchild. When Gwyneth was awake Lady Martha played with her. She and Emely's mother again reminisced about Felise and Emely when they were children.

"Remember how Benoit and Christian teased the girls?" Lady Martha said laughing.

"They were not nice," Emely's mother said also laughing.

"Benoit will never allow our children to tease each other," Marilee said.

"Of course he will," Lady Martha said turning to her daughter-in-law. "It is what children do. It teaches the younger children how to deal with difficult situations. If the parents are doing their job, they reprimand the older children, so they learn to treat others with respect."

"I cannot imagine Benoit teasing anyone," Lady Marilee continued.

"Oh, he did," laughed Emely's mother. "He and Christian both, Felise would burst into tears and made them stop. They were both very protective of her."

"And what did you do?" asked Lady Marilee of Emely.

"I did nothing. They were nobles and I was . . . am a serf. There was nothing I could do."

"I suppose is why you had a child without having a husband." Lady Marilee said in an unpleasant tone.

Both Lady Martha and Emely's mother gasp at the insult. Emely said nothing. Several seconds of silence seemed to help Lady Marilee understand she had been cruel. She had the sense to look down and continue her sewing. Several more seconds of silence followed before Lady Martha ask Emely about Christian's manor. Emely told her about the improvements to the village and the manor house and the school Father Francis began for the children who were all learning to read and write.

"Reading and writing?" Lady Marilee exclaimed. "What possible need have they?"

"It will give them a chance to better themselves," Emely replied.

"Better themselves? For what? They are serfs!"

"Lord Bryce and Lady Martha gave many of their serfs a basic education, reading, writing, simple math. Maybe some will go to the city and study law or medicine. They will have a chance to have a better life."

"They are serfs!" Lady Marilee said again with arrogant disdain.

"So am I," Emely said reminding the other woman in gentle tones. "And yet I am now responsible for a manor and its village."

"You are one person and when Christian comes home your services will no longer be needed."

"That is true but until then I am in charge and the children will be educated."

"Christian should have put Benoit in charge."

Emely studied the other woman. Now she understood Marilee's animosity. Benoit was a noble and a man. Christian should have left his brother in charge. Emely knew Benoit. He could be cruel. The manor might not have prospered under his guidance. It was also clear the other woman was jealous not only that Emely had had a child of her own but also of the responsibility Christian had given her. Emely ran Christian's manor while Benoit was still living under his father's rule. Emely was in charge of the manor house while Marilee was still living in someone else's house. It could not be easy to watch a serf get everything they both had been trained for. Emely turned her attention back to Gwyneth and smiled at the little girl's attempts at talking. She so wanted to be a part of the conversation.

Gwyneth and Emely stayed on a few more days. Emely felt she had been away long enough as there was still much to be done at Christian's manor. During the last few days Gwyneth and Emely were at Lord Bryce's Marilee said nothing. The night before Emely was planning on leaving, she let Lord Bryce and Lady Martha know she and Gwyneth would be leaving in the morning.

"I think it would be best if Lady Marilee and I traveled with you," said Lord Benoit.

Emely knew she had to be careful in dealing with him. He could cause her a lot of trouble if she spoke to him in a manner, he found offensive.

"I thank you for your generous offer. If we are to get to Lord Christian's manor by nightfall we must travel by horseback. It would be difficult for Lady Marilee. We would love to have you come with Lord Bryce and Lady Martha. the manor is very small, and our chambers are very . . . humble. There is only one other household serf and only one cook."

"Still, I would like to . . . see Christian's manor."

"Perhaps in a few weeks you could come and visit."

"We want to come now!" interjected Lady Marilee.

"I agree with Emely," Lord Bryce said. "We have been there," he continued looking at Lady Marilee, "you would not be happy."

"Father," Lord Benoit said turning to his father.

"Milord," Emely said trying to make him understand, "it is a small village, only twenty families. The manor house is wood. We were blessed last year with a good harvest, so we have enough food but . . . we do not have enough to feed more people than we have."

"Perhaps better management," Lord Benoit grumbled.

"No Benoit," Lord Bryce said. "Emely is taking care of everything as well as anyone could, even you."

Lord Benoit looked at his father and then his wife but said nothing more. Emely excused herself early and went to Gwyneth's chamber. She slept well that night knowing they would be home the next night. Lord Bryce and Lady Martha had been gracious and loving as always but dealing with Lord Benoit and Lady Marilee had been difficult. Emely longed for the peace of Christian's manor.

Lord Bryce and Lady Martha were up to see them off in the morning. Lady Martha had food packets made up for Emely, Gwyneth and the three men who would be returning with them. They again rode all day and were home at sunset. Sarah was there to greet Emely and have a hot meal ready. Gwyneth was down for the night, and Emely appreciated Sarah's thoughtfulness. They talked for a short time before Sarah returned to her hut. Emely sat at the table and looked around the main room and smiled. It was not grand, but it was home.

A letter from Christian was a bonus to being home. It was short as he gave only a short concise description of the sea voyage to Constantinople and the splendor the people lived in, the exotic and colorful clothing, and flavorful food.

CHAPTER 30

The next day Rand and Father Francis came and let her know what had been happening at the manor. She was pleased to hear there had been no problems in her absence. No repeat of the petty crimes from the year before when they had not expected Christian to return. She spent the day going through the village seeing for herself how everything was. The village craftsmen were working full time. Wool from the spring sheering was spun and woven. It looked like they would again have a good harvest. then the rain came. While they were on higher ground the fields were saturated. Animals had to be fed in shelters since the normal fields were soggy. Even the villagers stayed in unless they were forced to by need or want. Gwyneth was getting more teeth and was not her normal happy self. She whined every moment she was awake and refused to let Emely put her down for two or three days before a new tooth appeared. Two long weeks later the rain stopped. Emely went to work in the village to help clean up the mess the rain had made on the road going through the village. The stream had overflowed its banks and there were dead trees and bushes to be cleared. The wood would be dried and used for building or for firewood. Emely knew they had been fortunate. The damage could have been much worse.

When everything was cleared, Emely explored the area around the outside of the manor house, something she had not had time to do the previous year. She found the small flower garden Arianna had created at the back of the house away from the noise and disorder of the courtyard.

"Did Lady Arianna go often to her flower garden?" Emely asked at dinner that night.

"Flower garden? I did not know there was such a thing." Sarah said. "But I only came after Lady Arianna was . . . gone."

"Lady Arianna went there every day," Nelda said. "She would work for hours. When she was great with Gwyneth, she sat and read her bible or prayed."

The next day Emely returned to the garden. It was overgrown and weeds were trying to take back the soil, but the original arrangement of flowers and bushes was still clear. For the rest of the summer Emely went every day to the small garden and worked to return it to the order Arianna had intended. It was here Emely found Arianna's grave. She had been surprised to see the little mound and small cross with Arianna's name on it. Then Emely realized Christian had buried Arianna in the place she loved best at their manor. Restoring it would be Emely's way of honoring the dead girl who had given her life to bring Gwyneth into the world.

July turned to August and Lord Rene and Lady Gracen came to visit again. Emely had kept them aware of Gwyneth's progress and they had sent gifts for both Gwyneth and Emely. Emely had come to know Arianna's parents almost as well as she knew her own, Lord Bryce and Lady Martha.

Once they were settled, while Lady Gracen took care of Gwyneth, Emely showed Lord Rene around the manor. He questioned her about everything from how the spring planting had gone to how they had dealt with the rains and what they were hoping the harvest would be. Emely answered every question to his satisfaction. He was impressed at how well the manor was doing under her care. Over dinner their second night Lady Gracen ask about Christian.

"Have you heard of their progress?" Lady Gracen asked.

"Yes. He has sent two letters. He writes of their travel and the beauty of Constantinople. I have written him about the manor and Gwyneth's growth."

"You wrote him?" Lord Rene exploded.

"Yes. I want him to know all is well with Gwyneth and the manor," Emely said with a smile.

"Why should he care?" Lord Rene asked.

"He is Gwyneth's father. Would you not want to know of your child's progress?"

"He does not care! He killed," Lord Rene started to say but then saw the look on Lady Gracen's face and changed his statement. "He let Arianna die and cared not."

Emely looked at the man in front of her and could feel his anger. Then she looked at Lady Gracen and could see her pain. The Christian she knew was not uncaring.

"She died in childbirth?" Emely half asked.

"She died because he did not take proper care of her." Lord Rene snapped.

"She died because she was too young to have a child. She was only a child herself," Lady Gracen said. Her anguish at the loss of her child clear in the quiver in her voice.

"She was of marriageable age," Lord Rene snapped at his wife. Then a look of disgust came down his face. "My love, I am so sorry" he apologized to his wife knowing they shared the loss and the pain.

"You and Lord Bryce saw her body's age, but she was not ready." Lady Gracen uttered.

"She never would have been ready," he answered as he reached out to take her hand. "She was too . . . religious. She had to marry for her own protection. She crould have been helpless against those who would have taken advantage of her as my only heir. Bryce is my oldest and most trusted friend. No one would have taken better care of her than one of his sons."

"Why so soon?" Lady Gracen asked. "Why not wait a few more years?"

"Because death has no respect for age. Our sons were young but still they were taken from us. We could not wait. If I died, you and she would have been left to fend for yourselves. I could not . . . would not leave both of you unprotected."

"And instead, we lost her."

"We have Gwyneth," Lord Rene said. Then turning to Emely, he smiled. "And Emely."

"Yes, Emely," said Lady Gracen smiling at the young woman who had come to love them both.

Emely knew she could ignore Arianna's journal no longer. It had sat untouched in the cabinet this year. It was time for her to get to know Arianna. She waited until they left three days later.

The rest of their visit went uneventfully. Rand and Emely went with Lord Rene to the village every day so he could inspect the work of the craftsmen and the work in the fields. They had one incident of petty theft. Emely had to hear evidence on and determine a punishment if one was needed. Returning to the manor house, Lord Rene complimented Emely on her decision.

"Christian was wrong on many things he did here but leaving you in charge was a correct choice," Lord Rene said.

"Thank you," Emely said touched by the compliment.

CHAPTER 31

The morning Lord Rene and Lady Gracen left was warm and sunny. They hugged each other and promised to write often. Emely watched the little caravan leave the courtyard and then disappear into the forest beyond the village. She gave a sigh of relief once they were gone. She loved having them come for a visit, but it was a strain on their resources. Sarah did not come to the manor house when either of the lords were visiting, and Emely missed seeing her friend. The manor slipped back into a comfortable routine. Gwyneth seemed to grow each day and to talk more and get around faster. Emely checked their food supply. While the harvest was still going to be good the rain had damaged some of the crops and it would be smaller than anticipated. she was reassured they would have enough to get to harvest.

The daily work of overseeing the manor kept Emely busy but she was always aware of Arianna's journal. It took Emely two weeks before she went to the cabinet and got out the small book. Emely had put Gwyneth down for the night and sat under the torch in her room to read. The first date in the journal was a few months before her wedding. She must have been informed of the coming wedding day because there was a single entry, 'I am to be married to a man.' It was such a simple statement, but Emely believed there was much Arianna had not written that day. The next entry was a few days later. Arianna was lamenting her fate. She wished to be a nun. Emely stopped and stared at the words the young girl had written. Emely wondered if Lord Rene or Lady Gracen had any idea what Arianna wanted. Emely put the journal away. one entry had given her a lot to think about. She remembered the day David had been conceived. She loved Christian, had dreamed for so long of being his. The moment of pain had meant little while she was in his arms, and they were joined. She could only imagine how cruel it had been for Arianna. The loss of her innocence to a stranger. Emely believed Christian would have been gentle with Arianna. She had seen the look of horror on his face when he realized he had taken her innocence. He would not want to repeat that experience, but they had a responsibility to produce heirs. It took several days before Emely returned to the journal. The writings of a far too sheltered girl who had hoped to be a nun let Emely know the girl.

Summer turned to fall, and it was harvesting time. Everyone worked to bring in the harvest and prepare the manor for the coming year. Her list of tasks to be done never seemed to shorten. The first tapestry was completed. Lady Arianna dressed as she had been on her wedding day, her dark hair lifted by the slight breeze blowing that day. Her eyes dark brown shining as she looked off into the distance, a slight smile lifting her lips, she looked both serene and hopeful for the future. It was a vision of her, Emely knew Lord Rene and Lady Gracen would approve of even if it was not reality. Emely had it hung on one side of the wall behind the dais. Looking at it, Emely started planning its companion tapestry. It would be of Christian as he had looked the day he had left for the crusade. It was the last memory she had of him, and the one that sometimes visited her dreams.

The first snow came early and covered the village. Classes resumed after the harvest and the children were making progress in their reading and writing. Just before the snow cut the village off from the rest of the world, Emely received another letter from Christian. Days passed in slow succession. Emely read and reread Christian's letter from Constantinople. She also continued to read Arianna's journal. The contrast between the wonders Christian described and the dismal life

Arianna felt trapped in, was heart breaking. Emely had the joy denied Arianna of watching Gwyneth grow and become a child now she was no longer nursing. With the snow also came the usual increase in petty crime in the village committed by the same few people.

One day as she walked back to the manor house, she raised her face to the sun that had forced its way through the clouds. Patches of sunlight slid across the landscape. It was almost a perfect day, so Emely decided she did not want to be cooped up in the manor house. She made sure Sarah could watch Gwyneth and then had a horse saddled so she could go riding. Emely rode along the stream that flowed through the village until she was out of sight. Then deep into the forest. A small path wandered through the forest until it crossed the road to the village. Emely knew she would come to ride this path often in the future. When Gwyneth was older, she would bring her so the girl could play at the water's edge as she and Felise had when they were children.

The snow stayed and grew deeper with each passing storm. Tempers grew short and Emely heard problems in the village every week. Work had to be found to keep the village men busy. Emely decided the wall around the manor courtyard needed to be more substantial, a wall of field stone. Nearby clay deposits would work as mortar between the rocks. It was hard labor, and the progress was slow, but it was a project keeping everyone busy, and the petty crime stopped. By spring there would be ten foot sections completed on each side of the courtyard gate. It would take years, but there would be a strong wall to protect the manor house.

The Christmas holiday came, and after the Christmas morning mass everyone enjoyed the meal provided from the manor houses stores and appreciated the new clothing Emely gave everyone on Christian's behalf. The villagers seemed to appreciate Gwyneth's participation in the gift giving. Emely and the little girl were the focal points of their loyalty.

CHAPTER 32

1098

Winter came full force. It snowed for days and all work on the wall had to be stopped. The snow was now knee deep and no one ventured out if they did not have to. Emely and Gwyneth stayed in the manor house alone because it was too difficult for Sarah to come and bring her children. Father Francis came to dinner once or twice as did Rand during January and February. Emely and Gwyneth went to mass in the village church on Sunday mornings. Nelda had come every day, but Emely realized it was a hardship on the other woman and told her not to come. Emely ventured into the manor house storeroom every evening to get what she would need the next day to feed Gwyneth and herself. Once Gwyneth was down for the night Emely pulled out Arianna's journal and read a few entries.

Even though Arianna was the same age as Emely, the girl who kept this journal was so sheltered, she seemed much younger. Arianna had no exposure to a life not eased by others. Arianna did not care for possessions. In her mind she was married to Jesus, which she believed was her calling. She knew nothing of the world or the relations between men and women nor did she want to. Arianna spoke with childlike innocence of what the future held for her life married to a man. Often in her journal Arianna had prayed to the Virgin for deliverance from this torture she was enduring after her marriage to Christian. She never spoke ill of him and often expressed her forgiveness for his taking and using her body to satisfy his needs. Arianna had never hated Christian, and she understood what was expected of them and she knew she had to fulfill those expectations.

The most touching entry was the day Arianna had felt Gwyneth move within her for the first time and knew she was carrying a child. She wrote of her joy and excitement. In the following entries she forgave her father for forcing her into this marriage because she was bringing another soul into the world. The entry made Emely stop reading because it was so touching the way Arianna described Christian's reaction when she had told him she was with child. The beauty of her words describing his wonderment and reverence for both her and their child were more than Emely could bear to read. She put the journal away for several weeks knowing how happy he had been. She wondered if he would have been as happy to know of their child. even thinking the question she knew the answer, he would have been.

The first promise of spring came the first week of March. The snow started to melt, and people began to move around the village. Winter fought to retain its hold on the village dropping more snow two weeks into the month, but everyone knew it would not last and went about their business of preparing for spring planting. March turned to April and the snow was at last gone. Spring planting was done as was the shearing of sheep. The process of preparing the wool for spinning and weaving began.

It was the second week of July when another letter from Christian arrived, She put the letter away in the cabinet with Arianna's journal to be read when she was alone and could savor every word. They had left Constantinople and taken Nicaea and were now laying siege to Antioch. He did not write of the hardships and suffering they had endured or inflicted. He did tell her John, Michael, and all their men had fought with honor and courage. There had been few casualties in battle. Despite the few details, Emely sensed Christian felt there was little to boast about. He asked about Gwyneth, and her progress and he asked about her. He closed by saying he missed both of them and they were always in his thoughts. Reading his letter made Emely feel, despite the distance separating them, they were still together, living in each other's heart. She took hope he might love her but could not be so bold as to believe it was possible. She put the letter away with Arianna's journal and knew she would return to read it again many times.

CHAPTER 33

Christian July 1097

The Crusaders left Constantinople and traveled southward toward the Holy Land. Now they were in enemy territory and the advance toward the Holy city of Jerusalem was slow. Their progress slowed by battles along the way, sieges of towns, the loss of men but still they moved toward Jerusalem.

In May 1097, a year after he had left home, they began the siege of Nicaea. For a month they camped outside the city walls. The siege was dull, with men of action idle, tempers flared, and petty arguments became fights sometimes to the death. Christian and Michael were on constant alert to keep their men busy. The same could not be said for Drake and Piers. They were guilty of starting fights among their own men and then wagering as to who the winner would be. The wives and daughters of the serf Crusaders were not safe from the unwanted attentions and sexual abuse of men not their husbands or fathers. When the city was starved into submission weeks later, the carnage was horrific. Christian, Michael, and a few others were sickened by the evil supposed good Christian men could do.

A week after the fall of Nicaea, leaving behind a small contingent of men, most of the Crusaders began their march toward Antioch. Now they were at war, often fighting for every inch of territory, sometimes being pushed back from land already taken by the force of arms and deaths of good men. Their progress was slow, day after long, hot, grueling day of battle. It was during this march Piers foolishly led his men into an army of the enemy. Outnumbered by fifty or more enemies, Piers pressed forward until he was surrounded. Christian, Drake, and Michael were forced to rescue the reckless knight. By the time they could reach him he had taken multiple blows. He was curled up to protect his vital organs as the enemy abused his body with kicks and blows as Piers cried out for his mother. The enemy saw him as weak and dishonorable and continued their abuse until Christian and Drake were able to drag the enemy away. Piers lay broken in both body and mind, calling for his mother. Christian and Drake pulled Piers to his feet, but his legs would not hold him, and he had to be carried from the field. Even once to safety, he was incoherent and had lost control of his bodily functions. He was like a small child who could not care for himself and comprehended little of what was said or asked of him. He had screaming fits and other times when he sat for hours rocking and mumbling to himself. Other times he would try to run from anyone who approached him or hide under rugs or makeshift beds, peering out and then ducking back under whatever cover he could make for himself. Christian, Michael, and Drake decided they had to take Piers with them for his own protection. Until they were done with the Crusade there was no way to get him home.

They arrived outside Antioch in the fall and the siege began. Leaderless, Piers' men needed a knight to follow. Some chose to follow Drake and continue their drunken savagery toward local people. The rest, as shocked and horrified as Christian and Michael at such behavior, turned to Christian. Christian's men were leery at first but soon found these new additions to their ranks were longing for the discipline and fairness Christian's leadership provided. The two groups blended well together.

Now they sat outside Antioch. Days turned into weeks and weeks turned into months and still they sat outside the town. Drake's men searched the countryside looking for 'entertainment' in the abuse of the few locals who had either stayed or drifted back to their farms. The last few soon left again seeking the protection of the local lord. Christian and Michael's men were kept busy with daily drills, training, and maintaining their equipment and supplies. Still, they sat in siege of the city.

Eight long, bitter months later in summer, Antioch fell through the betrayal of one of their own. The walls were breeched, and the Crusaders entered the city. Their months of idleness turned again to the savage abuse and death of the citizens. many welcomed death. Their emaciated bodies attested to the starvation they had suffered. The Crusaders found nothing living in the city except the people as they had killed and eaten all other animals for food in their desperation. Christian rode through the city seeing the dead but lost all feeling of anger for their resistance or horror at the carnage. He felt nothing. the crusaders had little time to make the city livable for themselves because just two days after they took it, they themselves were under siege. For three long weeks as their meager supplies dwindled, an enemy army surrounded the city. The Crusaders in the city had to keep constant vigil so the walls were never breeched. They had to take cover at times as volley after volley of arrows descended on the city, killing men on the walls and in the streets. Another army of Crusaders finally arrived and freed the city. They brought food and supplies to people on the brink of desperation.

Christian was exhausted but relieved to get time without having to keep a constant watch on his men and the defenses. The night the siege ended, he sat again to write Emely. the words would not come. He could not tell her what he had seen. He could not be happy at the savage destruction they had brought. He wrote even less than before, only where they were, how well John was doing as second in command despite not having knight's training. Michael had earned the respect of his men for his valor, and he had earned Christian's loyal friendship. there was sad news. Two of their village men had died, a bitter loss because Christian had come to know and like all his men. Christian looked at the few lines he had written and knew he could write no more, it was too painful and appalling to admit what they had done to innocent people. He sat back and thought of home. It was well into summer, crops would be planted and starting to sprout, sheep sheered, repairs to huts from winter damage would have started. Gwyneth would be walking and talking by now. He smiled thinking of the child he barely knew but loved with all his heart. He pictured Emely as he had seen her that last day: warm, loving. How he wished to be back home, holding her in his arms. He could not tell her this. He was a warrior. He could die here tomorrow and even if he survived, he had little to offer her. Lord Rene could without hesitation make war on him when he returned and take back the manor. No, he could not tell her what was in his heart. She needed to find another and be happy.

Now was the time to rest and gather their strength. The months of laying siege to Antioch had depleted the men not only in body but also in spirit. Many questioned if being this far from home was worth the suffering and loss they had endured. For some the promise of riches once they took Jerusalem was enough, for others it was the promise of forgiveness of all their sins. for most it was their sacred duty to follow their knight. Christian and Michael chose to live among their men, keeping them battle ready but also sharing thoughts of home. They rested and rebuilt their bodies with the steady supply of food that was at last reaching them. They worked to clear the carnage they had created, making the city livable once more. It filled the months before they at last began their final march toward Jerusalem.

Six months after taking Antioch, the men and animals fed and healthy, the march began. It was January of 1099, almost three years since they had left home, and the end seemed to be in sight. They had only traveled a month when word arrived Antioch was once again under siege, and they had to turn back to relieve the city. It took seven precious weeks of fighting to reach and relieve the city before they could resume their march toward the Holy City.

CHAPTER 34

May 1098

Gwyneth had her second birthday and continued to make strides in her walking and talking. She was running and coming down the stairs. She also thought everything she could see was hers and would take playthings away from Eden, Sarah's little boy. He would grab the toy back and the howling would begin. Both children would be crying as they grabbed things away from each other. Gwyneth had two favorite words 'mine' and 'no' which she used often.

Emely was planning a trip to visit Lord Bryce and Lady Martha when in the third week of May a rider came to her. Lord Benoit had died. Lord Bryce's manor was in mourning for the loss of the heir. Emely made haste so she and Gwyneth could leave at first light in the morning to return with the rider. Like the year before, Emely rode with Gwyneth in front of her on her horse. They reached Lord Bryce's by nightfall and were welcomed both with warmth and sorrow. Lord Bryce looked pale, but Lady Martha was lost in deep mourning. Emely went to the older woman and held her while she cried for another lost child.

"He was jousting," Lord Bryce explained. "Something he did weekly. He and the other knights practiced their skills. I told him there was no reason to do so but he laughed and said they had to do something to amuse themselves."

"How is Lady Marilee?" Emely asked.

"Gone," said a saddened Lady Martha wiping her eyes. "She stayed a fortnight but when she was sure she was not with child, she sent word to her father asking for an escort home. Home! After all these years she was part of our family. She never thought of this as her home," Lady Martha said bitter at Marilee's rejection of the loving warmth this family had always given her.

"She is still of marriageable age," Lord Bryce said consoling his wife but citing the reality of the situation. "Her father will make a match for her to secure his borders. If Duran died and Felise came home, I would do the same."

"Felise would not come home. Garren is Duran's heir," Lady Martha reminded him.

"Garren is young. We know the young can die without warning."

"When the new baby arrives, please God it be a boy, the lineage will be more than secure," Lady Martha said.

"Like ours?" Lord Bryce said bitter at the loss of so many children. Then seeing his wife's face he softened his tone. "We have only one living son. He is off fighting in the Holy Land. If he dies, Garren and Gwyneth are our heirs. Our dream was not this. It matters not. Christian will come back to us. He must come back to us."

"He will," Emely said with faith she knew could be shattered. "He must. Gwyneth needs her father."

"Yes, she and Garren are our family now." Lord Bryce said. "Where is she?"

"It is a long trip for a two year old. She is in bed for the night."

"It is a long trip for a twenty year old," Lord Bryce said smiling at Emely. "Should you not be getting your rest?"

"I would rather sit with you and Lady Martha if you approve. I have missed you both. Tell me about Felise and Lord Duran. They are well. Happy?"

"Yes," said Lady Martha after a moment's thought. "I think they are happy now. Felise has come to accept, and I believe love Duran. He is a good man. He loves her deeply."

"I think he did from the beginning," Emely said remembering the care Duran had shown Felise from their first meeting.

They stayed and talked for a while longer but soon the long day had Emely yawning and Lord Bryce insisted, she go to bed.

In the morning Gwyneth was delighted to be passed around and played with by Lady Martha and her ladies. Lord Bryce took Emely on a tour of the manor and talked to her as an equal. She had learned so much about running a manor and asked him questions, sometimes surprising him. Emely and Gwyneth stayed a week, and each day was the same with Emely going about the manor with Lord Bryce while Gwyneth stayed with Lady Martha. Gwyneth got to explore the flower garden, feed the baby sheep and goats, and was adored by everyone in the manor house. Emely knew she would have a spoiled child when they got home. Everyone here let her do almost anything she wanted and when she was told no, she pouted in such an adorable way her grandparents gave in to her every wish. Even the morning they left for home, Gwyneth was pouting at having to be up so early and then be on horseback. She whined and Lady Martha tried to convince Emely to stay just a few more days.

"No, we need to get home. I have responsibilities there. We still have to visit Lord Rene this summer."

"How do you get along with him?" Lord Bryce asked, knowing Rene had forced Christian to go to the Crusades.

"Well. He has come to trust me and perhaps forgive Christian just a little," Emely said smiling.

"Forgive Christian?"

"Lord Rene blamed Christian for Arianna's death. I think he now knows she was just too young to be a wife. She was not ready."

"Is any girl?" Lady Martha asked.

"If you love the . . ." Emely started remembering her joy at being with Christian and then stopped.

"You loved the father of your child," Lady Martha said knowing there could be no other reason for Emely's protection of the unknown man.

"Very much. But he belonged to another."

"Who is he?" Lord Bryce asked, afraid both that she would and would not answer.

Emely looked at the man she loved almost as much as her own father. "I will not tell. It no longer matters. David is gone and I have a new life taking care of Gwyneth."

Once on the road, Gwyneth wiggled for the first few miles of the trip before settling down and snuggling into Emely's body to go to sleep. When she woke, Gwyneth was in a better mood and chattered and pointed at everything. She would sometimes go quiet and listen to the birds chirping in the trees and then make sounds back to them. Emely was enjoying the forest anew, seeing and hearing through Gwyneth's appreciation of it.

Back at Christian's manor all was quiet. Summer came with hotter weather and longer hours. Unlike the summer before, there was little rain, and the harvest was in jeopardy due to lack of water. Emely and Rand were looking for ways to get more water to the fields. They worked with the cooper to build a water wheel with buckets that would lift water from the stream running through the village into wooden troths directing the water to the fields and pastures where needed. With the heavy snowfall, the river feeding their stream was overflowing as was the stream. It took a week to get the water wheel built and working but there was great relief in the village when the first water reached the crops. Their harvest was saved and would again with hard work be abundant. Because everyone in their area was experiencing the same problem, Lord Rene and Lady Gracen did not come to visit in the summer. After an abundant harvest in the fall and work progressing on the manor wall, Emely decided she and Gwyneth would visit Arianna's parents at their manor. Like the trip to Lord Bryce's, it was only a day's ride on horseback. After Gwyneth was put down for the night, Emely sat and talked with Lord Rene and Lady Gracen. They ask about Lord Bryce and Lady Martha and expressed their sympathy for their loss. Emely knew they understood how devastating it had been since they had lost two sons themselves before Arianna had been born.

CHAPTER 35

Like their visit to Lord Bryce, Gwyneth spent her days with Lady Gracen and her ladies while Emely spent hers with Lord Rene. She told him about the new wall and the other improvements they were making to the manor.

"Why do you bother?" Lord Rene asked.

"It is our home. Lord Christian will expect to see improvements when he returns."

"Why? He cared nothing for the place. He will return to his father's now he is the heir. The place will be abandoned. It will return to the forest as it was before Bryce, and I had it built."

"No, I do not believe Lord Christian will leave, for quite some time."

"Why would he stay?"

"It is his home. He can be his own master, run his own manor. He will need time to be a lord again not just a warrior."

"He can do that at Bryce's." Lord Rene said bitter the younger man would have so much when all of his own children were gone. "He was always a warrior first. It is why he killed . . . let Arianna die."

"Must we talk of this again," Lady Gracen said as they walked into the great room of the manor.

"He cared nothing for her!" Lord Rene said bitterness at the loss of his child still a stab to his heart.

"She was too young!" Lady Gracen said with equal emphasis.

"Stop," Emely said going to stand between them. She had heard this argument before. She knew what Arianna wanted and how she felt betrayed by her father even as she forgave him and Christian.

"Yes, Lady Arianna was young," Emely said turning to Lady Gracen, "but so are all girls of marriageable age." Then turning to Lord Rene, she added, "Lord Christian was not to blame for her death. Women die in childbirth and after."

Lord Rene stared at Emely forgetting he often considered her and treated her as his equal. For a moment he saw only a serf who was speaking with disrespect to her better.

"How dare you?" he demanded.

"He is my lord. I have taken a vow of loyalty to him. A vow which requires I defend him. You would expect the same from any of your serfs," she defended.

Lord Rene continued to stare at Emely for several more seconds.

"She is correct," Lady Gracen said putting a hand on her husband's arm. "You would expect that. Emely has shown a great deal of courage in defending her lord."

Lord Rene looked at his wife and then at the girl in front of him. He had come to respect Emely because she did defend both herself and Christian. She had never before spoken Arianna's name. Then he realized his wife was right, he would expect his serfs to defend him if he were dishonored in their presence. He was not sure he would get the same loyalty as this girl gave Christian, however. He smiled.

"You are right, my dear. Emely, you are a good and loyal serf to your lord. I hope he appreciates all you do for him."

"Thank you," Emely said and then hugged the man she loved almost as a father.

Gwyneth and Emely returned to Christian's manor a few days later and prepared for the winter. Emely still went to the village every day and found time to ride along the stream. She often reread Arianna's journal, getting to know the other girl through what she had written. Her devotion to God and the saints she venerated. Emely read and reread careful finding meaning in the young girl's words: her fear of Christian, her love for her unborn child. Emely could almost hear the other girl speaking to her at times.

The first snow came late and work on the wall progressed faster than Emely could have hoped. They would be able to keep working as the harvest had been so good. The store houses were filled to over-flowing. Work on cloth making and the tapestry also went well. Christmas came and then the deep snow. By the new year, the manor settled in for the winter, cut off from the outside world.

The winter was less harsh and movement around the village was easy. By March, the snow was beginning to melt and in the second week another letter arrived from Christian. They had taken Antioch after an eight month siege; he wrote but gave little details. He also wrote that two of their villagers had been lost in the siege and asked her to notify the families. They were buried with the full rites of the church. Emely knew the two families well. One had been a younger son who had gone to seek his fortune, the other was a husband and father. His wife had been getting along with the help of the other villagers. Now she would need to remarry to give her children a father and protector.

Emely sensed Christian's sorrow at the loss of his men. She sensed he was changing from just a warrior to a true lord who took his vow of protection of his people seriously. They both were changing, would there be anything of the love they once shared left when they met again, if they met again, she wondered.

With spring coming so early, Emely was busy with the spring work, his letter was set aside until she had time to put pen to paper in May. She wrote, telling him of Gwyneth's progress and sharing short glimpses of the three year old. Then she stopped and looked at her words. She wanted to tell him how she longed to see his face, touch his hand, be warmed by his embrace, to speak of her love. she could not put words and emotions on paper. He was a lord, she a serf, there had never been nor would there ever be a future for them. She sat back from the table so her tears would not smear the ink. She closed the letter and sent it back the next day with the messenger.

Then she turned her attention once more to the manor and Gwyneth. The only way she could demonstrate her love for Christian was by making sure he would be proud of his manor when he returned.

CHAPTER 36

May 1099

Gwyneth was so much more aware of everything and played well with Eden. She seemed to carry on whole conversations with Emely. She loved being in the village and running around with the other children. She made friends with ease and was kind and loving. Emely was thankful Gwyneth was past the 'no' stage. Now her favorite word was 'why'. Emely wanted to be frustrated but she loved Gwyneth's curiosity, and it allowed Emely to see the world through the child's eyes. Gwyneth's questions made Emely think about things she had ceased to find fascinating and took for granted.

Spring planting was done, repairs on huts and common buildings started, and the new tapestry was hung. Emely could look around the manor and take pride in all they had and were accomplishing. Christian would return to a home and manor much more comfortable and welcoming then the one he had left. It was a surprise in June when both Lord Bryce and Lord Rene and their ladies arrived on the same day. Emely took a deep breath, reviewed their food supply with Nelda and had Sarah bring two girls from the village to help with serving and making sure the rooms they occupied were well maintained. The uneasiness between the two men was felt by all. Emely realized this was the first time they had seen each other since Christian and Arianna's wedding four years before. She remembered they had arranged the marriage because they had been such close friends most of their lives. Now one of their children was dead and the other had been forced to go fight a war thousands of miles away. The two ladies had been friends before their marriages and now were bonded over their mutual grandchild.

"Milady," said one of the village girls approaching Emely. "Should we prepare the tables?"

"Yes, please, Raine." Emely answered unaware as four pairs of eyes looked at her.

"Milady?" questioned Lord Bryce with a smile.

"What?" Emely asked, looking confused.

"She called you 'milady," he clarified.

Emely looked at him and then at the girl who was going through the door leading to the cookhouse. When had it happened, she wondered? When had they started calling her by the title and when had she stopped trying to correct them? Sarah had referred to her by that title almost from the beginning, but the rest of the villagers had taken up the title. Even Father Francis used the title.

"I . . .. I have asked them not to," Emely stammered looking at each of the nobles in turn.

Lord Bryce's smile deepened and then he started to laugh.

"Emely, you have earned the title," he said, pleased the villagers recognized and accepted this smart, kind, loving young woman.

"Yes," added Lord Rene. "Of all the things Christian did wrong, putting you in charge here was something he did right."

Silence filled the room for several moments as they all reacted to the first part of his statement.

"You were always meant to be a lady," Lady Martha said reflecting back on Emely's childhood. "Even as a child you always had a . . . sense of dignity. Often times more than Felise."

"We have come to know a warm charming woman," Lady Gracen said. We love her, we love you."

"I am not a noble. I am a serf," Emely said emphasizing her status.

"Only by birth," Lord Bryce said. "How you have lived your life, cared for Christian's manor, his home and most important his child, you are a lady. You have earned the title. I pray when you marry it will be to the station you deserve."

"I will never marry," Emely whispered.

"Emely!?" Lord Rene said in shock. "You must. You should have a husband who loves you, who will give you children of your own. Who . . . ." he stopped then seeing the look of pain on Emely's face.

"Emely?" he asked.

"I had a child of my own. I will never marry because of him," Emely said. The pain of David's loss still a wound in her heart. "I need to attend Gwyneth. Please excuse me," she said knowing she had to be alone with her still raw grief.

"Emely," said Lord Bryce

She ignored him turning and went upstairs to get Gwyneth up from her nap. The silence in the main room as she climbed the stairs spoke louder than if they had started talking about her. She leaned against a wall at the top of the stairs and took a deep breath. If Lord Rene had not known of her past before, he would now. He would have questions. She prayed Lord Bryce would answer them as best he could. Gwyneth smiled as Emely entered her chamber and all thoughts of her painful past were gone.

"You care not, my little love," Emely said picking Gwyneth up.

"Care not," Gwyneth repeated smiling in her sweet little child way.

Downstairs in the main room they could hear snippets of conversation as they left the chamber. When they reached the bottom of the stairs it stopped. The two ladies turned their full attention to Gwyneth. While the two lords watched. None of them looked at Emely. Conversation started again and was focused on Gwyneth. There was a hesitation in the conversation there had never been before. The older couples were more guarded about the topics they chose. It took several hours before everyone seemed to relax again, and Emely was grateful when they no longer seemed concerned. The conversation continued over the evening meal. Both Lord Bryce and Lord Rene seemed to enjoy the wine being served and began to remember the adventures of their youth; the battles they had fought and the cities they had taken. Reminiscing about one particular town, Lord Bryce smiled.

"Do you remember the girl?" Lord Bryce asked.

"The redhead?" Lord Rene responded also with a smile.

"Yes," said Lord Bryce with a deeper smile and a lifted eyebrow.

"Yes," said Lord Rene, his smile deepening.

"A redhead?" Emely asked with a wicked teasing smile.

"Yes" Lord Bryce started to continue and then saw his wife's face.

"She was not . . . good," Lord Bryce offered.

"What?" Lord Rene said then saw his wife's face. "No, not attractive at all," he offered.

"Ugly," Lord Bryce interjected.

"Bad teeth."

"Bad breath."

"Smelled."

"Pock marked."

"Vermin covered."

Emely was having trouble holding in her laughter as the two men tried to downplay this particular adventure.

"She was long before we met," Lord Bryce said to the wives.

"We were young," Lord Rene offered.

"Barely having our first hair."

"We knew nothing of women."

"Well, you certainly knew a lot about them by the time we met," Lady Martha said with a chill in her voice.

"A lot," Lady Gracen offered. "Perhaps a bit too much."

"And since the two of you seem to be enjoying your memories of that particular . . . person so much, I think you should stay up all night," Lady Martha said in a huff. "So, Gracen and I will share our room and the two of you whenever you decided to be abed you can share Rene's room."

The two ladies stood and went upstairs for the night.

"I think I should be abed also," Emely said. "Good morrow milords."

Upstairs she knocked on the door of the chamber Lord Bryce was to occupy. Lady Martha opened the door with a smile on her face and invited Emely in. Lady Gracen was there and smiling also.

"How are they feeling?" Lady Gracen asked.

"From the wine or their . . . ill-timed memory?" Emely asked laughing.

"I wonder if they think we are really angry," Lady Martha said with a smile.

"I hope they do." Lady Gracen said also smiling. "They need to be reminded we have feelings and are their equals, and they must respect us. We make their lives too easy."

"We however love them," Lady Martha said smiling at her friend.

"Yes, we do."

The next morning the two lords were feeling the effects of too much wine as Emely had the morning meal put on the table for them. She said nothing as she poured each a cup of morning ale. Lord Bryce looked up at her smiling but nervous.

"Were we fools?" he asked.

"You were men remembering your younger days," Emely told him.

"The ladies?" Lord Rene asked.

"Will be down shortly."

"Are they angry?" Lord Bryce asked.

"Would you be if they reminisced about . . . old loves?" Emely asked.

"Neither had old loves," Lord Rene said knowing both women had been innocence when first taken.

"No, we were their first, thankfully. The thought of another man with Martha . . .." Lord Bryce said then saw Emely's face. "Emely?"

"I must attend Gwyneth, please excuse me," Emely said.

"Emely!" Lord Bryce used a tone she seldom heard from him.

"Milord," she said with a sigh turning back toward him.

"No man of worth will care. If he loves you, he will not care!"

"I care. If I love him, I will not have him dishonored because of my past," she said with quiet conviction.

"No one cares about your past. You have lived an exemplary life."

"I care!"

"Emely."

"Please milord, we can keep having this conversation but neither of us will change our minds. I . . . made a choice and I will live with the consequences."

"You were taken against your will! I will always believe that!"

"I . . . I hoped for a future, but it was not to be."

"Who was he?"

"If I would not tell you when you banished me, why would I tell you now?"

"Emely, let me make this right."

"Will 'making it right' bring back my son?" Emely said with quiet annoyance.

"Emely?"

"I have work to do. It is time Gwyneth was up. Please excuse me," Emely said in a tone that allowed no further discussion and went upstairs.

For the rest of their visit, Lord Bryce avoided bringing up the past. Emely had Rand take the two lords around the manor so they could inspect all the work being done. She took the ladies to the small flower garden at the back of the manor house so they could enjoy the warm summer air. Gwyneth moved between the three women. She picked flowers and in turn gave one to each of them and then repeated the process twice more. Until Emely asked her to stop. Gwyneth made a face and picked another flower and took it to Lady Martha. Who smiled and said thank you as she took it from the little girl's hand. Then Gwyneth picked another flower and took it to Lady Gracen who also smiled as she took it. Gwyneth was on her way to pick another flower went Emely told her to stop. When Gwyneth picked yet another flower Emely knew it was time for consequences. She went and picked up the little girl and headed toward the house. It was nap time and some time away from her grandmothers' indulgence was called for. The ladies started to protest but Emely gave them a look indicating Gwyneth needed to stop when she was told to. The lords stayed a few more days, inspecting everything and giving Emely suggestions on more improvements to be done, although these came more from Lord Bryce than Lord Rene. Both men expressed how well the manor was doing under her management.

CHAPTER 37

As always Emely was pleased when they came to visit but was almost as happy when they left, and the manor could return to its normal schedule. She and Gwyneth were there to say their goodbyes the morning both couples left. The usual hugs and kisses were given, and both couples made Emely promise she and Gwyneth would come and visit them before the New Year. Then they were off. Emely and Gwyneth waving until both carts carrying the ladies were out of sight at the far end of the village and into the wood.

Summer progressed, sunny and warm. Rain came when it was needed followed by days of beautiful sunshine and gentle breezes. Emely rode every day and took Gwyneth with her. By the beginning of September, they knew the wood and stream well. The harvest was abundant, filling the storehouses. October came and went and still the weather remained warm. Even November was mild with warm days filled with sunshine and gentle breezes. The harvest celebration was a fitting revelry to an exceptional year's work. It stayed warm into early December.

It was mid-December; Gwyneth was down for the night when an insistent knock came to the manor house door. No one ever came this late at night unless someone in the village was dying and wanted Emely to witness their dying words giving what little they had to specific family members. Emely grabbed her cape knowing she would have to leave the house. She opened the door to find Rand, Sarah and Sarah's children standing on the top step.

"You are needed in the village," Rand said making it clear the issue to be dealt with was serious. "Sarah will stay with Lady Gwyneth."

"Sarah, take the chamber next to Gwyneth's so the children can be abed."

"Thank you, milady," said Sarah ushering the children up the stairs.

"Who is it?" Emely asked.

"There has been an . . . incident. You are needed to hear evidence," Rand said bitter at the crime.

"What? Can this not wait until morning?" Emely said stopping.

"No Emely, this cannot wait," Rand said. The look on his face even in the darkness of night told Emely this was serious.

"What . . ." she started.

"You need to hear the evidence," Rand cut off her question.

They walked to the church in silence. When they entered the entire village was already gathered. Emely and Rand moved to the front and as they approached Emely saw one of the male villagers bruised and bloodied. She was shocked. He looked like he had been beaten.

"Roland, what happened?" Emely asked but the man only hung his head and Rand drew Emely away and guided her to the altar.

"Emely, Lord Christian's designate, has come to hear witnesses against Roland accused by Jerod of violating Jerod's daughter, Elle, against her will. If you wish to be heard, come forward," announced Rand.

Jerod moved to the front of the crowd. Roland was shoved there by two of the larger village men.

"Jerod," Rand said, "tell us your tale."

"My daughter, Elle, she is but sixteen. Untouched and unknowing of what passes between a man and a woman," Jerod began. "She . . . she was walking in the wood, gathering berries. . .. She . . . she came home . . .." the man stopped as emotions overtook him. "She came home. Her tunic was ripped, her hair filled with twigs." He stopped again, closing his eyes, and shaking his head as if to clear the painful image from his memory. "She was bruised, bleeding down her . . . down her legs," Jerod stopped there, as his emotions won over his need to tell what he knew.

"She wanted it," Roland burst out. "She has been following me around for weeks. Flirting with me and every other man in the village."

"Silence," Rand ordered as the crowd began to grumble.

"She is only sixteen," Jerod said again. "She . . . she knows nothing. She is a friend to everyone. These are our friends and neighbors, so she smiles and greets them."

"She wanted it. She wanted me!" Roland burst out again. "I . . . I wanted to come to you, to ask for her. She said 'no.'" Roland continued but something in his desperation did not sound right to Emely.

"Where is Elle?" Emely asked.

"Outside with her mother," Jerod said.

"Bring her in," Emely requested.

"My lady," Jerod said. "She . . . she fears Roland. She screams and cries when she sees him."

Emely looked at Jerod and knew he was telling the truth.

"Everyone leave this place. Take Roland to Father Francis's hut while I speak with Elle here," Emely told Rand.

Rand grabbed Roland and dragged him toward the back entrance after telling everyone to leave. More grumbling came, but the villagers little by little moved out of the church. Emely sat on the top step of the alter platform. Elle and her mother entered by the main door and Emely saw a young girl with vacant eyes. She was trembling as they walked forward, and her mother spoke to her, comforting her.

"You may leave," Emely said to Tess, Elle's mother.

"My lady?" Tess said hopeful she could stay and comfort her daughter.

"I need to speak with Elle . . . alone." Emely answered the unspoken question.

Tess gave her daughter a hug and then turned and left.

"Elle please come sit with me," Emely said in calm tones.

The girl walked forward as if going to her doom and then sat with obvious discomfort next to Emely. Emely studied the girl for several seconds before speaking. It was obvious she had been taken, violated. Her eyes were haunted and moving looking for some unknown and unseen attacker. Emely could feel the tenseness in the young girl; she was ready to run from any sudden movement. Elle's hair still had twigs tangled in it, her tunic was torn halfway up her thigh, a bruise was starting to form on her left cheek, and there was a trail of blood at one corner of her mouth. Bruises were forming on her thin wrists.

"Elle," Emely said in a soothing voice. The child needed to feel safe and believed. "Can you tell me what happened?"

"I . . . I went to pick berries. I knew he was following me. He does to some of us girls. I . . . I thought he thought . . . I wanted help. We got to the berry patch and . . .." she started crying. "I . . . I . . .."

"Elle, have you bled your first?"

"Yes," came the answer and then Elle realized what the consequences could be. She screamed in terror and Emely took the young girl in her arms as she cried.

After several minutes, Emely could feel the girl's sobs slowing.

"Do you . . . wish to marry him?" Emely asked.

"No! I love another," came the swift response.

"Do you wish to marry the boy you love?"

"Yes, but . . . he is with Lord Christian."

"What do you want to happen to Roland?"

"I care not. I never want to see him again."

"And if you are with child?" Emely asked knowing that possibility had not occurred to the young girl.

"I . . . I . . . I" the young girl stammered.

"Your parents love you and know you are innocent. They will love you and your child."

"I . . .." the girl still could not speak.

"I will send Roland away," Emely promised. "Should he be whipped? Harmed?"

"No!" exclaimed the girl. "No."

"It will be so," Emely said giving the girl one last hug before she called in Tess and Rand.

Tess took Elle out of the church with instructions from Emely to help the girl clean up and get her to bed so she could try to sleep. Elle was not to be left alone. Emely then had Rand bring in the rest of the villagers.

Emely stood tall and straight as the villagers came into the church. Rand brought Roland back from Father Francis's.

"Roland," Emely began, "you are accused of violating Elle, daughter of Jerod. You claim she 'wanted' you. She says she did not and does not want you. She loves another. I have not the right to take your life as you have taken her innocence. Nor do I have the right to take your manhood as you have denied another of her innocence. She may even now be with child, your child, but if is to be you will never see the child or her again. Roland, I, Emely, guardian of the manor and people of our Lord Christian, do banish you from this village and manor. Rand will take you to the wood as you are and with what you have with you as of this moment."

The villagers murmured their discontent.

"This is what Elle wants," Emely said. "She is the offended. It is her judgement I only speak her wishes."

"She is but a child," Jerod said. "She knows not of the consequences."

"She knows. She is prepared for what may come. With the love and help of you and her mother and the entire village, she will find strength and peace."

"But" Jerod began but stopped when he saw Emely's face.

"This is my judgement given in Lord Christian's name," Emely said. "Rand, take Roland from this place but make sure he leaves Lord Christian's manor with no further injury."

"Milady," Rand said grabbing Roland and dragging him toward the door.

As the villagers grumbled, Emely moved toward the door herself.

"Go home," she ordered as she reached the door. "Those who took part in beating Roland are to come to the manor house in the morning. Your punishment will be pronounced then."

The grumbling continued.

"Lord Christian requires our loyalty, and it is his justice I speak. You may not pronounce punishment on each other. Which it is clear some of you have done this night," Emely said. "You will present yourselves at the manor in the morning!"

She left the church and walked distraught back to the manor house. Emely knew this was the worst case on which she had given judgement. She was saddened by what had happened to Elle and by the judgement she had to give Roland. She knew Christian's punishment would have been far worse. When one of his men had attempted to attack her, Christian had given the man twenty lashes.

In the morning three village men came to the manor house accompanied by Rand. They hung their heads as Emely studied them.

"Who struck the first blow?" she asked.

"I, milady," said Ned.

"The second?"

"I, milady," said Chase.

"And the third?"

"I, milady," said Owen.

"Were there others?" Emely asked.

"No, milady," Ned answered.

"Ned for the next week you will work in the mill. Chase for the next two weeks you will work in the blacksmiths. Owen for the next three weeks you will work at the tannery," ordered Emely knowing each job was worse in difficulty and smell than the one before.

"Milady?" Chase said. "Tis not fair."

"Ned acted in the heat of the moment. You and Owen had both the time to think and to stop Ned and yourselves. You chose not to do so, which means you are guilty of harming another villager than Ned is. Owen more than you, Chase."

"milady, how will our families live?"

"You should have thought of them before you beat Roland."

"But . . ." Owen started.

"No," Emely said. "Justice and punishment were not yours to give. You are excused."

Rand said nothing as he followed the three men out of the manor house. Emely knew he would make sure they fulfilled their punishment. She got Gwyneth up and they went about their day as usual. During the following weeks Emely checked on Elle and both were relieved when she had her usual bleeding. Elle was still distraught, fearing the other village men. Emely encouraged Elle to talk to her mother and told Tess to listen without judgement or comment. Elle needed to find a way to live with what had happened, but she needed all the love and support her family could give her. Emely hoped the man Elle loved would come home. He would have to be told what happened but if his love for her was true, he would not care. Emely realized she was hoping for the same thing she had rejected when Lord Bryce had said it about her. Emely knew it was more than the loss of her innocence which would keep her from marrying. She would never love anyone but Christian and she would not have him dishonored if he married a . . . a what? What had Lord Rene called her the first time he came to the manor? An easy woman, a kept woman, yes those were the words he used. She knew he regretted them now, but they had been his first belief, and they would be the first thoughts any other noble would have of her.

CHAPTER 38

November became December and still there was no snow. Emely and Rand talked daily about their concern for the following year's crop. Would there be enough water without the snow melting? They worked to maintain the irrigation system they had created so water could be diverted from the stream and river beyond if needed. It was almost Christmas time and Emely decided to take a chance and take Gwyneth to Lord Rene's for the holy day and the week after.

Again, a day's ride was all it took but unlike their summer trips, a steady wind blew. Even though Emely and Gwyneth were wrapped in thick warm capes and Gwyneth was tucked inside Emely's for extra warmth, the little girl caught a chill. By the time they got to Lord Rene's Gwyneth was warm but not from being bundled up. Emely took the little girl to Arianna's room that had been prepared for them and refused to leave the girl's sick bed until the child was feeling better. They missed spending Christmas Day with Lord Rene and Lady Gracen, but Lady Gracen came and brought some of her handmaids with her. Lady Gracen wanted Emely to come and visit, promising the handmaids would look after Gwyneth. Emely tried to refuse but it was clear Gwyneth was feeling better as she no longer felt hot to the touch, was hungry, and fidgety. Clear signs she was on the mend. Finally, Emely agreed to have two of the handmaids stay and went to the great hall for dinner.

"You do not look well," Lord Rene said to Emely with concern in his voice.

"I just need to rest a little," Emely said smiling half-heartedly.

"You need to rest a lot," Lady Gracen said in the caring tone Emely had come to know.

"And eat more," Lord Rene added. "You look . . . frail."

"I am . . . slim," Emely laughed. "I have never been frail."

"Still, you should eat more," Lord Rene repeated.

"What I should have done is not come," Emely said. "I put Gwyneth at such risk. How could I have been so stupid?"

"We are glad you came," Lady Gracen said with affection, patting the younger woman's hand.

"And now you can stay until spring," Lord Rene asserted.

"No," Emely said. "That is the bad part. We have to go home before the snow closes the path."

"You cannot risk going home!" Lady Gracen said worry for the girls safety in her voice.

"I must. I need to be home to run the manor. Even in winter there is much work to be done."

"Rand can supervise the work," Lord Rene said. "I have others supervise my other holdings."

"This is Lord Christian's manor, and I am responsible."

"Emely," Lady Gracen said in a cajoling voice, "you need to rest."

"We are going home tomorrow," Emely said making it clear she had made up her mind.

"But . . ." Lord Rene started to say.

"Tomorrow!" Emely cut him off and then laughed. "We have been through this before. Gwyneth and I need to be home."

"I will give you an extra warm cape," Lady Gracen said conceding they could not change Emely's mind about returning home.

"Thank you."

"Now eat more," Lord Rene said with a smile. "You need to put some weight on. You are . . . too slim."

"Yes, milord," Emely said teasing.

The evening passed with the usual conversation about Gwyneth's growth and beauty and how things were going at Christian's manor.

They left the next morning wrapped in a double fur cape. They started their ride home in the sun but shortly after the midday meal the first snow came and by the time, they reached Christian's manor there were several inches down. If she had waited even one day more, Emely knew they would have been forced to stay at Lord Rene's.

CHAPTER 39

Christian – February 1098

Christian and the others left Antioch marching toward Jerusalem. They fought small skirmishes along the way but none as bad of the battles they had already lived through. They moved quickly southward through barren countryside, abandoned by locals out of fear as stories of the savage carnage the Crusaders brought sent people fleeing in fear. The few skirmishes were with little pockets of resistance and often won in a matter of a few hours.

Then a few miles outside the Holy City they came to a stronghold of the enemy. Battle lines were formed and at the command, thousands of Crusaders moved forward like a wall only to crash into an equally strong wall. The clash of metal on metal as weapons were wielded with lethal force rang in the ears of the warriors on both sides. Christian, Michael, and Drake were all in the thick of battle. Christian was knocked from his mount. Michael came to his rescue and was himself knocked from his horse. They were a few feet from each other, fighting for their lives. The slash across Christian's leg was only a slight distraction to him. He kept fighting. He killed enemy after enemy but still they came. He looked to see Michael a few feet away fighting as hard. Christian felt relieved to have such a worthy companion at his side. Then he felt the stroke of metal cut into his cheek from ear to the side of his mouth. He tasted blood in his mouth. He turned to face his attacker, but Michael was already running his sword through the man but was unable to free his sword before he himself was attacked and fell to the ground. Christian was able to kill the enemy before looking to carry Michael from the battlefield. Christian reached the younger man as Drake and others came to fight off the last of the enemy. Christian looked down at Michael's blank unseeing eyes and knew the brave young knight was gone.

Drake dragged Christian away from his friend while Christian called out Michael's name over and over until the young man's body was lost in the sea of bodies of the dead and dying on the battlefield. Christian resisted Drake trying to get back to Michael so he could give him a proper burial. Drake had to knock Christian out so he could carry him back to a place where his wounds could be patched.

It was days later when Christian was well enough to visit the impromptu graveyard and find Michael's grave. Christian said his goodbye to the younger man and promised to get his belongings back to his parents. Christian went to the camp and found his men. The smell of death was in the air and a sense of loss. Two more of Christian's men had died in the battle. He looked at the anguished faces of the men he had brought to this place and shared their grief. Knowing they had killed more of the enemy then had themselves been killed was no consolation. It was all death, there was no honor in dying or in living.

"We came with a goal," he told the men under his command. "That goal is almost accomplished. When it is, we will go home! We have been too long without our families, our homes, without safety and peace. We are so close to our goal. Let us free Jerusalem, make sure it is secure, and then we go home as fast as possible."

Before John spoke there was mumbling of assent.

"We will follow you milord. Our losses have been less than some others because you have trained and prepared us. We trust you."

The men spoke their assent.

"Thank you," Christian said so all could hear. "It is my honor to be your knight. Now let us take back Jerusalem."

The men then gave a cheer before going back to their small fires. Christian watched them and said a silent prayer they would all make it home. They were good men and he wanted them to live long and happy lives surrounded by those they loved and who loved them. He had been forced to come on this journey but being with these men, fighting alongside of them had made him a better man. He would never again take even the simplest comfort as his right. He would value every man not for his status but for his contribution.

Months later in June they reached Jerusalem, but the city gates were closed as the people huddled within. Stories of the savage devastation the Crusaders had brought to Nicaea and Antioch had been carried here by the few survivors who had escaped. Now the siege began. Food ran low on both sides, and tempers flared. The Crusaders were angry at being denied their prize. The people in the city, terrified of what would happen if they failed. Six long, bitter weeks later the walls were breeched, and the Crusaders poured into the city spreading out as street by street and house by house fighting took the lives of warriors and innocents alike. Death knew no age, sex or religion, Christian residents died as quick as Jews and Muslims till blood flowed through the streets like water and bodies piled up. Almost a month later, the last of the city was secured and the Crusaders celebrated with a mass and feasts.

Christian waited a week to ensure the security of the city and to witness the crowning of the Crusader king of Jerusalem before he started to prepare for the long trip home. It was July and he calculated they could be home within the year if they wasted no time. He told the leaders. They agreed he and his followers were no longer needed. He ordered the supplies they would need and paid a ship's captain for their passage back to Venice. Once there he sent messengers ahead to pay for food and supplies along their way. Rested from the sea voyage, Christian and Drake pushed forward. With supplies ready when they reached cities and towns along the way, they traveled faster on their return. It seemed the closer they got to home the faster the men were willing to move. The sight of the Dover cliffs across the channel from Calis made them anxious for the crossing. Landing in Dover, the pace increased till men pleaded to keep pushing forward without sleep or food. Christian kept his followers on a sensible schedule with food and nightly stops. Some of Drake's men broke away and hurried forward. Their haggard bodies were found on the trails. Weak from lack of food and exhausted from lack of sleep, they had become easy prey for thieves.

The day they arrived in London, Christian had sent John and two trusted riders to the manor to let Emely know they were coming home. They were so close; Christian could almost smell the flowers Emely often wore in her hair. He could almost hear her soft voice telling him she loved him. He could almost see her sweet smile. Now even he pushed the men to move faster.

Four long years since they left, Christian rode at the head of the small army which had gathered under his leadership. When they emerged from the forest into the far side of the village, villagers came out to greet them. Reaching their individual family's hut, men left the ranks and ran to hug their mothers, wives, children. Some families cried when they realized their son or husband had not returned. Christian was not quite aware of the happy and sad scenes behind him as his eyes were focused on the manor courtyard gate.

The gates opened, and the manor house came into view. On the top step stood a small girl, her head held high and proud, a small replica of her mother. 'What a beauty she is' he thought before turning his attention to the woman who stood next to the stairs where she promised him, she would be all those years ago. Christian felt a tightness in his throat. He wanted to scoop her up into his arms and hold her for the rest of their lives. he knew he could not. Formalities of greeting had to be done, so he stayed astride his horse until he stopped at the foot of the stairs. When Gwyneth spoke, he knew he would die before he would let anything, or anyone ever harmed her. He loved her more than life itself.

CHAPTER 40

January 1100

Emely hoped to find a letter from Christian when she got home but none was there. She waited through January and into February but still there was no word from him. The snow did not come during the fall and early winter. Now winter came storm after storm. Soon the village was covered with two feet of snow. Movement through the village was by thin paths made by villagers as they repeated their daily chores. Sarah came every day and the two women worked on the third tapestry.

January turned to February and the snow still came as the village struggled to cope with three feet of snow. Much higher drifts covered the village. February brought a slight warming, beginning the spring melt allowing the villagers to come out and socialize again. Emely went with Rand to check every hut and family to make sure everyone had come through the winter safely. Only the oldest villager had died. there had been several births and the village celebrated with a feast. Winter, however, was not done with them and another storm hit the village and brought even more snow. The first week of March, winter seemed at last to lose its grip on the village as the temperature began its slow but steady warming. Winter yet again was not done with them. The first week of April brought one last blast of winter snow. Then it was over.

Spring came with everything changing almost overnight from white or light gray to the deep rich colors of spring. What had been snow covered paths became thick brown mud pulling at boots as people walked about their daily chores. Bare trees had the first buds of leaves, pale green and yellow. Newborn lambs, calves, and piglets frolicked in the meadows following their mothers. New life was everywhere.

Still Emely had received no letter from Christian and her fear for him increased. She sat to write to him hoping a letter would prompt a response. She wanted to know he was alive. She hoped he was safe and coming home. They knew nothing of the progress of the Crusade. The only news she had received was in the letters she had received from him, and they had been brief and without details.

During April it warmed a little more every day. The snow at last receded to the shadows and then was gone. The stream rose but did not threaten the huts nearest it. The river was higher than usual, but the flow of both the stream and river helped run the mill and bellows at the smith. May came bright warm and sunny. The laughter of children at play echoed through the village and even planting and repairing of huts from the effects of winter was done with a lighter sense.

Sarah and Emely took the little ones to the garden every day. It had become Emely's haven; her favorite place to be. She found herself often talking to Arianna as she took care of the flowers and kept Arianna's grave neat. She had the small wooden cross replaced with a metal one. Arianna's name was on the cross in brass. Emely had shown the grave to Lady Gracen the second summer they had come. She had cried while Emely held her but was pleased her daughter rested in such a lovely place. When Emely was not working in the garden, she often took Arianna's journal there, to read it yet again. She felt she knew the girl as well as she had once known Felise. They could have been friends under different circumstances.

Emely and Sarah spent hours in the garden watching the children run and play. Gwyneth knew she could touch the flowers and smell them but if she wanted to enjoy them day after day, she could not pick them. Eden was less respectful of the bright array as he ran through the flowers at will, despite Sarah punishing him every time. Even Gwyneth would scold her friend, but he only laughed at both of them. Emely always smiled when Gwyneth was protective of the flowers she loved so much.

It was mid-May after the midday meal when Sarah and Emely were in the flower garden talking about some small change when Sarah's face went white as she looked over Emely shoulder.

"John?" Sarah questioned as Emely turned to see what had brought the look of shock and awe to her friend's face. "John!" Sarah screamed as she ran to the thin man standing at the corner of the manor house.

Emely watched as the man braced himself for the blow he would receive when Sarah reached him. His smile was wide, lighting his face and his arms raised to welcome Sarah into them. The force of her embrace forced an audible gush of air from his chest as Sarah hurled herself into his arms.

"Sarah," the man whispered before kissing his wife, a kiss that continued for several seconds.

Emely hesitated before walking toward the couple not wanting to interfere in this special moment but knowing he would have some information about Christian. When she reached them, Emely still did not speak but John, conscious of her proximity, pulled his lips from Sarah's but did not loosen his embrace.

"Welcome home, John. You have been missed." Emely said, smiling at Sarah who still clung to her husband.

"Tis good to be home," John said trying to ease Sarah's grip on him.

"You bring news of Lord Christian?" Emely asked.

"Yes," John said finally getting Sarah to release her hold on him. "He is two days' ride behind me."

"Two days!?" Emely gasped.

"Yes, and he is not alone," John warned. "He brings Lord Drake, and the men of Lord Michael."

"Not Lord Michael?"

"We lost Lord Michael in Jerusalem," John said with regret. He had liked the young knight.

"He was a good man," Emely said with a sadden heart, remembering the young man from when they had left for the crusade from Lord Bryce's.

"Yes, he was," John agreed.

"Lord Drake?" Emely asked.

"From the north, a good warrior," John said with some reservation.

"Two days," Emely said thinking ahead. Then she looked up at Sarah still clinging to John and knew they needed some time together.

"Sarah, I am sure John would like to rest and clean himself after his long trip. Would you please take him to the chamber next to Gwyneth's? I will send up water and food. I will take care of the children so you can have some time together."

"Thank you, milady," Sarah said even as she turned and began to pull John away.

"Milady?" John said but had no time to question further as his wife was determined to have him all to herself as soon as possible.

Emely smiled as she watched them go. She had Nelda take food to them and carried a bucket of water up herself. She knocked on the door and waited until John, who was in only his tunic and leggings, answered the door. Sarah was hiding behind the far bed draping, but her tunic and surcoat were in a pile on the floor. Emely smiled as she put down the bucket of water.

"Take as long as you need," Emely said smiling at John who was red faced. "The evening meal can wait."

"Thank you," John said glancing at his wife. "This may take . . . .."

"I understand. You have a lot . . . to talk about," Emely said smiling deeper as John turned a deeper red.

Emely went downstairs and out to the cookhouse to talk to Nelda to make sure they would have enough food for the crusaders who would be visiting. She then went to the village to find Rand so he would know and could prepare empty land for the tent city the warriors would be creating. She also ask Rand to have the villagers come to the church that night. They would need to know what to expect from their 'guests' based on her experience at Lord Bryce's before the warriors had gone on the crusades. After the evening meal, John, Sarah, and their children accompanied Emely and Gwyneth to the church. Emely was very clear they would give the returning crusaders their full hospitality but none of the women were to go anywhere without a male escort. Farm animals were to be gathered into the manor house enclosure. Lambs, calves, and piglets were the priority to be protected as catching and killing them for food would be easiest to do and hide. Everyone ask about their sons and husbands, but John demurred saying Lord Christian was clear he, John, was not to say anything about who was or was not returning.

The next day was a flurry of activity. Emely made sure all the villagers had their new tunics of Christian's blue. The preparation of food began. There would be a feast worthy of any lord's manor. They would bring honor to Christian in all they did and provided. During the day when she was not needed to do other work, Emely rehearsed Gwyneth in the welcoming speech the little girl would make when their guests arrived. The child was only four but still she would be expected as the lady of the manor to formally welcome the knights to her father's manor. Emely made Gwyneth do the speech over and over until she did it without hesitation or stumbling over the words. After the midday meal Emely had the girl make the speech twice more and again after the evening meal. By the time she went to bed, Gwyneth did the speech to perfection and Emely praised her for the accomplishment.

"Emi," Gwyneth asked as Emely was tucking her into bed, "Will my father like me?"

Emely stared at the little girl who was always so sure of herself. She knew Christian only through the stories Emely had told her. Stories of when he had come home to Lord Bryce's after his training, stories of the tournaments he had fought in, stories of his courage. Most of all Emely had always told Gwyneth how much both Christian and Arianna loved her. How Christian had held her with such tenderness the first time, his joy at looking at her sweet face.

"Yes, my little love, he will like you. He will love you."

"I . . . want him to be proud of me tomorrow," Gwyneth said in a worried voice.

"He will be. There is nothing you could ever do which would not make him proud of you."

"I . . . love him so much."

"I know, my sweet. I know. Now go to sleep and dream of him holding you as he did for the first time. He will be so happy to see you."

"Good morrow, Emi."

"Good morrow, Gwyneth."

Emely stayed by the child's bed until she was sure the little girl was sound asleep. She went to sit by a window. She looked out over the sleeping manor. Only a few huts still had lights. Moonlight turned the village to silver. The white stone of the church glowed almost with an inner light, a beacon in the darkness to lead the weary travelers home to safety. Emely studied the village. It had done well under her care. She would give back to Christian a manor secure and improved from that he had put into her care. She looked at the road leading into the wood. They would come from there. It was where they would enter the village. He would lead them through the village, and they would be welcomed by the villagers clad in his blue, all cheering in welcome home. He would lead them into the manor house courtyard to the steps of the manor house. She would be standing in the same spot as he left her. That is where he would see her first, waiting as she had promised. It is also where she would see him first.

Tomorrow, he will be home tomorrow.

CHAPTER 41

May 1100

Emely stood perfectly straight, waiting. She took one last look around the manor house courtyard. Four village men stood looking out toward the village and the wood beyond. They were dressed in blue tunics with large white "Cs." They stood tall and straight guarding the manor house and courtyard. Emely could hear the cheering of the villagers as the Crusaders passed through the village from the forest beyond. She knew the greeting they were getting and smiled. Christian was getting the welcome home she had planned. Emely looked up at Gwyneth. The little girl stood on the third step of the manor house. Her eyes focused on the closed gate. Emely had made Gwyneth repeat her welcome speech once more this morning. She looked so grown up in her blue tunic and flowered surcoat. Her dark brown curls were topped by a little gold circlet. Her hair fell over her shoulders. She looked so calm, but Emely knew the child was trembling with excitement for this first meeting of her father. Gwyneth knew nothing of Christian but what Emely had told her. The little girl had created an image of her father which was almost bigger than any man could live up to. Emely smiled; little girls should believe their fathers could do anything. Emely took one last look around the courtyard as the cheering beyond the gate grew louder as the crusaders approached the manor house. She took a deep breath to calm herself and gave the signal to open the gate to the advancing Crusaders.

He was first. His horse reflected the excitement they all felt as it shook its head and tried to prance into the courtyard. Christian reined the animal in and forced it to a gentle walk. He stopped at the bottom of the stairs and kept his gaze on Gwyneth as the other nobles gathered around him. Once they were all in place and silent, Gwyneth gave her speech.

"We welcome you to the house of our father, good Lord Christian. Food and drink has been prepared and await you in the main room. Chambers have also been prepared so you may take your rest. We do this in our father's name to thank you for your loyalty and service to him. Please we bid you enter."

Cheering came from the men. Christian dismounted and removed his helmet. That is when Emely saw the scar and gasped. From the bottom of his right ear to the side of his mouth ran a thin red jagged line. He glanced at her when she gasped but only for an instant before turning his attention back to Gwyneth who now looked like the child she was.

"Are you my father?" she whispered.

"Yes, Gwyneth," Christian said through a mixture of sorrow that she would have to ask such a question and joy at her innocence.

"Papa," the little girl cried as she jumped into his arms. Her little arms wrapped around his neck as she clung to him. Christian wrapped his arms around the child he loved so dearly and held her close.

"My baby," he whispered in her ear.

The men cheered and Emely tried to keep tears of joy from falling. Then she took another deep breath.

"Milords, please enter the house of our Lord Christian," Emely gestured. "Land has been prepared for your men so they can set up their tents. Food and drink will be given to them from Lord Christian's cook house."

Christian took the hint and moved from the center of the stairs still holding Gwyneth who would not release her hold on him.

The nobles moved between them, thanking her for the welcome. Then Lord Piers came to where Emely stood.

"Am I home?" he asked in a timid voice. "I want to go home."

"Not yet milord," Emely answered as she studied the broken man in front of her.

She remembered the brash, flirtatious boy he had been at Lord Bryce's when they were leaving. Now he was trembling and needed help to walk.

"No, Piers," Christian added. "I have sent a message to your father. He will send an escort to take you the rest of the way home. They will be here in a few days."

"Father? Are you my father?" Piers questioned Christian.

"No, Piers. I am Christian. You will be home in a week."

"Home, am I home?"

"No, Piers not yet. A week," Christian repeated gently.

"A week?" Piers asked. "How long is that?"

"Seven days, seven sun rises and sun sets," Christian answered.

"What chamber should we take him to?" asked one of the men on either side of Piers.

"Top of the stairs far end of the hall the one on the right," Emely answered.

"Thank you. Will you send food up to us, please?" requested one of the men.

Emely indicated she would, and the two men helped Piers up the stairs.

Everyone had passed between them and only Christian with Gwyneth still clinging to his neck and Emely remained in the courtyard.

"Gwyneth" Christian said pulling the little girl away from him with reluctance. "Please go in and be hostess to our guests."

"Yes, papa," replied Gwyneth and then smiled her brightest. "Papa," she said smiling even wider. "I love you! I am so glad you are home at last."

"I love you Gwyneth and I am glad to be home with you also. Now go be hostess."

The little girl curtsied to her father, gave Emely one of her biggest smiles and then ran up the stairs and into the house.

Christian looked at Emely and smiled. He opened his mouth, but no words came.

"Welcome home Christian. You have been missed," Emely said reaching out to caress his scarred face.

He pulled away from her touch, but she moved closer and with loving care put her hand over the angry red mark as tears sprang to her eyes.

"Tis old," he said.

"Tis new to me," Emely answered. "Now you are home and safe. We will take care of you."

"It looks like you took care of a lot of things while I was gone," he said smiling at her for the first time.

"Tis what you gave me to do. After your guests have gone, we will show you everything."

The sound of rowdy laughter burst from the manor house.

"I think we should go in," Emely said smiling.

"Yes," Christian agreed as he turned to walk up the stairs.

Then he stopped realizing she was not beside him. When she stopped also, he put out his hand to guide her up to the same level he was on.

"We enter our house together," he said.

"Your house," she corrected.

"Our house, it would not be here if you had not taken care of our home!"

Emely smiled and took the hand he offered, and they walked up the stairs and into the manor house together. Inside the tables were piled high with food. Everyone had a large bowl in front of him. The two girls from the village who came to help were moving about the room refilling goblets with wine, mead, and ale. Two others were carrying in more bowls of food. Gwyneth sat up at the dais in the lady of the manor's chair. She sat, her hands folded in her lap, with no food in her bowl. She looked at the crowd of men in front of her almost as if she was afraid of them.

"Go to her," Emely said to Christian. "She needs you next to her."

"You?"

"I have work to do. We do not want to run out of food," Emely laughed.

CHAPTER 42

Christian smiled and walked to sit beside Gwyneth who's smile brightened when she saw her father approaching. He sat beside her, and they began to talk. He reached for food and put it in her bowl. Emely watched for a few seconds making sure the child was eating a little of everything he gave her. Gwyneth, like most of the village children, had favorite foods. If allowed Gwyneth would only eat those few things and Emely had never allowed that. Gwyneth was asking for a little of everything it appeared, and Emely was very proud of the child for not taking advantage of her father's lack of knowledge. Emely then went to the cookhouse where Nelda was commanding a staff of six additional helpers. Second platters of meats and vegetables were being stacked high to be taken to the tables.

"Nelda," Emely said, "do you need help? What can I do?"

"Take the vegetables," Nelda said before she realized who was speaking. 'No, milady. Let one of the girls do that," Nelda corrected herself in an instant.

"I can help," Emely said smiling as she grabbed a large heavy platter of vegetables and headed toward the door.

Emely delivered the platter of vegetables and then returned twice to the cookhouse for more platters. On her fourth trip she remained there working on cutting meat and placing it on platters. She was still there when Christian walked in. The silence in the cookhouse made Emely look up from her work as he walked toward her.

"You are needed in the manor house," he said in a low voice.

"I am needed here," Emely responded looking around at the food which was in many stages of preparation.

"You are needed in the manor house," he demanded in a gentle tone. "Now." He added in a tone allowing no disagreement.

"Yes milord," she answered in a demure voice but with a smile. She removed the apron she had tied around her waist. "Nelda, I am needed in the manor house," she said to the cook with a smile.

"Yes milady, I understand," the cook smiled back at Emely and then curtsied to Christian.

Christian raised an eyebrow but said nothing as he escorted Emely back to the house. Raucous laughter again greeted them as they entered. Emely first looked at Gwyneth who looked frightened of the men in front of her. Emely went first to calm the little girl followed by Christian.

"Perhaps Gwyneth should go to her chamber where it is a little quieter," he suggested.

Emely signaled one of the serving girls to her and asked her to take Gwyneth upstairs. Both girls looked relieved to be leaving. Gwyneth hugged Christian and Emely before leaving. Once Gwyneth was gone, Christian gestured for Emely to sit beside him on the dais. She took a few bites as she watched the village girls who were bringing food and drink to the warriors as they moved among the men. While most of the men were content to flirt with the girls, some half attempted to grab them. Two of the girls were able to fend off the slight attempts of the men but the third, Hope, who was not one of the usual girls who helped when the lords were visiting, was embarrassed by the unwanted attention. Her face was red, and she cringed whenever one of the men spoke to her. Drinking more, the men grew bolder in their comments and their attempts at grabbing the serving girls. Emely looked at Christian, but he was talking with the warrior closest to him. Emely heard the squeal over the loud talking and laughter of the men. She looked to see where the sound had come from. Hope had been pulled into the lap of one of the warriors who was trying to make her drink some wine. Emely looked to Christian again, but he still was not aware of the girl's situation. Emely rose from her place and walked with slow deliberation, forming a plan, to where the offending warrior sat still trying to force some wine into Hope.

"What is this? Lazing with a lord rather than doing your work?" Emely asked sounding angry.

"Oh milady," Hope said, tears beginning to fall.

"Get up! Go to the cook house. You will be more use there, rather than flirting with a lord," Emely continued still sounding angry at the girl.

"No," protested the man. "I want her to stay."

"My lord, she has work to do elsewhere," Emely said ignoring his desire.

"She has work to do here," he said leering at the girl he held tight in his lap.

"My lord," Emely said with an edge in her voice. "She is the serf of Lord Christian, and she has work to do elsewhere!"

The man released the girl who scrambled out of his embrace and ran toward the door to the cook house.

"Perhaps you would like to take her place," the man said reaching toward Emely.

"I also have work to do, milord."

"You are but a serf. Your work is whatever your betters wish it to be," the man shouted at Emely.

"Emely has no betters," Christian said with conviction as he stood behind her.

It was only then Emely realized the room had gone silent.

"She is a serf," repeated the man.

"She is the guardian of my manor," Christian said loud enough to be heard by all. "And under my protection."

"She is yours is that what you are saying," said the man with a nasty tone as he leered at Emely.

"Yes," said Christian with an irritated edge to his voice. "She is mine. And I Do Not Share!" The tone in Christian's voice told the man he would not be enjoying any of Emely's charms.

"Really, Dunson, did you not have enough women? Leave the girls alone. We are guests here," said one of the other men.

Grumbling came from the other warriors, some supporting the last speaker, others against him.

"You are welcome to my hospitality of food, drink and shelter," Christian said, "but not the women of my manor. Think of your mothers, wives, and daughters. Would you want them treated with such contempt?"

The grumbling continued but most were now in agreement with Christian. The man who had grabbed Hope looked none too pleased with the rebuke he had received from Christian.

"My wife is not as pretty," Dunson said as he sat down.

"Have more food," Christian said cajoling. "Make up for the times we were starving."

"More food," shouted several of the men nearby.

Emely took a deep breath and turned toward the cookhouse door.

"Where are you going?" Christian asked.

"I need to get more food for your guests," Emely replied. "I think it would be best if I did the serving."

"No, let the girls do it. These men respect me enough they will not abuse my hospitality. Come and sit with me. You have not eaten enough."

Emely let Christian guide her to the seat Gwyneth had occupied. He filled a bowl for her and watched as she took the first few bites. Then he turned his attention back to the warriors. He smiled as he watched the serving girls move about refilling food bowls and goblets. The men were loud and laughing, telling, and retelling stories of their adventures. Emely only heard snippets of their stories, but a picture began to form in her mind, the battles, the boredom, the feasts, the starvation, the women, the killing. It was not the picture she had had of the men going to fight a Holy war. After several hours of eating and drinking, the warriors at last seemed to have taken their fill. Several were very drunk and had to be helped up the stairs. Lord Drake and his second in command were given the room next to Lord Piers. Eight others were divided and given the two center rooms. Emely went and suggested to Gwyneth she come down to the main room with Christian. The little girl ran to Christian who scooped her up into his arms. The three of them returned to the main room as the girls cleared the tables. Lord Drake was still at the table and was not near as drunk as some of the other men had been. He watched the girls as they moved about the room.

CHAPTER 43

"Christian," Drake said as they came into the room, "you are a lucky man. Your manor well cared for, a beautiful daughter, and a beautiful woman at your side."

"Yes," Christian said smiling down at Emely, "I am very lucky."

"She is your woman?" Drake asked.

"She is . . . the guardian of my daughter and my manor," Christian answered with slight reservation.

"Not your woman?"

"We do not share a bed, milord. If that is what you are asking," Emely answered.

"What a waste," Drake said studying Emely until she was uncomfortable.

"I have work to do," Emely said turning toward the cook house.

The cookhouse was still a flurry of activity as more food was prepared for the next day. Emely put on an apron and started cleaning the bowls, an unending task as long as the visitors were here.

It was sometime later Christian again came looking for Emely. The silence in the cookhouse made her turn from her work to find him standing at the door watching her, a slight smile lifting his lips.

"Milord," Emely said as she walked toward him. "Are you in need?"

"Yes," Christian said with a slight teasing leer in his voice. "But nothing you can give me right now." Then louder so all could hear as Emely turned red with the image his words brought to her mind. "Gwyneth wants you."

Emely removed the apron she was wearing and followed Christian out of the cook house.

Halfway across the yard which separated the two buildings, Christian stopped.

"Emely, I . . . I do need something from you," Christian said unsure how she would respond to his request.

"Milord?"

"I . . . I have not held you," he said afraid she would refuse. "I would like to."

Emely stopped and looked up at the face she had adored for so many years, the face she wanted to touch. Then without thought she walked into his arms and rested her head on his broad chest. His arms wrapped around her and there they stood in the courtyard for several minutes. Emely closed her eyes and for a short time nothing existed except the sound of his heart beating under her ear and the tight band of his arms around her holding her close. She heard his contented sigh and knew at last he indeed felt he was home.

It felt so right to be in his arms, Emely thought. She had dreamed of this for so long. Now he was here, safe. They stood for several minutes before Emely knew they had to return to the main room. Gwyneth would be looking for them. Emely released herself from Christian's embrace with a great lack of enthusiasm, opened her eyes and smiled up at him. They turned toward the manor house. In the doorway Lord Drake stood with a smile on his face.

"So, this is the one you talked about so much," Drake said as they climbed the steps toward him. "The way you talked; I did not believe she was real."

Emely said nothing but gave Christian a questioning look.

"Emely is very real," Christian said smiling down at her.

"So, she is your woman, but you do not share a bed," Drake said still looking intent at Emely.

"Emely is the guardian of my daughter and my manor," Christian repeated his earlier explanation.

Drake stepped aside to let them pass into the manor house.

"He is a fool," Drake said as Emely passed him.

She stopped and looked at him in shock.

"I would bed you nightly," he said with a leer.

Emely's face went hot and red. No one had ever spoken to her this way before. She thought she should make some response, but no words came to mind. She moved past him with as much dignity as she could and went to Gwyneth. The little girl was telling Christian about her pony. It was long past Gwyneth's bedtime and Emely went and got the little girl who protested but with a stern look from Christian said her good morrows to the guests.

"Emely," Christian said in a low tone as she was turning to leave, "come back when Gwyneth is settled. Please."

"As you wish milord," Emely said with an appropriate curtsy.

For all the excitement she had had that day, Gwyneth went to sleep quickly. Emely tucked the cover close around the little girl's neck and kissed her on her forehead before leaving the chamber. Downstairs there were a few visitors still lingering in the main room drinking and talking quietly. Emely looked over the tables littered with the remains of the meal they had consumed.

"Our guests will want entertainment tomorrow. Perhaps you could help arrange a hunt or ride along the stream. They will need some air to clear their . . . befuddled minds." Christian said smiling.

"Of course, milord. Rand can guide them to the best hunting spots."

The rest of the evening passed quietly. Most of the men were abed sleeping in real beds under a roof for the first time in years. Emely was up with the sun rise and sent one of the guards who were still standing in the courtyard to get Rand so he could arrange the ride. When she turned back toward the manor house, Drake was there.

"You really took care of this while he was gone?"

"Yes, milord," Emely said walking past him.

"Will you go riding with us? Perhaps you could give me a private tour of this place."

"No, milord, I have work to do. My main responsibility is Lady Gwyneth. I must attend her needs."

"I have needs you could attend to," he said teasing.

"I fear I have not the . . . experience your needs might require," Emely said with a honeyed voice hoping to end the conversation.

"Oh, I would be happy, more than happy to give you all the 'experience' you would ever need."

"How long would that take, a day, a week, a month? Then you would be bored with me. You would cast me away. No milord, experience I need not."

"Oh, but that week, month, year would be so pleasurable for both of us," was his suave reply.

Emely was glad when they walked into the manor house, and she could join Christian and Gwyneth again. Christian gave her a questioning look with a glance toward Drake but Emely focused her attention on Gwyneth so she would not have to answer any question he might have. The morning meal was served, and Rand came a short time later and Emely explained what was needed. He left to make sure the horses were saddled and ready. Emely told Gwyneth their guests were going to go riding and asked if she wanted to go with them. Gwyneth looked at her father and asked if he were going and when he said he was, she said she wanted to go also. Emely took the child upstairs so she could change into something less formal and more appropriate for riding. When they got back to the main room, the lords were ready, and Rand came in to say the horses were waiting in the courtyard. The men filed out of the manor house following Christian and Gwyneth. Emely stayed behind to make sure everything for an evening meal would be ready. She was going about the main room straightening benches, picking up pieces of fallen food when she realized Drake had not gone with the others.

"Milord, do you need something?" Emely asked.

"Yes, but you are not giving it to me," he answered.

"Is there some entertainment I can arrange for you?" Emely tried to change the subject but realized her mistake when she saw his expression.

"Yes, but again you are not giving it to me."

"Milord, please excuse me I have work to do," Emely said trying to move past him.

"Christian would want you to 'entertain' me," he said as he blocked her path.

"Milord," Emely began in a curt tone, "please let me pass. I am needed in the cook house."

"You are needed here," he said reaching out to lift the end of her wheat colored hair.

Emely's patience with the man was at an end. "Milord," Emely said pushing his hand from her hair, "touch me again and you will regret it!"

"What can you do, a serf?" he said laughing until her hand slapped his face with a good deal of force behind it.

"That is what I can do," she said angry at his presumption. "Touch me again, and you will not like where I strike you next time! Now Let Me Pass!" Emely said as she walked around him.

Drake stood there shocked, his eyes wide and his mouth dropped open. Then he turned to watch her walk away, an amused smile lifting his lips.

CHAPTER 44

Emely went back to cleaning bowls in the cook house. She took her anger and frustration out on the wood, scrubbing it clean until the bowls were no longer smooth on the bottom. Emely sighed. She would have to take these bowls to the cooper to have them smoothed before they could be used again. Now she was angry with herself at letting Drake get to her. She would have to apologize to him.

"Milady," one of the girls said to Emely, "they are back."

Emely removed the apron and went to see Gwyneth. The little girl was holding Christian's hand as he talked with their guests. Emely could see Gwyneth was tired. Yesterday had been an exciting day, now a ride so early in the morning was a lot for a young child. Emely went and took Gwyneth's hand, but the little girl tried to pull away.

"Gwyneth," Christian said, "you need to go with Emely."

"I want to stay with you!" whined the child.

"Gwyneth," Christian said in a way which allowed no argument.

Gwyneth took Emely's hand and the two of them walked up the stairs. In Gwyneth's chamber Emely entertained the child by playing a game with her which was one of Gwyneth's favorites as a way to give the little girl some rest. Then Emely put her down for a short nap. While Gwyneth slept Emely straightened the room. When Gwyneth woke a short time later, Emely suggested they walk to the village to see Sarah and Eden. Gwyneth jumped up and ran to the chamber door. Downstairs, Emely let Christian know where they were going but refused his offer of an escort. They were almost to Sarah and John's hut when Emely realized they were being followed. She turned and found Lord Drake a few feet behind them.

"Milord, do you need something?" Emely asked.

He smiled but not the leer he had given her before.

"I was just taking a walk through the village. I want to check on my men," came the polite answer.

Emely was not sure she believed him but continued walking Gwyneth to Sarah's.

"Tis a well-kept village," Drake said.

"Yes. The people work very hard to maintain their huts and plots."

"I am sure as . . . guardian you help them any way you can."

"Yes, that is part of my responsibility."

"The manor house also."

"Yes."

"And you take care of . . . Gwyneth?"

"Yes."

"That is a lot of responsibility for one . . . so young."

"Women younger than I do the same and perhaps more."

They arrived at Sarah's. Eden was in the yard and jumped up to greet Gwyneth as Emely entered the yard. Lord Drake stopped at the gate.

"My lady," Sarah said coming out when she heard Eden call.

"Sarah, things are well with you?" Emely asked as John followed his wife out into the yard.

"Yes," Sarah said smiling back at her husband.

"Lord Drake," John said looking at the noble who still stood in the road.

"I am just walking with Emely," Drake answered.

Emely looked at him questioning but said nothing.

"May we offer you ale?" John asked.

"No, no thank you."

"Gwyneth wanted to play with Eden," Emely explained.

"Perhaps Gwyneth could stay here for a while and Emely could show me around the village," Drake suggested.

"Of course, Gwyneth can stay," Sarah said smiling as the children were already chasing the chickens.

"Emely," Drake said holding out his hand to her.

"Milord," Emely answered as she walked toward him. "I will be back in about an hour," Emely said to Sarah.

Sarah waved as Gwyneth and Eden ran around the yard chasing the chickens.

"Now what shall we look at first," Drake asked.

"I thought you were going to check on your men," Emely said.

"I would rather walk with you."

"Perhaps a visit to our church. You could pray for a safe and swift return to your manor."

"My father's manor and when he dies my older brother's manor. No, I am in no hurry to return there."

"Perhaps a pilgrimage to some monastery?"

"I have been on a pilgrimage for the last several years. My soul needs no more saving."

Emely had no more suggestions, so they walked without talking through the village to the edge of the tent village beyond.

"I should go back," Emely said.

"No come with me," Drake suggested. "You will be safe with me, and I do want to check on my men. Beside they would enjoy seeing someone as lovely as you."

"I should go back."

"No, come with me, please," Drake said taking her arm.

Emely looked down at his hand on her arm kend then up at him. He removed his hand with an apology. They walked into the tent village and were greeted by several men who were wearing Pier's yellow although not as bright as she remembered it. Then there were more men in dark green, Emely remembered that had been Michael's color. The last group of men were in light brown. They greeted Drake with slight bows and 'milord.' He spoke to each of the men, calling them by name, asking if they were getting enough food and drink, were the tents good shelter, did they have any needs. Emely was impressed; he did seem to care about these men and their welfare. He also introduced them to Emely, explaining she was the person who had made sure they were well fed and had wood for their campfires. The men thanked her and bowed to her. Drake, after talking to the men for some time, turned and took Emely's arm so they could return to get Gwyneth and return to the manor house. She glanced down at his hand on her arm and then up at him and he with only a slight hesitation removed his hand with a smirk on his face.

"You must know I will keep trying," he said.

She smiled; it was not the menacing touch from earlier, because he remembered and took note of her warning.

Gwyneth and Eden were sitting petting newborn lambs when Emely and Drake got to Sarah's. The little girl ran to Emely to show her the lamb which was almost as big as Gwyneth herself. Emely let Sarah know they were leaving and suggested she wait to return to the manor house until after the lords had left. Then the three of them, Emely, Gwyneth, and Drake, returned to the manor house. Gwyneth talked about the new chicks and how fluffy they were. They were approaching the manor house courtyard and Christian was walking with Rand. He looked up and smiled but frowned when he saw Drake walking with Emely and Gwyneth. He gave Emely a questioning look but said nothing.

In the manor house the midday meal was set out by the village girls. Emely left Gwyneth with Christian as she went to check on the cookhouse once she was sure there would be no repeat of the earlier unpleasantness. Nelda refused to let her do anything and sent Emely back to the manor house. The scene was less riotous than the day before and the girls moved more easily, one, Joan, even flirting a little. Emely asked her to go to the cookhouse as she was needed there to take care of the bread making. The girl was foolish and did not grasp how she could be compromised and discarded without a thought by the knights.

The girl left with a smile over her shoulder toward the visitors. Emely was going to have to make sure the girl was always under the watchful eye of an older woman until the warriors left.

As they were finishing the midday meal one of the guards came to tell Emely there was a small caravan approaching. The nobles, led by Christian and Emely, went to greet the new guests after Gwyneth was sent to her chamber. The rider in the front was an older man. He was followed by a younger man and two carts with four mounted men behind them.

"Lord Elwin," Christian said bowing slightly. "Welcome to my manor."

"Where is he?" demanded the older man. "All these years and he is still creating problems."

"Milord, may I suggest a goblet of wine and some refreshment before you see Lord Piers?" Emely asked with a welcoming smile. "We know you have traveled a great distance."

Lord Elwin looked at her before relenting.

"My men could use something," he conceded.

"Please milord, this way," said Emely gesturing toward the house.

In the main room one of the men who was attending Piers was filling a bowl to take up to their room. When he saw Lord Elwin, he went down on one knee without delay.

"Milord," said the man bowing his head.

"Willum," Lord Elwin acknowledged. "Where is he?"

"Upstairs milord. You . . . need to be prepared" the man said as he stood.

"Prepared? For what?"

"He . . .. It has been a long time, milord. Life was . . . difficult."

Elwin studied the other man for several seconds before his expression softened.

"He . . . is not well?"

"He . . . It was difficult."

"We will take some refreshment. I will be up later," Elwin conceded.

"Milord," Willum said bowing again before leaving.

Emely poured Lord Elwin a goblet of wine and made sure the food was within easy reach.

"There were horrific battles," Christian started, "A man was beside you one moment and the next his body was shattered, and you were covered with his blood and gore. The sounds of men and animals screaming as they died were everywhere. Fields after battles were seas of red blood, white bone, torn flesh, body parts of men and beasts. We survived but . . . none were . . . unaffected."

"That is what a warrior trains for," Lord Elwin said.

"Training does not prepare you for . . . the smell of fresh blood, the piercing sounds of a hundred men screaming, even the moans as they take their last breaths is . . .. "Christian stopped then as the memories and pain took over.

CHAPTER 45

The room had gone silent while Christian spoke, and the faces of the returning Crusaders reflected the truth of Christian's words. They had seen it, heard it, and lived it. From their expressions Emely felt what they had seen was far worse than Christian described. One by one, the men left the room to go out into the beautiful sunny day and enjoy the peace the manor offered. Lord Michael's men had announced they would be leaving in the morning. Lord Drake said he was thinking about doing the same. Now Lord Elwin was here, he would rest a day and then leave the day after. Christian sat with Lord Elwin while Emely went to see if she could be of any help in the cookhouse and as usual found work to do. When she returned, she got Gwyneth so the girl could spend the afternoon with her father. Lord Elwin was not in the main room, but Christian sat at the table staring into his goblet of wine.

"Papa," Gwyneth cried as she ran to him.

Christian scooped the girl up into his arms and hugged her until she squealed. He laughed and put her down.

"What shall we do this afternoon?" Christian asked Gwyneth.

"Ride to the stream and pick wildflowers," Gwyneth answered.

Emely knew this was one of Gwyneth's favorite outdoor activities.

"You will come with us?" Christian asked looking at Emely.

"No, thank you. The two of you need to spend some time alone," Emely said smiling.

"Come, papa, come," Gwyneth said trying to drag Christian out the door.

"You will be safe?" Christian asked glancing at Drake.

"Yes, I will be safe."

Christian relented and let Gwyneth pull him out the door. Emely turned and started to gather the used bowls from the table. Drake was next to her picking up goblets. He followed her to the cookhouse where his entrance was met with silence and stares. Emely said nothing hoping he would tire of the boring task and go find some other way to amuse himself, but it was not to be. Wherever Emely went, Drake was beside her. Every errand she went on he was there to carry things back for her. The whole time he asked her questions about the manor, Gwyneth, how things worked. He made jokes and told funny stories. He was amusing, charming, and attentive. Emely found herself liking him because he made her laugh. He also complimented her not only on what she had accomplished at the manor but on herself; how pretty she was, the soft curl of her hair, the faint blush on her cheeks, her slim athletic body, even on how fast she sometimes walked when she was embarrassed.

"Tell me of your father's manor," Emely said hoping to distract him from her.

"My father's manor," he started. "It is big, old, boring. No beautiful young women there," he added with a hint of a leer but then laughed. "My father and brother are the same, solid, cautious, humorless, no sense of adventure. They are content to be where they are, doing what they have always done."

"Not you," Emely said with a smile.

"Not me. I wanted . . . want more than a mundane life. I wanted to see the world beyond the manor boundaries."

"And now you have. So, what will you do for adventure now?" Emely asked teasing.

"Find a new war, new women," Drake answered as if those were the only adventures in the world.

Emely had no response, so they walked back to the manor in silence. When they entered the courtyard Christian and Gwyneth were returning from their ride. Christian gave Emely a questioning look as he helped Gwyneth off her pony.

"How was your ride?" Emely asked Gwyneth.

Gwyneth handed Emely the bundle of wildflowers she had picked and talked about the new duckling family on the stream and the family of rabbits they saw as they walked into the manor house. Lord Elwin was sitting at one of the tables looking pale and somewhat distraught.

"Milord? Can I get you anything?" Emely asked.

"No," he answered. "He is . . . so confused."

Christian went and sat by the older man and began to speak to him in hushed tones. Emely went to the cookhouse and started bringing the food for the evening meal. The crusaders were more subdued this night as if remembering the friends they had lost. Most drank far less than they had the night before and were in bed much sooner as they would rise early in the morning to begin the last part of their travel to their homes. When the main room was empty except for Drake and Christian, Emely helped the girls clean the remains of the meal they had shared. She went to the cookhouse to make sure there would be plenty of food to supply the crusaders when they left in the morning. Emely looked around the cookhouse, it was still a beehive of activity but soon they would be able to get back to their normal routine. Back in the main room Christian and Drake sat in silence sipping their wine. It was the relaxed silence of men who knew each other well, men who had shared horrible experiences and lived while all around them others had died.

"Come, join us," said Drake offering Emely a goblet.

"No, thank you milord. I must check on Gwyneth. Good morrow milords," Emely said curtsying.

She went up the stairs very conscious both men watched her go. In Gwyneth's room the child was still awake waiting to be tucked in properly. Emely told her a story of a brave knight saving a fair maiden as the little girl's eyes fluttered shut and she went to sleep. Emely tucked the covers closer around the child's neck before preparing herself for the night. She heard Drake and Christian come up and go into their chambers. Then the house was silent except for movement in Christian's room which was next to Gwyneth's. Later Emely heard the door open and light footsteps in the hall. Then Gwyneth's door opened and by the dim light Emely could see a man enter. She sat up.

"Emi," Christian said. "Is she asleep?"

"Yes."

He walked over to the foot of Gwyneth's bed and looked down at the child. He said nothing for a long time but smiled at the little girl. Emely said nothing as she watched him.

"I am keeping you up," he said at last smiling at her. "Good morrow, Emely."

He turned and left the chamber and Emely could hear his light footsteps in the hall then his door opened and closed. She heard his footsteps in his chamber and then the slight creak of his bed. Emely lay back down and was asleep in seconds. He was home and they were safe under his care. The weight of complete responsibility for the manor was lifted from her shoulders.

She was up at sunrise and down in the cookhouse overseeing the last of the preparations for the crusaders' leaving. Then the food for the morning meal was carried to the main room as the warriors were coming down. Christian moved among the men talking with several as he did. He sat not on the dais but among his friends. The conversations were quiet and the eating steady but not hurried as if they were lingering. Lord Michael's men stood and moved to the door. Lord Elwin and his men followed, helping Piers out of the manor house and down the stairs. Drake's men were the last to stand. He followed them out, but his horse was not in the courtyard.

"I am sending my men home, but I have decided to spend a few extra days . . . resting," he explained to Christian, but his gaze was on Emely.

The crusaders mounted their horses and after bidding Christian and Drake farewell, turned and left the courtyard. Lord Elwin had thanked Christian for the care he had given Piers. Then he too was gone. Drake, Christian and Emely returned to the main room to finish their morning meal. Rand came a short time later and began to tell Emely of a problem in the village that needed attention.

"Rand," Emely interrupted him, "Lord Christian should be taking care of these things."

Rand looked at Christian and back to Emely before turning to Christian and retelling the problem. It was a simple problem, but Christian looked at Emely a question in his eyes. She suggested a solution and he agreed. Rand left to handle the problem.

"I had forgotten how things worked here."

"You will remember," Emely said smiling.

"I need to talk to the families of the men I lost. Will you go with me?" Christian asked Emely.

"Let me get Gwyneth up and have one of the girls stay with her."

Emely went up and got Gwyneth who ran downstairs once she was dressed to greet her father. Emely and Christian left as Gwyneth sat eating. Christian took a small sack with him.

At the first hut the children were feeding chickens in the front and called their mother.

"Tolen was a good man," Christian said to the wife when she came out. "He was kind and helpful to the others. He was liked and respected. He fought well and died . . . honorably. He is missed by all who knew him. We . . . found these among his things. He would want you to have them and know they gave him comfort. He loved you and your children. I am so sorry I . . . could not bring him home to you. This bag contains some of the earth where he is buried. If there is anything you need, please let me know. If it is within my power, you will have it." Christian said handing the weeping woman two small bags.

Emely hugged the woman and held her as the children gathered around their mother.

"We thank you," the woman said at last. "He fulfilled his vow to you." she added.

Emely sensed the woman did not like Christian. Emely knew this family had come from Lord Rene's manor, so they did not know Christian well.

"Your loss is our loss," Emely said to comfort the woman. "We share your sorrow, all the village, Lord Christian and I included. He is a good lord and will help you all he can. Believe me!"

"I trust you milady," said the woman looking at Emely and then at Christian and back to Emely.

Emely gave the woman another hug and then she and Christian went to the next hut of a fallen serf. The scene was repeated at each hut. Christian brought each of the family something of the man's and a small bag of ground from where he had fallen and was buried. Emely held all the women as they cried. The families that had come from Lord Bryce's were less hostile and more trusting of Christian.

Christian and Emely walked in silence to the huts of the others who had gone with Christian. He visited each man letting his family know he had been a valuable warrior. When they reached Sarah and John's hut, Emely and Sarah hugged as Christian asked if John was ready to take up his responsibilities again.

"What of Rand?" John asked.

"He has worked very hard," Emely added. "Perhaps they could divide the work? We have cleared more land, and we could use more huts as I am sure there will be some marriages and new families."

"John?"

"It is a good idea," John said smiling. "How will Rand feel?"

"It has been a lot," Emely said knowing Rand had let some of his own work go unfinished. "He would probably like to be able to take care of his own field a bit more."

"As would I," John added.

"I will talk to Rand," Emely said then realized her mistake. "Lord Christian will talk to Rand," she corrected herself while the other three laughed.

Christian and Emely left and walked back to the manor house in silence. Drake was coming out as they entered the courtyard and invited Emely to go riding with him. She declined saying she had to take care of Gwyneth. Then rather than going riding he followed them back into the manor house. Gwyneth, seeing her father return, ran to him and he picked her up.

"It seems Lady Gwyneth is not in need of you," Drake said with a lifted eyebrow. "Perhaps you will reconsider riding with me."

Emely looked at Gwyneth and Christian before relenting. They had four years to make up and needed as much time together as she could give them. Out in the courtyard Emely was surprised to see her horse had already been saddled and was waiting for her. She gave Drake a questioning look.

"I hoped you would come," he said looking a little embarrassed.

They followed the stream until it emptied into the lake where he suggested they walk. New spring leaves rustled in the soft breeze coming across the lake creating a low hum. Drake was funny and charming, almost childlike in some ways as they explored the forest at the lake's edge. He picked wildflowers and handed her a bouquet.

"Tell me about the Crusade," Emely asked.

"No," came his short firm response. Then he looked at her and his face softened. "It was not the glorious cause we hoped it would be. Too many died."

"Did you lose many of your men?"

" Some, I will need to visit with their families when I get home."

"That is what Christian did this morning. Their families know they will spend eternity in paradise with our savior," Emely said.

"Eternity in paradise," he half laughed. "Some perhaps, most unlikely. There was nothing holy about what we did in Jerusalem or Constantinople."

"The pope promised."

"The pope was not there!" he said, bitterness in his voice.

They were silent as they were both lost in thought. The peace and beauty of the place somehow shattered by his words and the picture they evoked. Later they returned to the manor house. Gwyneth and Christian were talking with Rand. Christian looked up at Emely and Drake as they entered and looked less than happy. Emely passed through the main room and went to the cookhouse to bring back the midday meal. Now the crusaders were gone, Sarah and the children as well as John and Rand all came to the meal. The talk focused on manor events and what tasks needed to be done and how Rand and John would divide up the work. While they talked, Drake sat watching Emely, smiling as if he knew some secret about her. He no longer leered at her, but his constant study was disturbing.

A day turned into two then four then it was a week and still Drake stayed. He followed Emely everywhere and made her laugh, was charming and kind. She found herself liking him and even came to enjoy his blatant flirting with her even in front of Christian. It almost seemed at times as if he flirted more with her when Christian was around. He would reach out to touch her but always stopped himself before contact was made until she smiled at him indicating she would not react. While most of Emely's interaction with Christian was manor related and thus work, her interactions with Drake were fun and relaxing, at times playful. Finally, Christian's patience with the other man was at an end. They were at an evening meal a week and a half after their arrival and Drake's attentiveness to Emely was disturbing.

"When are you leaving?" Christian asked angry at the other man's obvious desire for Emely.

"When Emely agrees to leave with me," came Drake's answer.

CHAPTER 46

"What?" said Christian, Sarah, Rand, Father Francis, and Emely in unison then Emely added "No."

"With you as my wife, my father would give me my own manor. I will make you a good husband," Drake said smiling at Emely.

"No!" said Emely more emphatically. "We need to talk . . . in private," Emely added looking at Sarah, Rand, and the others.

"We should go to our hut," Sarah said rising. John, Rand, and Father Francis also rose. Nelda also left.

Cristian stayed studying Emely as if trying to figure out what she would do.

"In private," Emely restated looking at Christian.

"As your lord it is my responsibility to make sure you are safe and not pressured into a . . . situation you are opposed to," he replied.

"I will make you a good husband," Drake said again.

"I do not love you."

"You like me, that is a good start. Once we are married and away from . . . distractions," Drake said looking at Christian. "You will come to love me."

"No," said Emely again.

"I have not been a good man. with you as my wife I will strive to be a better person."

"Lord Drake," Emely started.

"Drake," he corrected.

"Lord Drake," Emely emphasized. "I am a serf and thus unworthy of you."

"You are smart, beautiful, warm, charming, and I believe passionate."

"I . . . do not want to marry. I am happy taking care of Gwyneth."

"You should have children of your own to care for."

Emely was silent for a long time before speaking.

"I had a child of my own," she murmured. "He died. Now I care for Gwyneth."

Drake studied her for a very long time before speaking.

"Where is your child?"

"He is at Lord Bryce's."

"Who was the father," Drake asked looking at Christian who had said nothing.

"It does not matter."

Drake again studied her for a long time before speaking.

"I care not of your past. I want you. I . . . love you," he said.

"No," Emely said. "I will not marry you."

"Emely," Drake said, "please."

"No!" Emely said standing and going upstairs.

She went to Gwyneth's chamber and put the little girl to bed for the night. she could find no peace within herself. She lay on her cot and stared at the shadows dancing on the ceiling from the single torch that lit the chamber. She was unsure of how long she had laid, a thousand thoughts going through her mind before the voices from the room below drew her out of the chamber and down the stairs. Both Christian and Drake had been drinking far more than they should and they were arguing about events that had taken place in Constantinople. Drake found these memories funny while Christian did not.

"That lion!" Drake said. "Alexis thought he could scare us with the beast. We made short work of it."

"I took no part in killing the animal," Christian said sadden by the destruction of the pet.

"You took no part in a lot of the sport we enjoyed," Drake said, distain in his voice.

"You mean the women," Christian said with scorn.

"Yes, the women," said Drake with a leering smile. "You, you were always with that girl. What was her name, Ali, Aleea?"

"Aliyah, her name was Aliyah."

"You had eyes for none other. Beautiful women abounded and you only had her."

"I did not 'have' her. We talked that was all," Christian said looking at Emely for the first time. "I never lay with her."

"Why?" Drake asked. "She was young, beautiful, and very much interested in laying with you."

"She was an innocent. Her dream was to join a religious order, to devote her life to God and prayer."

"What a waste!" Drake said.

"No what was done to her was the waste!"

"She was used for what a woman is meant to be used for," Drake said before taking another deep swallow of his wine.

"She was raped! Were you one of them?" Christian asked angry at the violation of the young girl.

"No," Drake answered looking Christian in the eye, so his honesty was not doubted. "I was otherwise engaged that night."

"If you had been, I would kill you myself right now."

"I swear," Drake said at last understanding how angry Christian was. "I was not one of them. I only heard what had happened days later."

"I found her body," Christian said, sorrow at the abuse the girl had suffered in his voice. "They just left her there in a pool of her own blood."

"Was it true? What was done to her?" Drake asked.

"Yes," Christian said. "They raped her, four of them, one after the other cheering each other on."

"Were you there?" Drake asked.

"No, I . . . I was in the high tower looking over the garden at night. I heard her screams. I heard their laughter. I tried to get to her but got lost in the maze of rooms and stairways."

"They killed her," Drake said.

"Yes. When they were done using her, they took a sword and thrust it into that which they had violated up to her heart and then pulled it up, gutting her as they would an animal."

Neither of them spoke. The horror of what had happened left no room for words. Emely turned and went back upstairs. In Gwyneth's chamber she looked at the little girl sleeping so peacefully. Emely thought of Arianna and her dream of joining a convent. Then she thought of a girl a thousand miles away who shared the same dream. Both never got their dream; both are now dead. She said a prayer for both girls. Sleep still would not come. Sometime later she heard footsteps in the hall and a door open and close. Emely knew it was Drake. She wondered where Christian was. He needed to sleep. She stood and pulled a surcoat over her night tunic and with uncertainty left the chamber. Down in the main room Christian sat, a goblet in his hand, he was staring into the low fire in the pit in the center of the room. She went and touched his shoulder, but he gave no reaction. She knelt before him and reached out and touched the scar on his face. He came back to her then.

"She reminded me of Arianna," he uttered. "She had that same . . . otherworldly look about her. She did not belong among the warriors or the peacocks of Alexis' court. Her family had rejected her because she would not marry the man they had chosen for her. I swear to you," he vowed, "I never touched her. I think that is when I came to understand why Arianna . . . hated me. She never wanted to be married to a man. Her heart and soul belonged to God."

"You did what you had to do. Both of you," Emely's sorrow for both Arianna and Christian bringing her pain.

"Where was God when Arianna needed saving . . . from me," he burst out. "Where was God when Arianna needed saving from her father? Where was God when Aliyah needed him to protect her? Is there a God? I found him not in Antioch or Jerusalem."

"Christian," Emely said shocked. "He . . . he is in our hearts."

"Not mine," he said bitter at what he had done. "I killed, raped, pillaged just like the rest of them."

"Christian, it was war. You did what you had to do."

"What I had to do? You of all people should be the last to comfort me, to forgive me."

"I . . .. It is late. We need our rest. Please," she said with a weak smile, "come up to bed."

"Emi." Christian said hoping they could be together.

"Rest, you need rest." She said ending any thoughts he had of being with her tonight,

He stared at her then put down his goblet, stood and pulled her to her feet. When they turned toward the stairs, they saw Drake standing there watching them.

CHAPTER 47

"I will leave in the morning," he said understanding the bond Christian and Emely shared.

"Drake," Emely said.

"I know where your heart lies," he said looking at Christian. "Do you know what you have?"

Christian said nothing as he looked down at Emely beside him. They all went upstairs, and Emely left Christian standing outside his chamber door. She heard his door and Drake's close as she closed Gwyneth's. She let the tears fall: tears for Arianna, tears for Aliyah, tears for all those innocence who had died at their hands, tears for the hurt she had caused Drake, tears for her lost son, tears for herself; tears, too many tears. She went to lay on her cot. Sleep came quick despite the turmoil she felt.

When she went downstairs in the morning, Drake was gone. Nelda said he had left at first light. Emely had wanted to say farewell. She hoped he understood and believed he did. Sarah came a short time later and life at the manor returned to normal. Except it was a new normal. Christian was taking on more and more of the daily running of the manor. John and Rand were overseeing the clearing of new fields and pasture areas. Emely had more time to spend with Gwyneth and overseeing the manor house and courtyard around it. She, Gwyneth,

Sarah, and Eden spent more time in Arianna's garden and the vegetable garden. She was planning a new tapestry to celebrate Christian and the others' return. May turned into June and the whole manor seemed to be fresh and green. Two of the returning crusaders married the girls they had left behind. Christian, Emely, and Gwyneth attended the weddings and shared in the happy occasions.

It was the second week in June when one of the Crusaders came to the manor house asking to speak to Emely.

"Modig?" Christian said seeing the man.

"Milord," Modig said looking from Christian to Emely and back again. "I wish to marry," he at length blurted out.

"You have my permission," Christian said.

"She . . . she will not consent," Modig said in despair. "She said she is unworthy."

"Elle, you are Elle's love," Emely said as both men looked at her. Each wondering how she could know this. "There . . . there is a reason," Emely murmured. "Let me talk to her . . . and Lord Christian. You will marry Elle. I promise," Emely said smiling at the hopeful young man.

"Milord," Modig said bowing before he left.

Christian turned and looked at Emely. What had happened to make a young girl reject an offer of marriage from such a fine man as Modig?

"Elle was raped. Since she is no longer an innocent, she feels unworthy," Emely explained to Christian.

"The man?" Christian asked.

"Exiled. Elle did not want his blood, but she also never wanted to see him again."

"What do we do?" Christian asked.

"You explain what happened to Modig and I talk to Elle. She loves him, she wants to marry him she just feels . . . unworthy."

"We talk to them tomorrow. I am sure Father Francis can schedule a wedding for Saturday."

"I am sure he can," Emely smiled.

The next morning Christian and Emely walked together to the village, greeting villagers as they went, stopping to talk to some. Emely walked through the gate at the hut of Elle's parents toward Elle who was feeding their chickens. Christian waited and smiled at the ease with which Emely interacted with the villagers. He turned and walked to the field where Modig was working.

Emely and Elle spoke for several minutes. Emely assured Elle Modig would still love her and wanted her for his wife. Elle tried to protest but Emely told her Christian was speaking to Modig. What had happened to her was not her fault and she should not feel guilty or give up her dream of being Modig's wife because of it. Elle kept protesting but Emely at last told her she would be married to Modig on Saturday. Elle looked at Emely with hope filled eyes, asking if Lord Christian would order Modig to marry her.

"If necessary," Emely said. "Does he have to order you to marry Modig?"

"No," Elle said in a small little voice. "Modig must understand . . .."

"He will," Emely promised. She knew Christian would help Modig understand and accept the loss of her innocence. While he would not be Elle's first, he would be her last as she loved him and wanted to be his wife.

Christian, Modig, and Jerod, Elle's father, came to the hut a short time later. Elle bowed her head and blushed as Modig came to her and again asked her to marry him. Emely had brought Tess out of the house so she could be a part of the happy event. Elle blushed a deeper red but said 'yes.' Modig picked her up and swung her around as they both began to laugh. Tess was crying and Jerod was smiling as were Christian and Emely.

"Saturday, we are to marry on Saturday," Modig said, and the smiles left the faces of Tess, Jerod, and Elle.

"We cannot be ready by then," Tess wailed. "She has no goods, no dress, nothing."

"We will ask all the villagers to bring one household item," Emely said already planning a successful start to the young couples' marriage. "That will give them their goods. I have a surcoat she can have as her dress. The manor house kitchen will take care of the meat if the villagers bring vegetables, fruits, and bread."

"Saturday," said Modig looking with deep love at Elle.

"Saturday," said Elle.

Emely had Sarah spread the request to the villagers. She worked with Nelda to make sure there would be meat for the celebration. Elle came to the manor house on Saturday afternoon and Sarah and Emely made sure the surcoat would fit her tiny frame. They also did her hair and put a ringlet of flowers on her head before walking her out to the courtyard so she would be lifted onto a horse to ride to her wedding at the village church. The whole village gathered on the commons after the ceremony. Food was plentiful, ale and mead flowed. The music was lively, and everyone danced. Christian and Emely both danced with the bride and groom who were both beaming. Laugher filled the village long after dark. Christian danced with Gwyneth as the little girl laughed. Then he asked Emely to dance. They moved among the villagers as they held hands in the long line of dancing people, coming together, moving apart, spinning, bowing, and skipping in dance moves they had both learned as children. Their eyes never looked at anyone else as they moved through the crowd until the music stopped and they were standing close. For Emely everyone else ceased to exist as she studied his face and looked deep into his eyes. He moved to lower his lips to hers.

"Papa, papa," Gwyneth squealed. "Come see the sweets."

"Saved again," Christian said laughing as Gwyneth pulled him away from Emely.

Emely felt her cheeks redden as she looked up and saw Sarah smiling at her. She turned to get a goblet of mead and then moved through the villagers chatting with them as she went. It was late when they left the celebration and walked back to the manor house. Gwyneth was asleep in Christian's arms. In the house Christian carried the little girl up to her chamber and laid her on her bed with great tenderness then stood back as Emely pulled the covers up to the child's chin. They stood side by side looking down at the child they both loved.

"I missed so much," Christian said.

"You will be here for the rest of her life," Emely replied happy to share this time with him.

"I meant David."

Emely stiffened and turned away from him. His hand grabbed her arm and pulled her back to face him.

"David! Our . . . "

"No!" Emely said. "My son. You were married."

"Emely, if I had known . . ."

"If you had known what, you would have defied your father? You would have risked a war between him and his best friend? Where would you have gone? Where would you have taken me, us? No, no," she added weary of once again having to think about what might have been.

"Emely."

"Good morrow milord," she answered dismissing him.

"Emely," almost asking her to comfort him as he reached out to touch her cheek.

"Please leave," she said resisting her need to console him. "Morning will be here soon."

"Emely," he requested again.

"Please leave," she begged. "Please," she whispered.

CHAPTER 48

With a deep sigh of resignation, he left the chamber. Emely changed to her night tunic and lay on her cot staring at the ceiling. It would have been so easy to go with him, to be with him. She wanted to but what would that mean for the future? No, they could not be together, not like that, perhaps never. She heard him go not to his chamber but back downstairs. She lay awake waiting for him to come back. It was sometime later when he had not yet come up, she wrapped a surcoat over her night tunic and crept down the stairs. He was sitting staring at the fire, a goblet in his hand tipped so the wine was close to spilling. She walked toward him, but he took no notice of her, lost in his own thoughts,

"Christian?" she said in a gentle voice as she reached out to touch his shoulder.

His hand came up and grabbed her arm but stopped at her cry of surprise.

"Emely," he said in shock, "what are you doing here?"

"You should be abed."

"Too many thoughts."

"Tell me."

"I am home and at peace. I . . . I have seen . . . terrible . . . ungodly things."

"Where? Tell me! Let me help you," she said kneeling in front of him.

"Constantinople, Antioch, Jerusalem. Jerusalem was the worst. May God forgive us for what we did there! If there is a god, but I think there cannot be. No god would allow such evil in his name."

"Tell me!"

"By the time we arrived the people had barricaded themselves in the city. The countryside was bare, no food, no shelter, no water, nothing."

"How long were you there?"

"Weeks, it could have been months or even years, there was no time, and there was only survival. We arrived in June and were at last able to take the city in mid-July. We killed everyone we could find, old people, babies were snatched from their mother's breasts and tossed in the air to see how many we could catch on the tips of our swords while the anguished mothers screamed in sorrow. We cared not. Women great with child were cut open while they still lived, and their babies torn from their bodies and hacked to pieces in front of their mothers as they lay bleeding to death. The streets were filled with blood and body parts. We hacked our way through the people even as some came begging for mercy. We showed no mercy. The Jews went to their temple for sanctuary, and we burned it down around them. The smell of burning flesh filled the air. Our horses were slowed by the depth of the bodies littering the streets as we pushed to the Church of the Holy Sepulcher where we celebrated a mass of thanksgiving and victory even as the stench of death and dying stung noses. We held for ransom a few survivors, but not before the women were used to give the Crusaders comfort and the men were abused and abased. Even some of the men were 'raped' to give those Crusaders who had the stomach for it satisfaction. We were the worst of humanity for a 'holy' cause."

Seeing her look of horror, he added, "I took no part in the rape. I thought of you, of Felise, of Arianna, of Gwyneth. I knew I would have died before I let anyone do that to any of you. Then I realized those would protect them were already among the dead or were being raped themselves."

"God was with you. He brought you home to us," she said trying to comfort him, reaching out to stroke his cheek.

"God had nothing to do with that hell. It was the devil's war, the devil's time."

"You are home. It is over," she said, still stroking his cheek.

"Is it? Crusaders are still there. How many more will they kill establishing their kingdoms? How soon will they call for us to come back and help them secure their kingdoms? There is nothing there to support them. Everything, everything must be shipped there from the merchants of Venice, Milan, the Papal States. When will the next 'holy' war begin?"

"You will not go!"

"No but our sons . . . "he stopped then seeing her face. "Our sons," he said.

"We have no sons," she said.

"We could. Come to my bed, be with me, and let me forget everything in your arms."

"No," she said. "You need to sleep. Tomorrow with the sunrise, the light of day will burn away the darkness of the night. Each day will diminish the memories and fill your mind with new memories, better memories. I will be with you but not in your bed."

"I want you."

"No, it cannot be. How would we explain it to Gwyneth, to the villagers, to Lord Bryce and Lord Rene? No, it cannot be," she said standing. "Be abed, milord, morning will be here soon." She left him then and returned to Gwyneth's chamber.

He came up a few minutes later, stopped outside Gwyneth's chamber door but did not knock. Emely heard his chamber door open and close and then the creak of his bed as it gave under his weight. She slept then but her mind was a jumble, and, in her dreams, they did all he wanted them to do, to be. In her dreams she saw their children as they raced through their lives and grew to be fine young people. In her dreams all things were possible. then she woke, and her real life was as it had been since she had come here and as it would remain. She dreaded going down, she dreaded seeing him. For the first time in her life, she did not want to see him, to be near him. She rose as she must. In the cookhouse everything was going slower than ever before as everyone dealt with morning headaches and sore muscles from all the dancing, they had done the night before. Emely put on an apron and helped wherever she could, then took the first bowls of bread and meat to the manor house. Once she had put them down, she went to get Gwyneth. The child's bright morning smile warmed Emely's day and made everything feel better. She could face him; they could go on as they had. She was content, he would have to be. She heard his door open and close and told Gwyneth Christian was up and going down. The little girl ran to the chamber door and was out before Emely could say anything else. Christian would be happy; there was at least one person who adored him without reservation as she once had. Down in the main room he sat at the table eating a piece of bread as Gwyneth asked him about going riding. He promised they would go later after he attended to some work in the village. Emely sat silent eating and watching father and daughter talk. Gwyneth always seemed to have very important things to tell her father. Emely smiled at the thought.

As they were finishing their morning meal one of the guards came in and said there was a little caravan approaching. Emely looked at Christian. Were there other Crusaders who would be stopping here on their way home? Had he known? They went to the front stairs as the lead rider came through the gates. Lord Bryce and Lady Martha had come. Emely smiled as Gwyneth squealed with delight at seeing her grandparents. Even Christian smiled to see his parents. Lady Martha slid off her horse and was in her son's arms before anyone could give any greeting. Lord Bryce was slower, but Emely could tell, no less pleased to see his son as he too hugged the younger man.

"Come in," Emely said. "We were at table but there is more than enough."

Everyone moved back into the manor house, Lady Martha clinging to her son's arm.

"Tell me everything," she said. "The places you saw, the people you met."

"Perhaps later," Christian said, emotion making his voice catch. "I just want to look at you, and you," he added turning to his father.

"Indeed," Lord Bryce said, "we want to look at you. You are . . . well?" Lord Bryce asked looking at the scar on Christian's face.

"Yes, I am well. Tis a story not for women to hear," he said knowing his father wanted to know the detail of how he got the scar.

"My baby," Lady Martha said the scar registering for the first time.

"Tis old," Christian assured her. "How are Benoit and Marilee?"

"You did not tell him?" Lord Bryce said looking at Emely.

"No, he needed to hear from you."

"Benoit is dead. Two years now. Marilee went home and married another. She is with child and very happy."

"Benoit dead?" Christian repeated. "That means . . .."

"Yes, you are my heir. When Rene and I are both gone you will be a powerful and important baron, one of the richest in the land."

"Not what I ever dreamed of," Christian said disliking the thought of losing any more people he loved.

"We pray there will be many years before that will come to pass," Emely said even knowing now he must marry to protect Gwyneth's inheritance. Without brothers to guide her she would be the target of many a fortune seeker. "Lady Martha, would you like to lay down for a bit? You must have started your journey very early this morning."

"Yes, that would be lovely. And please just call me Martha. You have earned the right."

"Martha," Emely said smiling. "Come Gwyneth and I will take you to your chamber."

The three of them went up the stairs while the two men sat in silence. Upstairs in their chamber Lady Martha gave a sigh. "How is he?" she asked Emely.

"Good, he is good. Taking on more of the manor work every day. The men who went with him honor him and have I think shared some of their experience with their families. How he led them, protected them, took care of them. He has shared little with me but slowly, slow in small reminiscence I have learned some of what they experienced."

"Was it bad?"

"Yes."

"The scar?"

"That he has not spoken of. It will take time."

"You have all the time you need."

They continued talking but changed the subject to Gwyneth, the manor and manor house, and the latest tapestry Emely was working on, Christian's homecoming. Lady Martha admired it and then Emely insisted the older woman lay down and rest. Gwyneth wanted to stay with her grandmother, so Emely left the two of them cuddled together. She went back downstairs. Christian and Lord Bryce sat staring into the fire pit talking quietly, two warriors sharing the battles they had fought: the killing, the blood, the stench.

CHAPTER 49

". . . it was outside Jerusalem," Christian was saying. "A band of Muslims was trying to escape with a message to the relief force which was rumored to be on their way. We caught them and one of them slashed me. Michael killed him and then was killed himself. I looked at my attacker's sword, my blood mixed with so many others. Then I looked at my own sword, covered in blood like his. In that moment, I saw him, them, not as heathens, pagans, non-believers but as men just like us. Only they defended their homes, their families, their lives. We were the ones who brought death and destruction."

"When we came here, we fought for the duke, for his right to the throne." Lord Bryce recounted remembering the days. "I came to the same feeling as you when I met your mother. The serfs wanted no part of the war we fought. They just wanted to live in peace, and we took that from them. We killed, stole land, and raped women. Then I met your mother and . . . I began to question what we were doing to innocent people. not before I raped her. Alain was conceived before we were married. I saw my child growing in her and knew I wanted to protect her and our child. She was great with child when we were married, and my punishment was the loss of that child. When he died, Martha and I grieved together, and I vowed I would never take another life. Benoit was God's gift to us, and I thought a covenant."

Father and son sat silent then. From her place on the stairs Emely crept back upstairs. Once at the top she made much more noise, coming back down. She wanted them to know they were not alone. Both men looked up and Christian gave a slight smile. She smiled back as she passed through the room and went to the flower garden to pick some flowers for Lady Martha's chamber. She stayed in the garden longer than she intended. She wanted to be surrounded by beauty and peace after the stories she had just heard. Finally, she laid a flower on Arianna's grave and took the rest to Lady Martha's chamber. They were awake and laughing when Emely went into the chamber. They went down and the mood in the main room seemed to lighten when they arrived. Lady Martha went to hug her son again and then her husband. Emely looked at them. The love they shared was so evident, even knowing how their relationship started. She knew now they were devoted to each other and their children and the life they had built together. Lord Bryce and Christian went to tour the manor while Emely, Gwyneth and Lady Martha worked on the tapestry. Lady Martha admired the two Emely had already completed. When the men came back, they shared the midday meal before Christian, Gwyneth and Lord Bryce went for a ride. Lady Martha and Emely continued to work on the tapestry along with Sarah who had come to help. The three women chatted about their children, their homes, and their households. It was an easy relaxing conversation that eased Emely's mind.

Lord Bryce and Lady Martha stayed for the rest of the week, spending every day with Christian, Emely, and Gwyneth. Then it was time for them to go.

"You must come home," Lady Martha said as she climbed into the cart for the trip home.

"Mother," Christian said, "I am home."

His mother looked at him disappointed then looked at Gwyneth and Emely and smiled.

"Yes, you are. You must come and visit us. We only get to see Emely and Gwyneth once a year. Emely has been so busy. Now you are . . . home the three of you must come more often."

"We will try," Christian said smiling. "I have to relearn a lot."

"Good," said Lord Bryce. "You will need to know how to run a manor and much more someday."

"Not soon father. Not soon."

The two men hugged, and Lord Bryce mounted his horse, and they were off. Christian, Emely, and Gwyneth walked behind the cart to the manor house gate waving as the cart passed through the village and into the wood beyond. Once they were out of sight the three turned back to the manor house. Christian went to the stable and got his horse so he could ride through the village and out to the field to check on its progress. Emely and Gwyneth went into the manor house to begin their day of lessons for Gwyneth. Emely was teaching the little girl how to read from a bible Lady Martha had sent the year before. Emely was also teaching the child her numbers.

June became July and with the new month came the summer heat. Field workers rested during the middle of the day because they collapsed from exhaustion and heat if they did not. The watering system Rand and Emely had devised a few years before kept the fields watered. Christian was impressed by their ingenuity. He also liked the wall they had built around the manor house courtyard. New huts were being built to house the new families the marriages of Crusaders and village girls had created. More fields were cleared to increase the village food supply. July became August and the heat remained. Christian, Emely, and Gwyneth went riding almost every day through the wood, so they were sheltered from the glare of the sun. Gwyneth loved to race them on her little pony and more often than not Christian and Emely let the little girl win. She laughed with joy when she reached their manor gates before them.

As they were riding, one day in the middle of August a small caravan emerged from the wood at the far side of the village. Lord Rene and Lady Gracen had come to visit. They were already in the manor house courtyard when Gwyneth came racing up to the gate, her hair trailing behind her, her eyes bright with laughter, smiling at winning the race yet again. Seeing the cart, she went a little faster, too fast, and stopping too quickly almost fell.

"Grandpare," she shouted as she slid from her pony and ran to greet Lord Rene.

He scooped her up and hugged her as Christian and Emely entered the courtyard.

"Grandmar," Gwyneth shouted as Lord Rene released her and she ran to Lady Gracen to give her a big hug also. "Look, papa is home!"

Christian and Emely dismounted, and Emely hugged both Lord Rene and Lady Gracen.

"You should have let us know you were coming," Emely said with a smile.

"We wanted to . . . surprise you," Lord Rene said giving Christian an unhappy look.

"Well, you have," Emely said feeling the tension between the two men. "Come in. We were riding and Gwyneth won the race home, again," Emely said with a smile and a laugh.

"We saw," said Lord Rene continuing the angry look at Christian. "You risk her."

"We ride almost every day," Emely said defending Christian before he could speak. "We know what Gwyneth can do. She was always safe."

"Did not . . . " Lord Rene started.

"Rene," Lady Gracen said, "We just arrived. Let us enjoy some time with Emely and Gwyneth before . . . before you . . . chastise Christian."

"As you wish, my love," Lord Rene said none too happily.

"Come in," Emely said gesturing them into the manor house.

Once they were inside, she left Gwyneth telling her grandparents with great excitement about Lord Bryce and Lady Martha's visit and how happy she was to have her father home. Lord Rene continued to scowl at Christian even as he smiled at Gwyneth and made the appropriate acknowledgements. Emely went to the cookhouse for food. She carried it back to the main room where Gwyneth's happy chatter continued unaware of the tension between her father and grandfather. Emely put the bowls on the table and went back for individual bowls. When she returned Lady Gracen was looking at Emely's latest tapestry along with Gwyneth. The two men sat at the table but said nothing to each other. The silence was telling. They did not like each other. Emely was glad they both had the good grace not to say anything in front of Gwyneth. Lady Gracen and Gwyneth came to the table and took some of the cheese and fruit. Lord Rene turned to Gwyneth and asked her about her pony. Gwyneth was eager to tell him about it and how she almost always won the race back to the manor house. She chattered on and Emely could feel the tension in the room lessening as they all focused on the little girl. Lady Gracen was the first to speak to Christian and ask him about his experiences at the Crusade. He minimized the events, telling her some funny stories of the places he had been and the people he had met. He told her of the life in the Crusader camps, the friendships and camaraderie the men had shared.

"There must be more than that," Lord Rene said. "I remember the fighting, the stealing, and the women."

"Rene!" Lady Gracen said glancing at Gwyneth who was wide-eyed.

"Those are not tales for Gwyneth to hear," Christian said. "You were a warrior as was my father, you know what happens."

"Yes, I know," said Lord Rene spitefully.

"As do I," said Lady Gracen looking at her husband with a look which said he should not continue.

Emely knew of the start of Lord Bryce and Lady Martha's 'introduction.' Had Lord Rene and Lady Gracen's been the same, Emely wondered.

"Grandpare," Gwyneth said wide-eyed, "you stole? Did you confess and get forgiveness?"

Lord Rene looked at the child and realized he had made a mistake.

"Yes, Gwyneth, I confessed and got absolution. I even returned some of the things I stole as part of my penance."

"Some things," Lady Gracen said smiling teasing at her husband.

Lord Rene went red as Lady Gracen laughed at him. Gwyneth looked questioning at them before Emely distracted her with a request. She should tell them about the weddings they had attended. Gwyneth was only too eager to tell them about how she had danced all night, how beautiful the brides had been; to tell them about the food, the music, and her favorite, the sweets.

The evening meal was served a short time later and then it was time for Gwyneth to go to bed. Emely took her up and stayed as long as she could justify doing so. She had no desire to return to the tension filled room she knew it would be now Gwyneth was away from the two men who seemed to be so angry with each other. She did, however, go with uncertainty back downstairs. She hoped with Lady Gracen and herself there they would try to be courteous to each other. It had been a long day and Lord Rene and Lady Gracen decided to go to bed early. Emely wished them a good morrow and Lady Gracen said the same. Neither Christian nor Lord Rene said anything. Christian sat staring into the fire in a position Emely had come to recognized all too well. He was probing his life and what he had done, wondering if he could have taken a different, better path. She knew such reflection was useless. She refilled his goblet of wine and got one for herself and sat beside him.

"He will . . . forgive you once he knows you better. You need to give him time," she counseled laying her hand on his arm.

"He . . . he thinks I killed Arianna. How could he ever forgive me for that?"

"You did not kill her! She . . . she died in childbirth. It happens. He does not know you. Let Gwyneth and I show him the man we know, the man we love."

Christian looked at her hoping her words were more than a simple platitude. "You love me?"

"I . . . I . . . You are my lord, of course I love you as any loyal serf would love their lord." She explained.

"No, Emely. Do you love me?"

"I . . . I . . .. Please ask me not. I . . . I . . . I love Gwyneth. I love the people here. I love this manor, this village, the life you have given me when I only wanted to die. This is how . . . why I love you." She stammered.

"Emely," he said still hopeful she still felt as she once had.

"I must be abed," she said standing and moving away from him before he could ask again.

"Emely," he said grabbing for her hand, but she eluded him and rushed up the stairs and into Gwyneth's chamber, bolting the door behind her.

She heard him come up a short time later. He knocked on the chamber door.

"Emely," he whispered.

"Go to bed, milord. Tis late," she answered.

"Emely," he said again.

She did not answer this time. She touched the door as she would have touched him and felt his presence on the other side. Several minutes later she heard him walk down the hall to his own chamber, his door open and closed. The house was silent. She slept fitfully, and morning came all too soon. She was up at first light and down in the cook house. She stayed until she knew she could stay no longer. She had to get Gwyneth up and there were duties she had to attend to. The morning meal was served and then Lord Rene and Christian went to tour the fields. Lady Gracen helped Gwyneth with her reading and numbers while Emely worked on the tapestry.

CHAPTER 50

With each day that passed the two men seemed to be getting along better. They could speak to each other without hostility. Emely was relieved they found some understanding. She took Lady Gracen to Arianna's garden often and they enjoyed the colorful flowers and shade of the trees. Lady Gracen and Gwyneth put flowers on Arianna's grave and the little girl was enthralled at the stories Lady Gracen told of when Arianna was growing up; how kind she was, how funny, how loving. When Lady Gracen told Gwyneth how excited Arianna had been when she learned she was to be married, Emely knew Arianna had never shared her true wish with her mother. Perhaps she knew it would make no difference. She was betrothed and could only live the life her father had planned for her.

Lord Rene and Lady Gracen had been with them for ten days. The anger of the early days had passed. Christian and Lord Rene talked now and even found humor in the same things. They teased the women and Gwyneth, they drank and told clean versions of their war experiences, at times they shared looks that said there was much more to the story then what they were saying but because the ladies and Gwyneth were there, they could not tell the whole truth. It was after the midday meal when Christian said he was going riding and ask the others to join him. Lady Gracen declined as did Gwyneth who wanted to stay and go to the garden with Lady Gracen and hear more stories about her mother. Lord Rene also declined as he had some stories of Arianna's youth also. Emely, however, had not been riding since the day Lord Rene and Lady Gracen had arrived and wanted to exercise. Later their horses were ready and Christian and Emely rode away toward the stream to follow the path they often took.

It was a perfect day; a warm breeze danced through the trees moving the leaves to make ever changing patterns of sun and shadow. They rode far down the stream along the bank, talking of meaningless things but almost knowing each other's thoughts. They stopped at a favorite inlet and dismounted so they could walk a bit and let the horses munch on the green grass close to the edge of the stream. The breeze pushed and pulled Emely's hair into her face and away again, making her laugh even as she pushed it back. One particular strong breeze blew her hair over her face, Christian was beside her and lovingly pushed it away tucking it behind her ears. His hand lingered on her face as he smiled down at her. Looking up at him, her laughter and smile faded, replaced by the memory of another day they had shared by water. She hoped he would kiss her. Christian remembered that day also. The loved they had shared, the feel of her in his arms. He lowered his lips to hers with hesitation to savor a quick kiss before he lifted his head and waited for her reaction. It came as she stood on tiptoes to bring her mouth back to his, igniting a fierce need in both of them. His arms were around her pulling her closer and he deepened the kiss. Desire sprang forth in both of them; the tension between them exploded as they sought to satisfy their growing need. The kisses became deeper, more probing. They tasted and savored each other. It took another strong sharp breeze hinting at a coming storm to break their hold on each other.

"We should get back," he said regretting they could not find pleasure together as once they had.

"Race you," she laughed relieved they had been prevented from succumbing to their desires. She ran and jumped on her horse before he had a chance to react. She was going at a full gallop down the path they had taken so many times before. He was gaining on her as she glanced back at him, laughing. She never saw the branch that knocked her from her horse. She only felt the nothingness of flying through the air before she crashed to the hard rocky ground. Pain, unlike any she had ever known before ripped through her side as she screamed in agony.

He was there beside her helping her to her feet, but the pain kept her limp on the ground. Then he touched her to see where she had fallen, she screamed again. He looked at his hand in horror as her blood was seeping through her tunic and surcoat.

"We have to get you to the house," he said knowing he was going to hurt her, but they had to get to help.

"I . . . It hurts," she cried.

"Emely, I have to pick you up and get you on my horse." he said lifting her even as she cried out.

He lifted her onto his horse and then pulled himself up jostling her with his movements. He urged the horse forward but slowly, but every movement hurt and while he held her in place she whimpered in pain. They came out of the wood onto the road leading to the manor house, and he held the horse back from racing home as was their custom. Villagers stopped and stared as they passed. Emely leaned against him feeling safe in his embrace despite her pain. Passed the church, passed the gate and into the manor house courtyard. Shouts and horses whining in protest of their hurried treatment filled the air. Emely heard Gwyneth crying and Lady Gracen trying to soothe the frightened child.

"What happened?" demanded Lord Rene as Christian reached the manor house steps.

"She fell," Christian explained as he dismounted and turned to pull Emely into his arms.

"Fell!" shouted Lord Rene. "How?"

"I will explain later. Now she needs to be in bed and attended to. Lady Gracen, Sarah can help you," Christian said carrying Emely into the manor house and up the stairs to Gwyneth's chamber.

Once there Christian lowered Emely to the bed and then stepped back as Lady Gracen and Sarah moved forward. Emely saw their faces go white and knew the wound was serious.

"We have to get her clothes off," Lady Gracen said. "You need to leave," she continued turning to Christian.

"I . . ." he started.

"Go," she ordered pointing toward the door.

Christian lingered before walking backward out of the room as if afraid if he left, she would be gone from him.

"Emely," Lady Gracen said, "Can you help us? Lift your arms."

Emely tried but pain coursed through her, and she cried out. Lady Gracen pulled a small dagger from her belt and began cutting the surcoat and tunic beneath away from Emely's body. Lady Gracen went even whiter when she saw the wound. then set to work.

"Sarah, get me wine."

Sarah dashed from the chamber and was back in seconds.

"Here drink this," Lady Gracen ordered Emely.

"No,"

"Emely drink this!"

Emely complied and took a sip of the strong wine.

"All of it," Lady Gracen ordered. "This is going to hurt. The wine will help dull the pain."

"I . . ." Emely started but saw Lady Gracen was not going to accept anything less. Emely drank down the rest of the wine and the second goblet Sarah gave her.

Lady Gracen put thread in a needle, washed away as much blood as she could and then began sewing up the gash on Emely's side. Each stitch pulling the jagged flesh together was a hot poker shoved into Emely. She moaned but did not cry out. She did not want to let Lady Gracen know how much pain this was causing her. Finally, it was over. The gash was stitched back together and bandaged. Lady Gracen made Emely drink two more goblets of wine. Once the wine took effect and Emely dozed off. The two women left the chamber.

It was dark when she woke. Loud voices were coming up from the room below. She could not make out all the words but knew it was Lord Rene and Christian arguing. She sat up. Pain made her pause before she stood. More pain but she had to get to them, to stop them before they said things to each other which could never be forgiven. She took one step and then a second. Despite her great discomfort, she made her way to the chamber door. Opening the heavy door was the worst but she did it and moved with care along the hall to the top of the stairs. She went down the stairs with extreme care as the voices grew louder and angrier.

"You killed her. Today you tried to kill Emely!" Lord Rene shouted.

"No," Christian shouted back. "Arianna died in childbirth."

"You do not deny you tried to kill Emely today?"

"I would never do anything to harm Emely!"

"Just like you would never do anything to harm Gwyneth? We saw the first day, your disregard for her safety."

"I would never do anything to harm Gwyneth or Emely."

"You killed Arianna!"

"No, you are as much to blame as I am. She never wanted to marry me, and you forced her. She hated me and you for that."

Stunned silence filled the room except for the sound of Gwyneth crying.

"You killed Arianna. You tried to kill Emely today and it is only a matter of time until you kill Gwyneth," Lord Rene said with icy vehemence. "We are taking the girls home with us. They will be safe from you. You will never see either of them again!" Lord Rene shouted.

"No," said Emely from the stairs but not loud enough for the angry men to hear her.

"You are not taking anyone anywhere," Christian shouted back.

"We are and there is nothing you can do to stop us. This whole village will help us save them from you."

"No," said Emely louder but they still did not hear her.

"This is my manor, and I am the lord and law here," Christian shouted back at Lord Rene.

"You think after what they saw today the villagers will let you stop me?"

"NO!" Emely shouted from the stairs drawing everyone's attention to her. "No, Gwyneth and I are staying here, at this manor."

"Christ's blood," Christian said jumping up and hurrying toward her. "What are you doing out of bed?" He said as he scooped her up and started up the stairs.

"Down!" she ordered.

"Up," he said.

"Down!"

"Emely."

"Down! If you take me up, I will come down again."

He gave a sigh but took her to one of the benches and sat her down gently.

"Gwyneth," Emely said holding out her arms. The little girl ran to her and threw her arms around Emely evoking a small gasp.

"Gwyneth," Emely said with loving concern. "I never told you your mother and father loved each other. I told you they loved you."

"Grandpare said papa killed mama," Gwyneth cried.

"No, he did not. Your mother . . . she was an angel come to earth. She wanted to be married to Jesus. Do you understand?"

"Jesus died," Gwyneth said.

"Yes, but special ladies called nuns are married to him in special ceremonies. They live among other women in convents and spend their days in prayer."

"So, she would not have married papa and she would not have given birth to me?"

"True. But once she knew she was to give birth to you, she was so happy. She dreamed of the day she would hold you, all the things she would show you and teach you. She loved you from the moment she knew you existed."

"Where is she now? Does she still love me?"

"Her body lies in the garden, you know that. Her soul, her spirit, they are with you. She watches over you all the time. She keeps you safe."

"I miss her," Gwyneth said sadly.

"I know," Emely said. "I miss her too."

"Did she love you?"

"No, she never knew me. I know her, and I love her because she gave me you to love."

Gwyneth gave a big sigh and turned to her father and grandfather.

"You should love each other because she loved me, and I love both of you."

"It is late. You need to be in bed," Emely said smiling. "Sarah, will you take her up." Emely knew she would have to explain how she knew what she knew about Arianna. She gave the little girl one last hug before Sarah took the girl up to her room.

The silence in the room was heavy as all of them waited until they heard the chamber door shut. Emely rearranged herself as best she could on the bench and waited for the questions.

CHAPTER 51

"Why do you think Arianna wanted to be a nun?" Lord Rene asked.

"She wrote it in her journal," Emely explained.

"Journal, what journal?" he asked.

"She kept one. Had for years it seemed," Emely said. "I found it when I was cleaning her room."

"No, why would she . . .." Lord Rene started then looked at Lady Gracen who had gasped. "Gracen?"

"Yes, she kept a journal. I found some of them after . . . after she died. They were in a chest."

Lady Gracen came to sit by Emely.

"I knew she was not happy about the marriage," Lady Gracen said "but I thought she was like any young girl, afraid of the unknown. I believed she would . . . adjust as we all have had to over the years."

"She did," Emely said reassuring the other woman. "When she knew she was to have a child. She . . . never accepted Christian as her husband," she said but continued with haste when she saw the expression on Lord Rene's face. "I do not believe she would have accepted any man. She wanted to be married to Jesus and the church."

"Why did she not say something?" Lord Rene questioned.

"Because she loved you," Lady Gracen answered. "Everything she did was to please you, to somehow make up for not being the son you wanted."

"I loved her," Lord Rene said, hurt the daughter he loved so dearly thought she was not treasured and adored. "I loved her every day of her life!"

"You would have loved a son more," Lady Gracen said.

"I . . .."

"No, I do not believe she felt she was less important because she was a girl," Emely said to comfort the distraught man. "She just wanted a different life. If she had been a boy, perhaps she . . . he would have wanted to be a priest or monk."

"That would not have happened," Lord Rene said without hesitation.

"No, it would not have," Christian said, "because you needed an heir. You would have betrothed a son to Felise perhaps. No only child would have entered the religious. I will not allow Gwyneth to do that either. Now she is heir to both your lands and my father's she must marry and have children of her own."

"Until you have a son," Lord Rene corrected.

"Gwyneth will always be heir to your lands," Christian said. "I will make sure of that. It is only right."

"You will split your inheritance?" Lord Rene asked.

"Your lands are not mine. They were Arianna's and when the time comes, they will be Gwyneth's."

The two men stared at each other, a new respect forming.

"Will you let me see her journal?" Lady Gracen asked Emely.

"Yes, of course."

"Now you should be back in bed," Christian said as he moved to pick Emely up.

"Yes, milord," Emely said starting to laugh but pain went through her.

"Bed and broth," Lady Gracen said standing to fill a bowl for Emely.

Upstairs Christian took Emely to Arianna's chamber not Gwyneth's. He told Sarah she could go home and put Emely on the bed with great care as Lady Gracen brought the broth. Gwyneth, who had been sitting by the fire came to the side of the bed and Emely signaled her to join her on the bed. Gwyneth climbed on causing Emely to grimace, but she made no sound and let the child cuddle with her. Lady Gracen also sat on the bed and watched as Emely ate the whole bowl of broth. The older woman then helped Gwyneth prepare for bed and tucked her in next to Emely. Lady Gracen was preparing to leave so the girls could sleep,

"Arianna's journal is in the cupboard underneath the bottom board," Emely told Lady Gracen who found it and took it with her.

"It needs to stay here. It is Gwyneth's now. When she is older, she can read it for herself and know how much Arianna loved her."

"I will send the journals we have. Gwyneth should read those also, to know of Arianna's childhood."

The rest of their visit was uneventful. Emely came down every day but spent most of her time on a bench working on the tapestry. Christian and Lord Rene went out every day to tour the manor. They began to like each other and began exchanging teasing comments. There was, however, always a reservation, a concern that one wrong word or phrase might lead to an argument. Emely and Lady Gracen were happy and relieved the two men were getting along so well. On their last night, Lord Rene surprised all of them by asking Emely if she and Gwyneth wanted to go home with Lady Gracen and him. The silence filling the room was oppressive until Emely spoke.

"Why would you ask that?"

"You need to rest more so your wound can heal," Lord Rene said trying to sound like he was not planning to take the girls away from Christian. "We would like to spend more time with Gwyneth. Christian needs time to reestablish himself as lord of the manor, and . . . well we want to look after you."

"Lord Rene, Gwyneth and I love you, but this is our home. We have had this conversation before," Emely answered gently.

"You need to rest," Lord Rene repeated.

"And I would rest being jostled in the back of the cart along the path through the forest? No, we stay here. I promise to take care of myself."

"I will take care of Emely," Christian said.

"You . . . have work to do," Lord Rene reasoned.

"I will take care of Emely!"

"Christian be reasonable. You cannot be out on the manor and here in the house making sure she . . . is careful."

"I will take care of Emely!" said Christian showing his anger.

"Christian . . .."

"Rene!" Lady Gracen snapped at her husband. "Emely wants to stay here. She has made this her home. We cannot force her to leave, nor can we force Christian to let her go."

"But . . .."

"Stop!" Lady Gracen ordered. "They have made up their minds. Now you must accept their decisions."

Lord Rene looked none too pleased, none of them agreed with him, but he had the good grace to relent. When they left in the morning, Emely again assured Lord Rene she would rest and take care of herself. Christian assured Lord Rene he would take care of Emely. The small caravan left after hugs all around and promises Christian, Emely and Gwyneth would visit them soon. They walked to the courtyard gate to wave as Lord Rene and Lady Gracen left through the village and into the wood beyond. Life returned to normal as Emely healed little by little.

CHAPTER 52

August became September and then October. They took in the harvest and prepared for winter. In November they held the harvest celebration. Everyone was happy. The new families were in their new huts and some of the new brides were beginning to show they were carrying new lives. There were also losses. The one that touched Emely the most was Rand's wife dying in childbirth.

They had been married since before Emely had first come but had not been blessed. Now, at long last they were to have a child, but it was not to be. The birth had been long and hard and the child when it came was small and lived only a few minutes. Tandy knew of her child's birth but not of his death a few minutes later when she became incoherent and slipped into a deep sleep before dying herself. They were buried together, mother and child. John took over Rand's responsibilities for a few days, but Rand wanted to work, and John and Christian eased him back into a full workload. December came and again the weather remained mild with no snow to enclose the village. With the field work done for the year, Christian decided it was time for them to visit Lord Rene.

They left early in the morning as was Emely's habit and arrived just after dark. It was a happy time for all as Lord Rene seemed to accept Emely and Gwyneth would be leaving with Christian when he returned home. The acceptance between Christian and Lord Rene grew as the two men came to accept each other and their relations with Arianna. It was agreed after a week they would return home but in a surprise for Gwyneth and Emely, Christian announced instead they would be going direct to Lord Bryce's. They took an extra horse with them to carry the additional supplies they would need to spend one night in the forest. The next morning, they were off. On the road they spent a night in the forest, Christian set up a small shelter for Gwyneth and Emely while he slept under the stars. They were fortunate the snow still did not come. They spent another week at Lord Bryce's and then returned home in time for Christmas.

The snow came on Christmas morning and the village woke to a white landscape. Gwyneth was so excited she wanted to go play in the snow. So, after they attended mass in the village church with the rest of the village, Christian and Emely gave Gwyneth permission to go and frolic with her friends while the adults greeted each other and exchanged Christmas greetings. Everyone had the day off as all the food had been prepared the day before. Tables were set up in the church for the Christmas feast everyone contributed to. It was an annual party, made all the better because the Crusaders were home and safe. With the New Year came more snow closing in the manor.

CHAPTER 53

1101

The snow continued through January and into February, laying layer after layer of white on the manor. February was much the same as snow forced everyone to remain indoors as much as possible. People only left the warmth of their huts to do their daily chores and care for their animals. Christian tried to go to the village every day to check on the people and talk to Rand and John. Everyday Emely and Gwyneth worked on Gwyneth's reading and numbers. Emely encouraged Nelda to stay at her hut rather than coming to the manor house. Emely took care of making their meals in a large pot set in the fire pit. Sarah had stopped coming at the New Year when the snow got so deep. Now everyone was safe and as warm as their huts would allow. In the evenings Christian, Emely and Gwyneth played games or sang songs or found some small pieces of work to do. It was a comfortable time. Once Gwyneth was in bed Emely would work on the tapestry while Christian found some work. They would talk, remembering stories from when they were young. He told her of his training, his experiences in battle, she was sure he made them sound far less gory than they had been. She told him about Gwyneth as a baby and learning to walk, talk, and all the other firsts he had missed. They never talked about her life at Lord Bryce's when she had been exiled to the village. They never talked about David because she would change the topic whenever he questioned her about what had happened. The most she would ever say was he could see how their villagers lived and it had been no different at Lord Bryce's for her. Their lives were comfortable and relaxed in the cocoon the snow created around them. March brought more snow as the layers grew deeper. Then there were days of bright sunlight as warmer breezes weaved through the manor. People came out to enjoy the warmth and see and talk to neighbors. Children ran and played, having snowball fights. Christian and Emely went to the village to check on everything and everyone. One sunny day turned into two and then three and then it was a whole week. The hope was spring had made its arrival.

It had been yet another sunny warm day. Emely, Christian and Gwyneth had spent it in the village visiting and planning for the work needed to be done. The evening meal finished, and the villagers gone home for the day, Christian and Gwyneth were playing a board game while Emely worked on the tapestry. The knock on the door was unusual but not extraordinary. Villagers came at times to inform them of some occurrence in the village. Emely went to open the door. Outside winter had once more come to the village and Sam, one of the villagers stood there.

"Lady Emely," he started, "there . . . there is sickness in the village."

"Who?" Emely asked grabbing for her cape without pause.

"Robert, Joseph, Misty, and Reed"

"When? I saw all of them today."

"Came on sudden, milady."

"What is it?" Christian asked as he walked toward the door.

"Sickness in the village," Emely answered. "Nothing serious. I will be back shortly. Please put Gwyneth to bed and I will see both of you in the morning," she assured him before going out the door.

Emely went to each of the huts and found the same thing. The sick person was hot to the touch but shivered as if standing in the cold. They had muscle aches, a cough and breathing difficulty. Emely would not have been concerned if only one villager had been ill but four in just a few hours indicated more would become ill in the next few days if not hours. She could do nothing for them except suggest rest and fluids. By the time she was leaving the last of the original four huts two more villagers were ill. She went to them in turn and found the same thing. Now her concern was Gwyneth and Christian. Had they been exposed to whatever was sweeping through the village? Could she be sure she would not bring the illness back with her if she returned to the manor house? She had to be sure they were safe and there was only one way; she could not go home, nor could they come out until the illness had passed. Emely walked to the courtyard gate but did not enter.

"Close and lock the gate," she ordered the guards on the wall. "Let no one pass in or out," she said emphasizing the last.

"Milady?" one guard questioned.

"There is sickness in the village. Lord Christian and Lady Gwyneth must be protected."

"My family?" another guard said.

"No one from your family has taken ill yet, Benjamin. I will let you know if that happens," Emely added.

"Milady?" asked the first.

"I am sorry, Paul. Your eldest son is ill. I will let you know if there is any change. Now, please close and lock the gate. Protect Lord Christian and Lady Gwyneth and yourselves." Then as an afterthought she added, "Pray for us, all of us."

The large gate doors swung shut and Emely heard the wooden bar put into place, sealing her out, and them in. She could now focus on taking care of the ill in the village without having to worry about Christian or Gwyneth. She turned back to the village and went to the church. She would take her rest there until the illness passed. Father Francis was waiting for her with pillows and blankets and a mattress. He used these to make a small sleeping spot for her in a corner by the altar. He had also brought her candles so she would have light. They talked for a short while and then he left for the night. Emely lay down and tried to get some rest, but she was worried about the villagers. It was long after the sun had set when sleep overtook her, and morning came much too soon. The morning brought three more cases and half of the huts in the village had at least one family member ill. The healthy took care of all the chores of those who were ill. Father Francis and Emely agreed to continue the children's lessons so they would have some time in the fresh air and away from the illness of their huts. By evening there were five more cases. Emely ate when she could, where she could, as she went from hut to hut visiting the sick. Among the latest to become ill was Elle who was expecting her first child. Emely saw the look of concern on Modig's face and tried to reassure him that because Elle was young and in otherwise good health, she and the baby would be fine, but she was not as sure as she tried to make him believe. She greeted the children coming in for their lessons as they surrounded her. The sad part was the number of children who were not coming to the lessons. Some had to do the chores of their parents, who were ill, but some were ill themselves. Going from hut to hut none of the ill seemed any better this morning and some seemed worse. The next three days passed the same, a few more ill each morning and one or two more ill in the evening. By the fourth day every hut in the village had at least one family member ill and in some of the huts there were two or even three family members ill. Neighbors shared food with those who could not prepare food for themselves. Then the first villager died. It was a shock no one had been prepared for. One of the original four, Reed, died during the day on the sixth day after the first became ill. The other three seemed unchanged and one of the two who had become ill when Emely first came to the village seemed to be getting better. Who would get better and who would not was unpredictable. How many in a family were sick also gave no indication as to who would die and who would live.

CHAPTER 54

On the twelfth day after she came to the village, Holt, Sarah's oldest son, did not come for lessons. Emely hurried to Sarah and John's hut. Holt was ill. Sarah was giving him a chicken broth and the rest of the family was eating the chicken they had killed that morning. Sarah was trying to stay calm but everyone in the village knew Reed had died, and a pall had come over the village. By night fall another of the original four, Misty had also died. Over the next three days four more died. With the ground frozen there was no way to bury the bodies so an animal shelter was used to store them until the spring thaw would allow them to be buried in the village graveyard at the edge of the village. Even as some died others became ill. Modig was already ill when Elle died. Emely sat with him as he cried over her body and the loss of not only her but their unborn child. He had seen war and men at their worse, but he had not been prepared to lose his beautiful young wife. He died three days later as much from a broken heart, Emely thought, as from the illness. They were together now. Then Holt died and John became ill. Emely sat with Sarah and did what she could to ease her friend's suffering. Death surrounded them and hut after hut experienced loss. The bodies were piling up in the animal shelter. Then three weeks after it started, a day passed when there were no new illnesses. One day becoming two and then three. The illness was not done, however. John died on the fourth day. Emely sat again and consoled her friend as Rand and another villager took John's body and put him with the rest of the lost. A week passed and there were no more new sicknesses. Villagers were still dying, twenty lost, strong men, children, and women young and old. Who would be lost next was unknown. Then a month after the first illness a day passed when there were no deaths. The weather warmed, the snow began to melt, and people began to emerge from their huts. They talked to each other but at a distance.

It took two days before Emely realized if the snow was melting the bodies would also be warming. She went to the shelter and knew while they still could not bury the dead because the ground was still frozen, they had to do something. Emely hated what she knew had to be done. She knew the living would hate her, but she had no choice because a new kind of sickness would be among them if the bodies were not disposed of quickly. She found Rand and two other men and told them to bring all the bodies to Modig and Elle's hut. While they did that, she went from hut to hut getting buckets filled with oil. She watched as the last of the bodies were put in the hut. Several villagers came to watch but said nothing. Once all the bodies were inside Emely handed Rand one bucket and the other man the other bucket and told them to pour the oil on the hut. They both gave her a questioning look, but she stared straight at the hut and with shrugs they did as she had ordered. Once they had poured the oil on the hut, she used the torch she had lit from one of the huts and put it to the hut. While the twigs and straw were damp from the snow the oil lit, and the hut began to burn. Father Francis came to her side as she walked to the road.

"What are you doing?" he demanded.

"There is no choice," Emely answered without looking at him.

"They are good Christians. They must be buried in sacred ground!" the priest protested.

"We cannot wait until the ground is thawed."

"Lady Emely!"

"We . . . I had no choice."

"I must bless them."

"Do it from here."

"I . . . They should be blessed individually with Holy oil and prayers said over their bodies."

"Do it from here!"

Villagers had gathered around them. Emely ignored the murmuring of the crowd. She continued to stare at the burning hut ignoring them. The fire was an inferno, the heat forcing Emely and the others to back away from the flames consuming the hut and everything inside. Emely turned from the hut at last and saw the looks on the faces of the villagers. Their expressions ranged from anger to shock to sorrow. Then she looked up and saw Christian on the wall around the manor house courtyard. She moved through the crowd that parted sluggishly. She walked toward the wall, her eyes never leaving his face. She saw his concern.

"Emi," he called as she approached.

"I had to burn the bodies," she explained.

"When are you coming home? Gwyneth does not understand why you are gone."

"I will come home as soon as I am sure it is safe."

"How many?"

"Twenty."

"God have mercy on their souls. How many still sick?"

"Five but no new sickness the past week. I think it is over. I need to wait just a few days more."

"I miss you," he said wanting her to return home to safety.

"I miss you," she said smiling up at him. "Soon, I promise soon. I must go and check on the five remaining. Give my love to Gwyneth. Tell her I miss her and want to hear all her lessons when I come back."

While they talked the snow came again. It was the first week of April when the village should have been beginning the spring planting. When the first sprouts of the winter plannings should have been coming through the ground. When the village should have been coming back to life after its long winter's nap. She turned back toward the village and walked through the falling snow to the church. Father Francis was there waiting for her. He said nothing but the expression on his face told her he was not happy. She cared but not enough to argue with him. She had done what had to be done. She sat for a little while resting and preparing for what she knew she would face as she traveled through the village to visit the last of the sick. They would forgive her in time but for now they were angry. She went to each of the huts where someone was ill. They were in different stages of the illness, but all were recovering and would soon be well enough to resume their lives. She went again to Modig and Elle's still burning hut. She stood and stared at it remembering each of the people inside, people she cared about. They would not build another hut on this site, she decided. They would erect some kind of memorial to those they had lost.

The snow came but lighter, in big fluffy flakes. Then a few days later it stopped. Emely walked through the village, but her legs felt like they were carrying stones, her body ached as did her head. She did not remember when she had last eaten but was not hungry, then came the chill. No matter how she wrapped her cape around her she could not get warm. She was walking through the village and saw Christian again on the manor house wall. She started to walk toward him so they could talk but each step seemed harder to take than the last. She was tired and the wall seemed to move away from her. She put out her hand to reach for him, but it was not the wall she felt but the last of the white snow as she collapsed.

CHAPTER 55

"Emely," she heard him yell as she turned over to look up at him on the wall. It was the last real thing she saw before darkness closed in around her.

Christian watched her walk slowly toward him and knew she was ill. Even from the distance between them he could see she was pale. He would insist she come home once she was close enough, they could speak. He realized her steps were slowing as she struggled to walk. He could see her effort on her face. Then he saw her collapse, face down into the snow. She rolled over so her eyes could stare at the sky. Then he saw them flutter close as she tried to stay conscious.

"Emely!" he called to her as he saw a flicker of recognition and then she was lost to a deep sleep.

"Open the gates," he called as he hurried down the steps.

"Milord?" one of the guards said.

"Open the gates," Christian called again.

"Lady Emely . . . "

"I am the lord here and you will do what I order!"

The two guards looked at each other but then opened the gate without delay.

Christian was out and to Emely's side.

"Emi," he called but got no response. He lifted her into his arms and turned toward the manor house.

She was floating through darkness then entered the light. It hurt her eyes and she tried to shield herself. Then she heard the child's voice. The child was crying and calling her name. Emely became conscious enough to realize it was Gwyneth. Christian had lifted her from the soft snowy bed and brought her into the manor house.

"No," she said. "Sick."

"Hope, take Gwyneth," Christian ordered. "Bring broth to my chamber," he continued as he climbed the stairs.

"No, sick," she protested again.

He paid no attention to her. In his chamber he put her on his bed and pulled her cape off as she whined, she was cold. He pulled the furs over her and took the bowl of broth from Hope.

"No one comes in this chamber," he said. "Put food outside the door and knock so I know it is there."

"Sick," Emely protested again as he fed her the thick hot broth. It was the last conscious word she said for several days.

She was floating again. She was floating in the river by Lord Bryce's. Christian came and they floated together, locked in each other's arms. She whispered his name and he whispered hers. She was wrapped in the cocoon of his warm arms. Then he was gone, and she was floating alone. Angry voices demanded a name. She could not see anyone, but she knew those voices: Lord Bryce, Lord Rene, and Benoit. Behind them stood Christian saying nothing, watching her. They kept saying it over and over, 'who, who, who.' She would not tell them. Then she was floating again but heavy and sinking below the water, gasping for air as she fought to come to the surface. On the surface, the voices demanded a name. She could only get peace beneath the water, but she could not breathe there. She was heavy and her body felt big, great with some inner weight. Darkness fell and she was alone but still felt heavy. Clouds of mist surrounded her, but a small beam of light appeared and grew.

"Mama" said a child's voice as a young boy emerged from the cloud. She knew this was David. David as he would be now. David with his father's hair the color of fresh cut wood. David with his father's green eyes. David, tall and slender, dressed in Christian's blue. David.

"Mama, I miss you."

"I know baby, I miss you too," Emely answered.

"Papa would have loved me if you had told him," said the young boy's voice but not with anger or reproach.

"I . . . I could not tell."

"Mama, who was my father?"

"David, David!" Emely cried.

"Tell him. He needs to know."

"David, I . . . I cannot."

"Papa needs to know. Please tell him."

"David," Emely cried, then knew she had to say the words she had carried in her heart for so long. She had to say them out loud even if Christian never heard them, she had to say them.

"Christian, you have a son. We have a son!"

"He knows mama. He knows and he loves me. He loves me and he loves you. You need to go back to him and to Sissy."

"Sissy?"

"My sister, Gwyneth. They need you."

"David, I want to be with you. To take care of you."

"You are with me. I am with you. they need you. Go back, mama, go back," David said as he faded, and she was left alone again.

"Please God, do not take her," she heard Christian pray. "She is loved by so many. She has suffered so much at the hands of those who should have protected her. Give her back to us so we can care for her as she needs to be cared for. You have so many angels and saints with you; leave this angel here among those who love her. Please God, do not take her, please!" he said begging a God she knew he did not believe in anymore. Then she was in darkness again and there were no more voices.

Emely opened her eyes one at a time to the soft light of a single torch lighting the bed chamber, Christian's bed chamber. Weight on her hip and a hand covering hers woke her. She turned her head to see him sleeping. His head lay against her hip, his hand on hers. Emely smiled and moved her hand from under his to touch his face. He looked old and tired. She stroked his cheek and lifted her hand and gasped when he opened his eyes. She had not meant to wake him. He smiled at her, and her regret passed. She smiled back.

"You are awake," he said softly.

"I came back to you," Emely said smiling at him. "David sent me back to you and Gwyneth."

"David?"

"Our son. He told me to come back to you and his sister. He calls her sissy," she added with a laugh.

"David," he said the name with deep love. "You need something to eat," he said shaking off the sadness.

"I . . . I am not hungry."

"You need to regain your strength," Christian said standing and leaving the room.

CHAPTER 56

A few seconds later Sarah and Hope came in with a bucket of warm water and a clean tunic of fine white linen. They helped Emely wash the dried sweat from her body, changed the bed linen, brushed her tangled hair, and helped her back into the big bed before getting her a large bowl of vegetable soup. Emely took a first hesitant sip and then a second and third. Before she realized she had drunk the whole bowl. The effort had exhausted her. Hope took the empty bowl out of the chamber as Sarah helped Emely slip down into the covers. Emely drifted off to a dreamless sleep and woke hours later. The sun was up, and the torch was out. She sat up and Sarah was at her side instantly.

"He wanted to know when you are awake again," Sarah said as she left the chamber.

Christian came in a few minutes later smiling at her sitting in his bed.

"What?" she asked, smiling back at him as he came to sit beside her on the bed.

"The image of you in my bed kept me warm many a night while I was away," he answered still smiling. "I always imagined I would be in the bed with you, not caring for a sick woman."

"I will leave," she said starting to throw the covers off.

"Emi, I am teasing you," Christian said stopping her. "You need to rest more and regain your strength. Now, Gwyneth wants to see you. She will not believe you are better until she has. Ready? She is going to bounce in here."

"Yes," Emely said eagerly. "I have missed her so much!"

"You were warned," he said smiling as he walked toward the door. "Gwyneth," he called out the open door.

"Emi!!" the little girl shouted as she ran into the room and jumped on the bed to throw her arms around Emely's neck. "Papa would not let me see you because you were sick. He would not let anyone in the chamber."

"I was sick but now I am better, and you can see me every day," Emely smiled.

"The snow is gone," reported Gwyneth. "Everyone in the village are out and working. there are so many people missing."

"Gwyneth, they died. They got sick like I was sick, and some died."

"No! So many?"

"Yes, so many," Emely said pain at their loss still raw. Whole families were gone, Elle, Modig and their baby, John, and Holt, all the others, friends, all gone.

"Gwyneth, go downstairs and do your lessons," Christian said from the door. "Emely needs to rest."

"Papa, no," Gwyneth whined.

"Gwyneth!"

"Yes, papa. I can come back later?"

"Yes, you can come back later," Emely said smiling at the child.

"I need to be up," Emely said to Christian after Gwyneth had left. "I am sure there are things I need to be doing."

"No, there is nothing you need to do. You need to rest a few more days before you even think of leaving this room let alone bed."

"Christian, please I need to do something."

"I will have some sewing brought up to you. You are not getting out of bed for at least two days. I like having you in my bed," he added smiling. Then seeing her blush, added, "even if you will not let me join you."

She said nothing but thought to herself 'if only you knew how much I would like you to join me.' she shook off the thought. It could not be.

He left and a few minutes later Sarah returned with another bowl of broth. She was followed by Hope who was carrying an arm full of sewing. The two women separated out the things to be worked on as Emely drank her broth. Then they sat talking in low tones as they worked. Sarah was much quieter than in the past. Emely knew there was no way to console her friend, only time would ease the pain.

"How long was I ill?" Emely asked.

The two women looked at each other before Sarah spoke.

"Eight days. Lord Christian never left you and would allow no one in."

"He must have been exhausted," Emely said. "And after I woke that first morning?"

"You slept the rest of the day and all night. He stayed with you then also."

"The village? How are the sick?"

"Better, everyone . . . who survived is better," Sarah added.

"Sarah, I had no choice," Emely explained.

"I know. Father Francis has blessed . . . the place. It is now a second graveyard. We have put up . . . markers for each of them."

"Sarah," Emely said the tears for her remaining friends as well as her lost friends.

"They are with the saints," Sarah said with confidence was as much self-assuring as assuring to Emely.

The warm April sun had come out at long last and the last of the snow was gone. The village had returned to the busy planning and tending their fields. Work consumed the spring months. Emely and the other two women worked in Christian's bed chamber for the next three days before Christian would allow Emely to come downstairs. He insisted on helping her down. He also insisted she sit and work on the tapestry and let everyone else do any moving around that needed to be done. Three days later, Emely made sure she was up before him and went downstairs and out to the cookhouse to check on everyone and everything there. Nelda greeted her with warmth and then shooed her back out saying Lord Christian would dismiss her if she let Emely stay. Emely grabbed a bowl of bread as she went out the door, laughing as she went at Nelda's half angry yelling at her. In the main room, she straightened up the tables and benches and gave the room a thorough inspection to see what cleanup had not been done while she was away and ill. Christian was not happy with her when he came down but knew better than to argue. The next day she moved out of his bed chamber and back into Gwyneth's much to Christian's displeasure. Later that day she walked to village for the first time, with Christian accompanying her at his insistence. She put flowers from the garden among the crosses representing each of the lost.

CHAPTER 57

May came beautiful, sunny, and warm. Emely was back to full health and the village was thriving. The loss of the winter seemed unreal until Emely looked at the faces of the villagers and so many were missing. Gwyneth and Christian went riding every day. Emely wanted to go but Christian refused until a particularly warm day in the first week of May. He had ridden with Gwyneth in the morning but agreed to let Emely ride with him in the afternoon. With the understanding there would be no races like the summer before. Emely agreed, she would have agreed to almost anything to be on a horse again and out enjoying freedom.

They rode along the stream as they had so many times before following it to the river beyond. They followed the river to their favorite inlet and dismounted so they could walk a bit and let the horses munch on the green grass that was close to the edge of the stream. Christian had a sack of light food for them to snack on and a skin of wine. They sat in comfortable silence until she yawned.

"We should go back," Christian said standing and putting his hand down to help her to her feet.

"No not yet. I have not been out for so long. I want to enjoy this beautiful day."

"Emi."

"Please?" she said in the same begging voice Gwyneth sometimes used.

Christian burst out laughing and sat down beside her.

A short time later Emely leaned against Christian as the warmth of the day made her drowsy. He readjusted and she cuddled deeper into him and slipped an arm around his waist, and he wrapped an arm around her shoulders. It felt so right to be in his arms like this. Like they had always been together and always would be. It felt right when he lifted her face and lowered his lips to hers in a quick kiss before he lifted his head and waited for her reaction. It came in a hurry as she wrapped an arm around his neck and pulled him down to her again. She deepened the kiss this time and he responded. Desire sprang forth in both of them; the tension between them exploded as they sought more. The kisses became deeper, more probing as he lowered them to the ground. They spread out their bodies next to each other. His tongue probed the sweetness of her mouth, and she probed the strong depth of his. His hand found her breast and even through the cloth of her tunic and surcoat he felt the hard peak seeking more. He moved so his body was covering hers. She could feel his need and the warm dampness between her thighs.

"It has been so long," she whispered.

"Too long," he replied moving his lips to her neck and nibbling the lobe of her ear.

"Please," she begged.

"No!" he said without warning and moved off her and stood.

"Christian!?"

"No, I will not leave you with another child."

"Leave me? Where . . .. "

"Get up. We need to go back to the manor," he ordered.

Emely stood, the heat of embarrassment replacing the heat of passion. She walked to her horse and was on and heading back to the manor before he could help her. Once they were back at the manor house he stayed on his horse.

"I am going away for a week or two," he announced.

"What? Where?"

"I need to see my father."

"It is late. You will not get there before sunset." Then seeing the determination in his face, she added. "Wait and go in the morning. We can pack food for you. If you leave now, you will have nothing."

She could see him thinking and then he relented.

"In the morning," he said dismounting. "Emely, forgive me. I let . . . I should not have taken advantage of you that way. It will not happen again, I promise."

"I wanted to be joined with you," she said as heat went through her body just remembering their few minutes together. "You do not have to leave because of me," she added.

"Yes, because of you I do have to leave," he said.

Emely turned and went into the manor house and straight through to the cook house. She needed to be away from him. She could not look at him for some time. How could she stay now? In the morning before he left, she would ask him to ask Lord Bryce if she could come back to his manor. She would still be able to see Gwyneth a few times a year but could again build a new life for herself. Perhaps she would find a man who would understand and forgive her past mistake. Perhaps she could have the life she always should have had as a simple village woman, wife, and with good luck someday a mother. She wanted children. She loved Gwyneth with all her heart, but she wanted to have children of her own with a father who would love her and their children as she loved Gwyneth, as Christian loved Gwyneth. The rest of the day and evening passed in tense silence between them. Gwyneth must have felt something because she was unhappy with everything and demanded their attention. When Emely put Gwyneth to bed she did not return to the main room, and a short time later Emely heard him come up and go into his chamber. Then the house was silent. Emely lay awake and relived the time they had spent together over and over until the tears came. Of course, he would not be with her. He would marry again and would not want her and a possible child around his new wife and children. Yes, she needed to go back to Lord Bryce's so both of them could build a new life with new people. She would not, could not say a new love because she knew part of her heart would always be with Christian and Gwyneth. Then at last sleep came. She had decided.

She was up early and planned to prepare a food packet for him and to ask him to talk to Lord Bryce about her. She was too late, however. When she went to the cookhouse to prepare the food, Nelda told her Christian had already been there and taken food with him. He was gone, already. Emely now felt even worse. He was so desperate to be away from her he had left long before most of the manor was even awake. He said a week, maybe two. She had that long to prepare herself for whatever announcement he might make as to a future wife Lord Bryce might arrange for him. Marilee had a younger sister as did Duran, perhaps one of them, to help secure Lord Bryce's manor. She would wait and prepare Gwyneth for her leaving for she would not stay once she knew he was to marry again.

CHAPTER 58

The time passed slowly. Each day dragging along. She had gotten so comfortable having him there. Just to be able to look up and see him sitting there in the room, she had made so comfortable, was wonderful. Even Gwyneth was feeling his loss and was not her usual happy and loving self.

"Rider coming," came the call from the manor house wall.

Gwyneth ran out to greet her father. Christian slid off his horse and scooped Gwyneth up and twirled her around in his happiness to see her.

"Did you miss me?" Christian asked.

"Oh, papa, I thought you were gone forever."

"I tried to explain it was only for a short time but . . ." Emely explained.

"I promise you, Gwyneth, I will never leave without telling you again."

" You should never leave me again!"

"Okay, I will try never to leave you again. Next time, every time I have to leave, I will take you with me."

"And Emi. You cannot leave without Emi."

"I will not leave without Emi" he said using the childhood name as he smiled at Emely.

Emely smiled knowing he was only saying what Gwyneth wanted to hear. He would have to explain to Gwyneth when the time came why Emely was leaving without them. That, however, would be for another day and time.

They settled back into a routine perhaps not as comfortable as it had been before but simple and easy. Christian acted as if nothing had happened between them, and Emely knew that was for the best. She would carry the memory and it would warm her many a night but that is all it would ever be: a memory. The week passed then two and while Christian was attentive to her, he made no move that would suggest he had any romantic thoughts toward her.

Emely, Sarah, and the children were in the flower garden. The children were playing and running through the flowers as they always did. Sarah and Emely were doing some sewing when the children stopped and stared at the garden entrance. Both Sarah and Emely turned, and Emely was surprised to see Felise standing there.

"Felise," Emely called as she stood and walked to hug her friend. "What are you doing here?"

"We have never come and now Christian is home, we wanted to see his manor. I wanted to see you. I was so stupid the last time I saw you. I . . . I have missed you so much," Felise said hugging Emely. "And I heard you had been ill. I wanted to see if you were better."

"I am so glad you are here. You have to tell me everything. How is Duran?"

"He is . . . wonderful. I . . . I cannot believe how happy I am with him."

"Nor can I believe how happy I am with her," Duran said coming into the garden followed by Christian.

"Lord Duran," Emely cried as she curtsied to him.

"Lady Emely," he said bowing.

"I am not a lady," Emely said laughing.

"Mother and father say you are," Felise said. "They say you have done wonders with this place."

"Not their manor but we love it," Emely said smiling at Christian. "How long are you staying?"

"A few days perhaps a week," Lord Duran said. "Now Christian you were going to show me your wood."

"Yes," said Christian leading the other man away.

"Come sit. Tell me about your children," Emely said leading Felise to the bench. "This is Sarah."

"I remember Sarah. It is nice to see you again and to see you are friends."

"Lady Emely has been very good to me," Sarah said.

"Emely was always good to everyone," Felise said smiling at her friend.

"How are your sewing skills?" Emely asked trying to change the subject.

The other two smiled but said nothing more about Emely. They talked of their children, the recent illness, and the losses which brought tears to their eyes. Then Gwyneth and Eden ran through the garden, laughing. They were joined by Felise's two older children, Garren and Elise. The men returned and after dinner the two couples, Duran, Felise, Christian and Emely sat talking and laughing long after dark. There was none of the tenseness of their last meeting. Emely kept thinking how right this felt to be among friends, people she loved. If this was to be their last time together, she would be happy it was so pleasant.

Early in the afternoon of the next day Lord Bryce and Lady Martha arrived with the explanation they had heard she had been ill, and they came every year. Gwyneth squealed with excitement and Emely started to think about their food. Nelda assured Emely their stores were able to handle the extra people. The men went off hunting while the women sat in the warm May sunshine sewing. evening again after dinner the now three couples sat talking. It was an easy relaxed time filled with laughter and reminiscing. Lady Martha told stories about Christian, Felise, and Emely as they were growing up. Some of the stories about Christian, Emely had never heard, and she could tell he was a little embarrassed by some of them. Some of the stories about Felise and Emely were new to Christian. Felise and Emely were laughing at the stories about them as much as the others and even added some things they remembered.

With no new visitors, the next day was quiet and peaceful. In the evening, there was talk about all the work that needed to be done to give the manor permanence.

"Why?" Bryce questioned. "You will be moving home, once I die."

"I think not father. My home is here now. Gwyneth's home. She is also Rene's heir so we should stay here between the two manors."

"This manor is far too small for how powerful and important you will be."

"No this is home," Christian said firmly. "When the time comes, after I am gone, my eldest son will get your manor, Gwyneth and her husband will get Rene's, and I think I will leave my second son this manor. I want it to go on independent of the other two. Independent as . . . Emely has made it."

Emely looked at him when she heard her name. She met his smiling gaze and was confused and a little hurt. Some other woman's sons would benefit from all she had done to improve this place. With a deep sigh she reminded herself as a serf she had no say in the matter. Now she was even more determined to go to Lord Bryce's as soon as Christian was married. Her work here was done. Christian was now in full control of the manor; Gwyneth was old enough Emely was not needed to care for her so intently. She was glad this place and the people would not be abandoned. They had built such a wonderful community here. They had been through so many good times and bad times. They had come to rely on and support each other.

It was late when everyone went up to their chambers. The next day after the midday meal, Christian ask Emely to go riding with him. She refused, remembering the rejection of the last time they went riding. He insisted, in fact he ordered her to go with him. She started to question him, but he only said she needed the exercise. She had been working too hard and staying too close to the manor house. Their horses were saddled in the courtyard when they walked out. Emely reluctantly got on her horse and followed Christian out of the manor courtyard but rather than the road through the village to the stream he led her in the other direction. Into the wood where they had not ridden before. She had been down this path many times and knew it led to a beautiful clearing filled with early summer flowers. He helped her off her horse and watched as she walked through the field, her hand sliding over the rainbow assortment of flowers.

"Emely" he said behind her as he rested his hands on her shoulders before turning her to face him.

He took her face in his hands and lowered his lips to hers, soft at first, then as desire grew in both of them and she responded, his need for her demanded her full response. Her arms were around his neck as they probed each other's mouths seeking to be united.

"We need to be joined," he whispered, and he came again to probe her sweet mouth.

"I . . . "she hesitated then relented. "Yes, Christian, yes," she moaned as her desire for him overwhelmed all rational thought. If she was to go, she would have this one last memory of him. She knew it sealed her fate. She would never marry because her heart and body would always be his. She would have this one last time to savor the touch and taste of him.

Their joining was intense and passionate. They both said the three words they had wanted to say for so long. They laid in each other's arms without speaking for a long time as she cuddled into him. A slight breeze brought the renewed scent of the wildflowers and relief from the warm sun on their exposed bodies.

She dozed off in his arms and knew if she died in this moment, she would be happy.

"Emely," he said waking her, "we must go back."

"No, not yet" she pleaded sleepily.

"Yes, my love, we must."

"Yes," she said pulling from his reluctant arms.

They dressed and walked back to the horses hand in hand. He lifted her up as she looked back at the place. She would never come here again. This time and place were too perfect to be spoiled by coming here without Christian. They rode back to the manor house in silence.

CHAPTER 59

Several more carts were in the courtyard indicating they had more company. In the manor house Lord Rene and Lady Gracen were sitting with Felise, Duran, Lord Bryce, and Lady Martha. Gwyneth was playing in one corner with Felise and Sarah's children. Sarah moved among the nobles serving them, making sure they had all the food and drink they wished. Emely greeted them then tried to slip away to the cookhouse, but Christian stopped her and insisted she come and sit with them. She tried to be as inconspicuous as possible and as soon as she could she slipped away to the cookhouse but there too she was blocked. Nelda met her at the door and refused to let Emely enter. Nelda assured Emely they had plenty of food for the guests and she should go and be with the nobles. Emely went back to the manor house and Christian was at the door waiting for her.

"You need to stay here," he said smiling. "I need you to protect me from Rene."

Emely smiled. She knew the two men had become close and wrote often. She went and sat among the people who had become her family over the years. She would miss them when Christian married, and she left this place. They had the evening meal and after the children were in bed, the men sat playing chess while the women worked on their sewing and the tapestry was almost finished.

"You will need to start a new one soon," Felise said. "Perhaps Christian's wedding."

The room went silent as everyone turned to stare at her.

"We all know he will have to marry some time," Felise said defensively. "Gwyneth needs brothers and sisters, all children do."

"That is not a topic I wish to discuss," Christian said his anger at his unthinking sister in his tone.

"Really Christian, you must be thinking of marrying again," Felise insisted.

"Felise, stop!" her father ordered.

"Really, why are you all ignoring this reality?"

"Felise! Stop!" her mother ordered.

"Really!" Felise added with a huff.

Emely smiled. This was the Felise she remembered from their childhood. Felise wanted what Felise wanted and was willing to harass anyone and everyone till she got what she wanted. When she looked at Christian, she could see he was not happy with Felise. He would not look at Emely. She was sure he regretted their afternoon together.

"Enough!" said Christian looking at Emely. "I will marry when I am ready to and have found the right mate."

"It is late," Emely said. "I bid you all a good morrow," she said standing.

"Emely," Christian said also standing and walking with her to the stairs. "Sleep well," he said when they reached the bottom of the stairs and then kissed her on her forehead.

She smiled up at him, but it was a sad smile. They had only said what she knew to be true. She had trouble sleeping at night reliving their time together but with visions of him marrying someone else. She had seen it happen before; she knew she would not want to see it again. She would be gone before he married again. She would find someplace far away from him, from all the people she loved.

Morning came too soon, and Emely got up and went to the cookhouse but again she was denied access by Nelda. In the manor house, as they ate the morning meal, Felise suggested they have a celebration since they were all together, Christian was home safely, and Emely was well again. Everyone was excited at the prospect.

"We must make ourselves beautiful," Felise said, always one to enjoy a good celebration.

The women all went upstairs to prepare themselves. Emely was busy making sure they all had hot water to bathe, clothes to dry themselves and help dressing. When Felise, Lady Martha, and Lady Gracen were all prepared they turned their attention to Emely. They fussed over her until she was laughing at their over attentiveness. Emely saw a new gown of Christian's favorite blue laid out on the bed and fresh flowers on the table. The ladies helped Emely dress in the gown. They arranged the flowers in her hair. Finally, they stood back and admired their handiwork.

"Someone else wants to help," Lady Martha said going to the chamber door. She waved to someone and a few seconds later Emely's mother came into the chamber.

CHAPTER 60

"Mother," Emely cried going to hug her mother. "When did you get here? Why are you here?"

"We came a few days ago but wanted to wait for the . . . celebration to see you."

"We? Is father here?"

"Yes," her mother answered. "He is downstairs. Are you ready?"

"Ready?" Emely asked before looking at the other women who were all smiling happily.

Then she realized what the celebration was going to be. She sighed. She would not let this happen.

"We cannot keep . . . people waiting," Felise said taking Emely's arm and leading her from the chamber.

Downstairs Emely's father stood dressed in his best and smiling at her with all the love fathers had for their beloved daughters. He took her arm from Felise as she and the other women left the manor house. He led her out and down the outside stairs and helped her mount a white horse. He led the horse toward the closed gate. Then the gates opened and beyond Emely could see the village decorated in flowers. The villagers lined the road leading to the church and cheered her as she passed. Emely smiled at her friends even as her heart was breaking. She had to talk to Christian. She had to make him understand why they could not marry. She saw him standing at the church doors smiling at her. He never looked more handsome, and her heart melted. She wanted this but knew it could not be. Her father helped her dismount and led her up the church steps. Reaching the top, he kissed her forehead and then handed her hand to Christian who took it thanking the older man.

"We must talk," Emely whispered to Christian.

"We will have the rest of our lives to talk, my love."

"No, we must talk now!" she insisted.

"Emi, I love you. I have always loved you."

"I will not let you be shamed because of me."

"What?" he said. Then realized what she was referring to.

"Emi, no one cares."

"I care. People who do not know . . . us will care you married a . . . a woman who had a child without having a husband. Lord Rene once called me an easy woman. That is what others will think and they will think less of you. I will not have you be degraded on my account."

"Emely you may be with child now," he whispered so only she could hear. "I will not have you and our child unprotected."

"I . . . I," she stammered not knowing how to answer that.

"Father Bernard, Father Francis," Christian said loud enough for all to hear. "I wish to make my confession."

"My son?" Father Bernard said.

Christian never took his eyes off Emely as he knelt before her.

"Bless me father for I have sinned. It is . . . too long since my last confession. I now confess to you and before this assembly the child this girl bore was mine. I took her innocence and then left her to punishment, exile, and the death of our child. I beg her forgiveness. I ask of you absolution for my sins and will endure any penance you proscribe for me."

"We can absolve your sins, but forgiveness should be granted by Lady Emely," said Father Bernard.

"And we think penance should also be given by Lady Emely," said Father Francis smiling.

"Emi?" Christian said looking up at the girl with tears sliding down her cheeks even as she smiled lovingly down at him.

"I forgave you the first moment I held Gwyneth," she said through happy tears. "For without David I could not have taken care of her."

Christian stood, still watching her intently.

"As to penance," Emely said with a wicked teasing smile. "I will come up with something. Perhaps a lifetime of loving me?"

"Tis no penance," Christian said smiling at her. "But a life of happiness."

"Can I call you mama now?" asked Gwyneth.

"Yes, my darling daughter, you may," said Emely picking up the little girl.

"May I give you, my blessing?" asked Lord Rene smiling at Emely and Christian.

"We would be honored," said Christian shaking the older man's hand before Rene pulled Christian into his arms for a fatherly hug.

The priests said the wedding mass there on the steps of the church so the whole village would be part of this joyous joining.

EPILOGUE

Christian and Emely had four more children, two sons and two daughters who lived to adulthood, married and were happy because all were allowed to marry someone they loved. A descendant of Lord Christian and Lady Emely was among the barons who forced King John to sign the Magna Carta. Another fought with Henry, Earl of Richmond, as he became King Henry VII. Another was among the nobles who welcomed William and Mary after the Glorious Revolution.

ABOUT THE AUTHOR

Jan has been married to her college sweetheart for over fifty years and they are the parents of two smart beautiful daughters. Jan has been writing for most of her life. Having ADD as a child meant that she was often off in her own make believe world, making up stories. Now she spends days sitting in a comfortable chair reading or writing. At home when there is not a book in her hands Jan sews, crochets, and knits. Afghans are her specialty.

Jan has traveled across the United States and the world visiting fifteen states and four foreign countries. She and her family lived briefly in both London and Paris. She has flown over both the North Atlantic and the South Pacific.

NOTE FROM JAN KELLY ANDERSON

Word-of-mouth is crucial for any author to succeed. If you enjoyed *The Lovers' Crusade*, please leave a review online—anywhere you are able. Even if it's just a sentence or two. It would make all the difference and would be very much appreciated.

Thanks!
Jan Kelly Anderson

We hope you enjoyed reading this title from:

www.blackrosewriting.com

Subscribe to our mailing list – *The Rosevine* – and receive **FREE** books, daily
deals, and stay current with news about upcoming
releases and our hottest authors.
Scan the QR code below to sign up.

Already a subscriber? Please accept a sincere thank you for being a fan of
Black Rose Writing authors.

View other Black Rose Writing titles at
www.blackrosewriting.com/books and use promo code
PRINT to receive a **20% discount** when purchasing.